UNITING

The Souls

SOULS OF CHICAGO #6

I0563651

ANNABELLA MICHAELS

Possible trigger warnings: This book contains situations of child abuse, physical violence and substance abuse which may be disturbing to some readers.

OTHER BOOKS BY ANNABELLA MICHAELS

Souls Of Chicago Series:

Feeding the Soul, Book 1

Music of the Soul, Book 2

Protecting the Soul, Book 3

Renewing the Soul, Book 4

Constructing the Soul, Book 5

DEDICATION

To Allison, thank you for being my friend, cracking the whip, encouraging me and talking me off the ledge more times than I care to admit, but most of all, thank you for Tompalooza. I can never thank you enough for all that you do.

PROLOGUE

Isaac

I SMILED AS I LOOKED AROUND AT THE NEW BUILDING AND everyone gathered there for the grand opening. The new Agape House was much bigger than the old facility and we'd be able to help so many more kids. Lately, we'd seen a rise in teens that had been kicked out of their homes or needed to run away to escape an abusive parent, or were just living in such terrible conditions that they needed a helping hand. Whatever their reason for coming to the center, they all had one thing in common, they were all members of the LGBTQA community.

It hadn't been that long ago that I was one of the teenagers that needed the center. I didn't allow myself to think about the circumstances that had led me to seek refuge at Agape House very often, choosing to focus on the positive things that had happened since I first walked through those doors instead.

Agape House had changed the course of my life, just as it had done and would continue to do for countless other teens, and it was all because of the man standing next to me. Matt was the first face I saw when I walked through those doors so many years ago. I'd been wary of him at first, which was completely understandable given my situation, but after getting to know him as a teen and then working with him as an adult, I found it laughable that I'd ever been afraid to be around him. He was an amazing man with a huge heart and a kind soul. He would give the shirt off his back to anyone in need, yet rarely shared any personal information about himself. I gazed up at Matt as he looked out over the crowd with a small smile on his face that got wider when he caught me looking at him.

"This is really something, isn't it?" I said.

"It sure is. It's still a bit mind-boggling that someone would take such an interest in my little center and want to help in such a big way. This new building will change everything," he replied.

"Well, they're a great group of people for sure, but I bet none of them would have fallen in love with the center if it wasn't for you and the work you're doing to improve the lives of those kids. You're the heart and soul of this organization," I told him, speaking passionately because it meant that much to me.

"I don't really do all that much. It's the kids who are the heart of the center," he replied modestly. I shook my head with a smile. That was typical Matt, always deflecting any praise away from himself.

Matt was an amazing boss who genuinely cared about the kids that came to his center. He did his best to provide care for each LGBTQA youth that walked through its doors, but it had become a constant struggle to keep the program running while trying to maintain the old building that threatened to crumble around them. Government funding had become scarce, so Matt was forced to rely on donations and various fundraisers just to remain afloat, but that barely covered the cost of the daily operations.

Just when things started to look their bleakest, music mogul, Lachlan Edwards stopped in one day to look around. He'd heard about the work the center was doing from his fiancé, Rylie, who'd begun volunteering at the center as part of his recovery program from drug and alcohol abuse. Lachlan had been so impressed with Matt's program that he'd immediately offered to build a new facility for the center.

Lachlan, Rylie, and several of their friends—including the entire Greene family who had taken turns volunteering at the center ever since I could remember—worked quickly to put together a plan which would not only provide a new location for the center, but also allow us to help more youth than ever before. Lachlan and the band, Carter's Creed, had used their connections to raise awareness, and enough funding to ensure that Agape House would be able to keep running for the next hundred years at least.

I looked out over the room and smiled as I watched our friends who had helped make the new center a reality. Giovanni and Caleb were kneeling on the floor talking animatedly to their daughter, Sarah, as if they were telling her a story. Carter had his hand in Ryan's back pocket as they talked to Lachlan and Rylie. Every so often, I'd see Ryan glance down at his husband, giving him a very heated look and I could only imagine what Carter was doing with that hand.

Landon and his husband, Micah, were talking with Landon's parents and I watched as Micah reached up and put his hand on the back of Landon's neck, letting him feel their connection. And then there was Morgan and Akio, who were standing in a corner, talking quietly. Every once in a while, they'd glance down at the rings on their fingers and then give each other a look that was so intimate that I knew, for them, they were the only two people in the room.

"I hope I find a love like that someday," I said wistfully, not referring to any one couple in particular. As far as I was concerned, they all had found the kind of love I'd like to have; the kind that lasts forever and defies all logic.

"I hope you do, too," Matt murmured quietly and I thought I detected a hint of sadness in his voice. My heart ached at the thought of anything hurting Matt.

I glanced over at him and opened my mouth, but then shut it right away. I could tell that there was something in Matt's past that haunted him and I wished that he would open up and let me in, but I knew, better than most, how painful it could be to revisit the past, so I let it go. I was still watching Matt when suddenly his back straightened and his eyes grew wide. He looked startled.

I turned my head to see what had caused his reaction and my heart skipped a beat when I saw the gorgeous man walking towards us. He was tall, even taller than Matt, with broad shoulders and biceps that would probably rip the sleeves of his shirt if he were to flex at all. He was wearing black dress pants and a gray polo shirt, making him look both stylish and sophisticated.

He had beautiful ebony skin and full lips and his eyes were…his eyes were zeroed in on Matt and the look he was giving Matt could only be described as…hungry. I quickly looked at Matt and saw that his attention was still focused on the man. The look in Matt's eyes was a mixture of heat and confusion and something else that I wasn't quite sure of, but if I had to guess, I'd have to say…guilt?

My stomach knotted as I continued to watch the two men. There was an electric charge in the air that I'd felt on a few other occasions, but now it seemed stronger and I wasn't sure if it was coming from the two of them or if it was my own reaction.

Just as the stranger was about to reach us, he turned his eyes on me and those warm brown eyes widened just a fraction and then heated further. I could feel my body starting to respond to him, which surprised me because I had only ever reacted that way to one other man. His eyes bounced back and forth between Matt and me and he looked just as confused as I felt. When he was standing in front of us he spoke and his voice was rich and deep and it caused goose bumps to break out across my skin.

"Which one of you is Matt?" he asked.

"I am," Matt answered gruffly and then cleared his throat. He looked nervous and I could see sweat beading above Matt's brow. The stranger moved his head and my legs turned to jelly as I became the focus of his attention.

"Then you must be Isaac." He smiled, showing a row of perfectly straight teeth. It was a friendly smile, warm and inviting and my instincts kicked in, letting me know that he was safe.

"Yes," I said weakly. I tried to think of something else to add, but the synapses in my brain were too busy misfiring.

"It's nice to meet you both," he said, sticking his hand out to shake first Matt's hand and then mine.

He stared at Matt as they shook hands, but Matt pulled away quickly, looking down at his hand as if he'd been shocked. He looked back up at the stranger in confusion. He shook mine next and I watched as his large hand engulfed my smaller one. It was warm and soft and I felt a current of electricity that traveled from my hand all the way up the back of my neck and out the top of my head. I looked at him in surprise and he was staring back at me, his head tilted to the side and I could see the questions behind those eyes. Unfortunately, I didn't have any answers as to what was going on.

I looked to Matt, because he'd always been the one I turned to, but his eyes were going back and forth between the stranger and me. He paused on me and when he looked at me, it was as if he were seeing me for the first time. His tongue darted out to wet his lips and I felt a stirring in my groin. That wasn't anything new, but the way he was looking at me was. I felt off kilter and I wasn't sure what was going on with me or with Matt who had always been the strong and steady one of the two of us. Who was this man and what did he want?

"What's your name?" I asked. His brown eyes turned to me and my skin heated under his gaze.

"My name is Hudson."

CHAPTER
One

Isaac

I PUNCHED THE BUTTON ON THE COFFEE MAKER FOR THE hundredth time, but no amount of begging, pleading, or cursing was going to get the thing to turn on. I groaned as I unplugged it from the wall and tossed it into the trash can, making a mental note to pick up a new one as I stumbled into the bathroom and turned on the shower. Hopefully, the water would be enough to wipe the remnants of sleep from my mind until I could make it into work and get a cup of coffee.

I showered quickly then wrapped the towel around my waist before walking out to my bedroom. I stood in front of my closet, deciding which outfit to wear. I chose something quickly and began getting dressed then I took the sheets off the futon that I used as a bed and folded it back into a couch position. I placed the sheets on the shelf in the closet then glanced around, making sure everything had been put away. Not that I ever had company, but I took pride in my home and I liked to keep it neat and organized.

My apartment was nothing fancy by any stretch of the imagination. It was tiny and cramped, with the kitchen, living room and bedroom all in one space. The only room that was separate was the small bathroom. There were holes in the walls left by the previous tenants, the heat didn't work properly in the winter and I was constantly having to clean up the white dust that would fall from the plaster ceiling whenever the neighbors above me walked through their apartment. I knew most people would consider it deplorable living conditions, but to me, it was safe, it was home, and it was mine. It was filled with things that I had earned on my own, working a job I loved, and no one could take that away from me.

I checked the time on my watch, knowing I needed to get a move on if I didn't want to be late for work. I slid my phone and wallet into my pants pockets and locked the door behind me then raced down the stairs and out the front door. I got to the L train just as it pulled up and quickly paid and climbed on, the doors swooshing closed behind me.

As the train began to pull away from the station, I slid my phone out and brought up my reading app. I'd argued with Matt when he'd given me the phone, telling him that I didn't need anything that fancy and that I had a prepaid phone if he needed to get ahold of me. However, he'd insisted, saying that with the new center, I was going to be taking on a lot more responsibility and that I would practically be able to run the entire office with my new phone. He'd explained that it was a business expense and had already been accounted for through the funds that Lachlan had set up.

I'd finally agreed and then I'd spent hours learning all the things my new phone could do. I'd been surprised when I'd seen the reading app already loaded with a full library of books, but when I'd questioned Matt about it, he'd just shrugged his shoulders and said that he knew I liked reading and that the phone didn't have to be used strictly for business. I still remembered the way my eyes had stung. It was the most thoughtful thing anyone had ever done for me.

I let the book I was reading transport me far away from the noise and the smells of the train until an announcement rang out over the speaker system, alerting me that my stop was coming up. I closed the app and shoved the phone back in my pocket and then stood, holding onto the metal bar until the train came to a complete stop.

The sidewalks were crowded as I walked the three blocks to work and neared the area of the city that used to be nothing but old abandoned textile factories, and was quickly being revitalized as the warehouses were sold for office and housing use. I smiled when I saw the building stretched out in front of me, the sign above the door reading *Agape House—A safe place to call home*. I had been running the front desk at the center ever since I graduated from high school and I couldn't imagine ever wanting to work anywhere else.

I opened the front door and was greeted with the sounds of laughter and lively conversation. Some of the teens that came to the center only needed us for a few hours a day. For them, we offered a safe environment where they could hang out with kids their own age that were part of the LGBTQA community. We also helped them with tutoring, mentoring, and applying for colleges or jobs to get them started out on the right path.

For some kids though, Agape House was their home. Many of the teens that came through our doors had been kicked out of their homes or had run away in order to avoid abusive situations. Matt worked closely with the police and children's services in those situations, making sure he went through all the proper legal channels so that the teens could remain in his care until everything could be resolved. Often times, the parents chose to sign custody over to the state rather than work on fixing themselves. When that happened, the teens either went into foster care or stayed at Agape House until they could be adopted out. Unfortunately, the chances of them being adopted once they were teenagers were very slim.

That was one of the reasons that Matt and I had been so excited to move to the new facility. The previous building only had space for thirty-five residents, but the number of kids needing help had been growing each year. It had torn us up to do it, but we had gotten to the point where we were going to have to start turning kids away. When the building's contractor, Morgan Greene, developed the plans for the new center and told us that we would have enough room to house over one hundred kids, it was like a dream come true.

A month after opening the doors of the new facility, there were nearly sixty-five LGBTQA teens that called Agape House home and from the sounds of it, every single one of them were in the kitchen. I made my way down the hallway and opened the large set of double doors to the kitchen, the noise level reaching a fever pitch as I stepped inside. I thought it was a beautiful sound though, because it was the sound of kids enjoying themselves as they ate a healthy breakfast before they left for school. I wondered how many of them had ever had that before they came to the center; probably very few, if any.

I waved to several of them that called out my name as I made a beeline towards the cooking area of the kitchen in search of coffee. I gave Gladys a quick kiss on the cheek as I stepped behind where she was standing at the stove. Gladys had been in charge of the kitchen since before I showed up all those years ago and I'd taken to her right away.

She had a no-nonsense attitude when it came to how she expected things to be done in her kitchen and she had a list of rules that were to be followed by the kids that ate there. They all were expected to be kind to each other, use their manners, and clean up after themselves as if it were their home. Those rules went right along with Matt's list of chores that each kid was given on their first day at the center. There was rarely any argument about it because most of the kids were just happy to be able to stay there. I know I had been anyway, and the rules they had set in place for me had made me feel safe and secure. As if by being able to contribute something, I could safeguard my spot at the center.

"I saved you a bowl of oatmeal," Gladys said as I filled a large mug with coffee and doctored it with cream and sugar.

"With brown sugar?" I asked, smiling at her hopefully.

"Of course, I know what you like, sweet pea," she answered back, an indulgent grin on her face.

My heart warmed at the endearment. I knew that she loved each and every one of the kids that came through her kitchen, but it never failed to make me feel special when she called me that or set food aside for me, adding something extra that she knew I liked. She was the mother I'd always wished I'd had.

I chatted with her for a while as I warmed my breakfast in the microwave and then I thanked her for the food and made my way out of the kitchen and sat down with a group of kids as I ate. I was just finishing up when I heard some of the kids calling out Matt's name. My head whipped up and my heart leapt in my chest when I saw my boss walking through the maze of tables.

Matt stopped to talk to a table full of kids and I took the time to admire him. He looked very handsome in his khaki dress pants and light-blue button-down shirt which showed off his broad shoulders and narrow waist. His dark curls looked soft and silky, but they also looked longer than usual which surprised me because he was always meticulous with his appearance and never let his hair get too long without scheduling a trim. It just went to show how preoccupied he'd been. In fact, he'd been acting strangely ever since the night of the center's grand opening.

I'd always had a bit of a crush on Matt, but it wasn't until I got a little older and began working for him that my attraction had really developed. Unfortunately, Matt had never shown any interest in me, not that I'd seen him show an interest in anyone. Matt was a very private man who never discussed his personal life.

That night, however, I'd seen the flare of desire in his eyes as he'd watched Hudson moving towards us. I'd felt jealous at first, but then he'd turned to me and the look in his eyes was different from the way he normally looked at me. I wasn't quite sure what that look meant, and unfortunately, I hadn't had an opportunity to try and find out because Matt had left shortly after Hudson introduced himself and I hadn't seen him the rest of the evening.

Someone had come up to me shortly after that wanting to discuss the new center and I'd grudgingly turned away from Hudson to talk to them. When I'd turned back around, the sexy man was gone. My eyes searched the crowd, but it was like he had vanished. I'd been shocked by my reaction to Hudson because up until that point, Matt had been the only man that had ever made my heart race, not that I had ever let him know that.

Still, to suddenly find myself attracted to both of them had been disconcerting. I'd been left feeling completely confused by it all, but I hadn't seen Hudson again after that and Matt had been avoiding me ever since, unless it had to do directly with our work at the center.

As if he'd heard my thoughts, his head lifted and his gaze caught mine from across the room. I could see his brows furrow slightly as he looked at me, but then he turned his attention back to the kids he'd been talking to. My shoulders slumped and I let out a low sigh. I was going to have to try and find a way to talk to him so I could figure out what was going on. If I'd done something wrong or upset him in some way, then I wanted to know about it so I could try to correct it. Matt was too important to me to just let it go.

I said goodbye to the kids at my table and told them I'd see them after school then I picked up my dishes and walked over, placing them in the sink. After refilling my coffee mug, I made my way back down the hall so I could get started with my work.

"Good morning, Isaac!" Allison said as I walked towards my office.

I smiled at the vivacious brunette sitting at the front desk. Matt had hired her to run the front desk shortly after we made the move into the new building. He'd explained that since I knew more about the center and the direction he wanted to take things than anyone else, that I was the perfect person to be his assistant.

I'd been speechless when he'd shown me to my very own office right next to his and I'd stood there for a long time, tracing my finger over my name engraved in the gold plaque on the door. I'd had to swallow several times around the lump in my throat before I was able to tell him thank you, but the soft look he'd given me told me that he knew how much the gesture had meant to me.

The center still relied heavily on volunteers from the community, but with the attention that had been drawn by having Carter's Creed involved, the number of people willing to help had risen considerably. Matt had increased the permanent staff though to include more kitchen help, an on-call pediatrician, and of course, Allison. The only position that hadn't been filled was a therapist who would be willing to come in as needed to talk with the teens and help them work through some of the things they were dealing with.

I'd just sat down at my desk when there was a knock at the door. I looked up to see Matt standing there with a tentative grin on his face. I wished I knew why he'd started acting so differently around me. I smiled at him, trying to put him at ease, but his eyes widened and he dropped his gaze to the floor. I sighed.

"Have I done something wrong, Matt?" I asked quietly.

"No, not at all. Why would you think that?" He sounded surprised as his eyes shot up to mine.

"Because you've been acting really strange lately. Almost like you're avoiding me or something," I told him, shrugging my shoulders casually so he wouldn't know how worried I'd been. I watched him carefully as his shoulders slumped and he reached up to pinch the bridge of his nose.

"I'm sorry, Isaac," he said with a sigh. "You haven't done anything wrong at all. I've just had a lot on my mind."

"Is there anything I can help with?" I offered. The smile Matt gave me that time was more genuine.

"No, it's something I have to work out on my own, but thank you. I actually stopped by to see if you had time to go over some ideas I had for a project that I'd like to get the kids involved in; kind of a way for them to give back to the community that's helped them so much," he explained.

"That's a wonderful idea. I have time right now," I told him.

"Great! Do you mind coming to my office? I have all of my notes in there," Matt said.

"Not at all," I told him. I stood from my desk, stopping to grab a notepad and a pen before following him next door to his office.

I sat across from Matt as he explained his idea for the kids at the center to help with a community beautification project in which they would spend a couple of Saturdays each month cleaning up and making repairs to neighborhood parks and local playgrounds. I, of course, thought it was a brilliant idea and Matt became more animated as we began planning how we could turn the idea into reality.

I could see him becoming more relaxed the longer we talked and I was glad that he had asked me to help with the project. Matt and I had always worked very well together and I was relieved to find that whatever had been bothering him wasn't going to get in the way of that. Neither one of us stopped talking until we were interrupted by a knock at the door. We both looked up as Allison pushed it open and peeked her head in.

"Oh, I'm sorry. I didn't realize you were in a meeting," she apologized.

"That's alright, Allison. What's up?" Matt asked kindly.

"There's a gentleman here to see you. He said he's interested in the therapist position," she said. Matt looked at me excitedly and we both grinned at each other.

"Send him in, please," he told her. She nodded her head and then disappeared back down the hallway. We both stood and I grabbed my things, intending to make myself scarce, but Matt stopped me be-fore I could leave. "If you have time, I'd like you to stay. Choosing the right therapist is a big decision and I'd really appreciate your input on who I hire."

"I'd be happy to," I agreed.

I couldn't help the grin that spread across my face. It meant the world to me that he valued my opinion. Matt held my gaze and for just a second, I thought I saw the same look he'd given me the night of the grand opening, but we were interrupted once again when the door opened and I turned my head, my jaw nearly hitting the floor when I came face to face with Hudson.

CHAPTER
Two

Hudson

I FROWNED AS I WATCHED THE RETREATING FORM OF THE YOUNG woman walking down the hallway. Micah had told me that Isaac worked the front desk at the center and I'd be lying to myself if I didn't admit that I was a little disappointed when instead of Isaac, I'd been greeted by Allison's bubbly personality. It wasn't her fault, she was a charming girl with a bright smile, it just wasn't the smile that I'd been looking forward to seeing. I shook my head. That wasn't the purpose of my being there, I reminded myself, although I still couldn't help but feel excited at the prospect of seeing the two men that had invaded my every thought since the night I'd first laid eyes on them.

After listening to Rylie and Lachlan go on and on about the work being done at the center, I'd decided to check it out for myself during the grand opening. I looked around a bit, wanting to see what all the fuss was about and I had to admit, I was thoroughly impressed. It was obvious that a lot of thought and consideration had gone into the space, making sure that the kids who went there would feel welcomed and at home.

I'd wandered the halls, thinking how lucky the young people of Chicago were to have a place like that to turn to and wishing that every city in America would offer places of support for their LGBTQA youth. Too many teens were being turned away from their homes each year, many of them living on the streets, getting hooked on drugs and being forced into prostitution just to try and survive.

I'd returned to the party, determined to help in any way possible and anxious to meet the person responsible for starting such an incredible program. I met Micah and Landon on my way back into the main area and when I asked them who I should speak to, they'd pointed to two figures across the room saying that the dark-haired gentleman was Matt, the owner of Agape House and the other was Isaac, the front desk manager. They told me that either one would be able to find some way for me to volunteer.

I'd made my way slowly across the crowded room and my steps faltered when Matt and I locked eyes. He was gorgeous with his thick dark curls and smoky gray eyes, which widened as he stared back at me with a mixture of surprise, curiosity, and heat. I felt inexplicably drawn to him and I moved closer, even more determined to meet him when movement to the left of him caught my attention.

My eyes had darted to the person standing at Matt's side for just a second, but then froze there as I'd taken in the stunning young man who must have been Isaac. He was nearly a foot shorter than me with light-brown hair that was a little longer on the top than the sides with blond highlights streaked throughout.

I found myself being drawn to him the same way I'd been drawn to Matt and it left me feeling disoriented. They were both stunning, but how could I have such a visceral reaction to two different men in a matter of seconds? My mind felt foggy, but my feet continued to move me in their direction until I'd ended up standing right in front of them. Everything seemed to disappear around us until it was as if we were the only three people in the room.

"Which one of you is Matt?" I'd asked as if I didn't already know the answer.

Somehow, I'd managed to make it through introductions, but my heart was racing the entire time. I tried to think of something else to say, but it was as if my tongue was tied in a knot. My eyes kept darting back and forth between the two men, taking in the slight crease between Matt's eyes and the freckles dotting the bridge of Isaac's nose. I'd had the strongest urge to kiss each and every one of those freckles while finding a way to make Matt smile. *What the hell was wrong with me?*

Matt turned to look at Isaac and I saw the same mixture of emotions playing across his face when he looked at the younger man as he'd worn when he'd looked at me, and I felt disappointed as I wondered if there was something going on between the two of them already. If so, I'd have no choice but to walk away. Before I had the chance to find out, however, Matt suddenly said something about needing to talk to the mayor and then he'd spun on his heel and disappeared into the crowd.

I'd turned to Isaac who was wearing a confused expression as he watched Matt walk away. He'd shifted his blue eyes to me then and opened his mouth as if to say something, but someone came up to him, wanting information about the new center. I felt completely unbalanced by everything that had happened so when another person walked up to join the conversation, I took the opportunity to slip away. I needed air and to get my bearings so I could try and make sense of the strange situation.

I'd spoken to Lachlan and Rylie for a few minutes and then made my way outside where I leaned against the building, taking in several deep breaths while waiting for my heart to quit racing. I stared down at my hand which still tingled from where my skin had touched theirs when we shook hands. It was shaking and I grabbed it with my other hand to steady it. After several moments, I'd pushed off the wall and forced myself to move towards my car.

I'd almost convinced myself on the drive home that night that I'd imagined the entire thing, but I woke the next morning with both of their names on my lips and my cock rock-hard and begging for release after the dream I'd had. I knew that I wouldn't find any peace until I was able to see them again and figure out what the hell was going on. I'd tried to be patient and give them time to get settled into the new center, but I also genuinely wanted to become involved and help out in any way I could. When Lachlan mentioned that Matt might have been looking to hire a therapist, I'd decided that that sounded like the perfect opportunity.

So, there I stood, trying to appear calm as I waited for Allison to return and tell me if Matt would have time to speak with me, and wondering what would happen if he did. Part of me expected that when I saw each of them again that there would be no spark, that I'd discover in the light of day that I'd made more out of my reaction to them than was really there.

"Matt can see you now, if you'd like to follow me." I nearly jumped out of my skin at the sound of Allison's voice right next to me. I'd been so lost in my thoughts that I hadn't seen or heard her walking back towards me.

"Thank you," I said, returning her friendly smile.

I picked up my briefcase and followed her down a long hallway. I couldn't help looking in each open doorway that we passed, hoping to get a glimpse of Isaac, but he was nowhere to be found. My heart was pounding against my rib cage and I rolled my eyes at myself, not sure if it was nerves or anticipation that was causing me to react so out of character and I reminded myself once again of the main reason I was there. Allison stopped in front of the last room just as a phone started ringing in the direction we'd just come from. She turned to me with a startled expression.

"I'm sorry, I need to get that. You can just go on in, Matt's wait-ing for you," she said with a wave of her hand as she rushed back towards her desk.

I watched her leave and then turned to face the closed door. I straightened my shoulders and took a deep breath as I turned the knob and let the door swing open. My eyes widened as I came face to face with both of the men who'd left me so rattled after that night and I found my body reacting the same way to them as it had that first time.

Matt stood behind his desk, a wary expression on his handsome face. His gray eyes looked tired, as if he'd had too little sleep, but he still managed to look stunning. Isaac stood on the opposite side of the desk closest to me, and while he looked surprised, I also caught a glimmer of excitement in his bright blue eyes.

"Hudson, what are you doing here?" Isaac asked and my heart stuttered at the sight of the smile spreading across his face. It was open and friendly and showed off a set of straight, white teeth and I felt my lips curl up in an answering smile.

"Lachlan told me that you were looking for a therapist," I answered.

"You know someone?" He looked at me hopefully. There was something so warm and inviting about Isaac's personality and I felt my smile widen as I looked at him.

"Yes, me," I told him.

"You're a therapist?" My eyes darted to Matt as he sudden-ly spoke up. His face was still guarded, but I could see his curiosity shining through. Before I could respond, he spoke again. "Oh, I'm sorry, please, come in and have a seat."

Isaac gestured to the seat next to his and I watched his Adam's apple bob as he swallowed hard. I stepped closer, my large frame dwarfing his smaller one and my arm brushed his as I moved to sit down. My skin felt warm where we'd touched and I heard his sharp intake of air; I was definitely not the only one who'd felt it.

We took our seats and I noticed Matt staring at Isaac and again, I wondered what he was thinking, but he brushed it off quickly and turned his attention to me. I pulled a file out of my briefcase and laid it on Matt's desk, letting him sort through my credentials.

After several minutes, he leaned back in his seat and crossed his arms, making his shirt stretch tightly across his broad shoulders and chest. I heard a sigh next to me and I had to fight back a grin when I glanced at Isaac and caught him staring at Matt with a look of pure longing. Matt seemed completely oblivious to our ogling however, as he chewed on his bottom lip, apparently lost in thought.

"Well, Dr. Westley, I have to say, I'm quite impressed, but I'm not sure we could afford someone of your caliber on our payroll," he said slowly.

"Please, call me Hudson, and, I think you misunderstood. I have my own practice and I'm not looking to leave it. I would, however, like to volunteer my services a few evenings each week to the kids at your center," I told them.

"Volunteer? You mean you want to provide therapy for free?" Isaac asked.

"Yes, exactly." I smiled at him and nodded my head.

"Why?" Matt asked. His head was tilted as he studied me through narrowed eyes. I could tell he was protective of the kids in his care and I respected the fact that he was choosing their future therapist carefully. I looked him directly in the eye as I gave him an honest answer.

"I grew up in this city and I know how rough its streets can be. I was fortunate to have been raised by a grandmother and an older sister who loved and accepted me no matter what, but I knew several kids who weren't as lucky and I wished there'd been a place like this for them to turn to." I looked at both men as I spoke.

"I think that Agape House is not only an amazing and inspiring place; it's necessary. Our youth need to be shown love if they're going to learn how to love themselves as well as others. I want to volunteer my time with your program because I believe in what you're doing and I want to be a part of the positive changes you're making for the next generation of the LGBTQA community." It was quiet for a few seconds as Matt stared at me and then Isaac broke the silence.

"Wow! You should have been a politician," he said. Matt and I turned our heads in his direction and I chuckled when I saw the look of awe on his face.

"No, thank you. I have no desire whatsoever to enter into politics." I gave an exaggerated shudder and he and Matt both laughed. The previous tension in the air was gone as we smiled at each other. "In all seriousness, I would really like to volunteer at the center if you'll have me."

I had to fight to keep eye contact with Matt as he considered my offer because my attention kept getting pulled down to where he was working his bottom lip between his thumb and forefinger. He was much more serious than Isaac, but I found myself equally as interested in getting to know him as I was the younger man.

"I'm not sure how much time you have to devote to the program, but I was hoping to have a therapist available at the center at least two evenings a week as well as being on-call for any emergencies that may arise. It would be a big commitment," Matt explained. I let my gaze drop back down to his mouth then slowly moved it back up to meet his gaze.

"That won't be a problem. I'm available most evenings, given the fact that I'm single," I informed him.

"Oh, I wasn't…" Matt's eyes widened and he began to shake his head.

"I know you weren't, but I thought you should know. Both of you," I said boldly, turning my head towards Isaac. He stared at me unblinking, as if he were trying to piece together my words, and I could see his pulse pounding at the hollow of his throat.

My hands fisted in my lap as I fought the urge to pull him

towards me so I could press my lips to the pale flesh of his neck. His eyes darkened as they heated and I smirked at him. I loved the way he responded to me. We turned our attention to Matt who was watching us closely. I saw the flair of interest in his eyes, but it was gone a second later. He cleared his throat.

"I appreciate your offer...to work with the children," he clarified quickly. "We'd be honored to have you as part of our team." Matt went over the paperwork that I would need to have on file before I could begin and then stood and thrust his hand out in front of him, effectively calling an end to the meeting.

Isaac and I followed suit and I shook Matt's hand, a zip of electricity flowing from his hand to mine and traveling up my arm, leaving goose bumps in its wake. Matt pulled his hand away quickly and his brows furrowed as if he couldn't make sense of what he'd just felt. He glanced up at me with an almost pained expression and I wondered what had happened to put that look on his face.

I turned to Isaac who stuck his hand out with a shy grin. My lips pulled up as I looked at him and I felt the same shockwave as we shook hands. He looked up at me through thick lashes and my cock twitched inside my pants. I wouldn't mind seeing him look up at me as I fed my cock through those full, pink lips. His pale skin flushed as if he had read my thoughts and I smirked at his reaction.

"I'll be in touch as soon as I have my background check completed," I told them. Matt nodded, but I noticed he wasn't really paying attention because he was too busy staring at Isaac who was staring at me. I winked at Isaac and then stepped out of the office, closing the door behind me. I was still wearing a smile on my face as I made my way out of the building and to my car.

CHAPTER
Three

Matt

M Y LEGS FELT SHAKY AND I SAT BACK DOWN IN MY CHAIR, afraid they were about to give out on me. The door shut behind Hudson and Isaac turned to me with a small smile. His cheeks looked flushed and his blue eyes looked brighter than usual. I felt the same strange fluttering sensation in my stomach that I'd been feeling lately whenever I looked at him and I wasn't sure what to make of it.

"Well, it looks like we have a new therapist," Isaac said excitedly.

"Yes, it does. That's good…for the kids," I replied quietly. Isaac tilted his head at me, the look on his face changing quickly to concern.

"Are you unsure about Hudson working with our kids? Because you need to be sure, Matt. Choosing a therapist is a big decision." My chest felt warm when I heard Isaac refer to the kids at the center as *our kids.* I knew that what we were doing at the center was more than just a job to him. Isaac put his heart and soul into Agape House and he loved the teens that came to us for help, but it still meant a lot to know that he felt like they were his own, just as I did. I saw the worry in his eyes and I didn't want him to get the wrong idea.

"No, I don't have any concerns about Hudson's ability to work with the kids. His portfolio was very impressive and he had several referral letters in his file, including two from Lachlan and Rylie. I'm not sure what their connection to him is, but if they were willing to refer him to us, then that's good enough for me. I know they would never let anyone around the kids that they didn't feel was the absolute best," I assured him. I watched as his shoulders visibly relaxed.

"Then what was wrong? You seemed agitated when Hudson left," Isaac pressed.

"Nothing was wrong, I just have a lot on my mind. I have a million things to do today. In fact, I probably should get started on those if I don't want to have to stay here all night," I told him, gentling my dismissive tone with a small smile.

I didn't want to hurt his feelings, I just needed some time by myself to figure out what the hell was going on with me. I couldn't make sense of the sudden onslaught of emotions that I felt every time I was in the room with the two of them. He cocked his head to the side as he studied me and I forced myself not to squirm under his knowing gaze. I'd known Isaac for six years, working closely with him for five of those years and sometimes when he looked at me, it was as if he could see my every thought.

"Okay, I'll let you get to work," he said, making his way to the door. I watched him open it, but then he looked over his shoulder at me. "Hudson seems like a nice man, don't you think?"

"Yes, he does," I answered honestly.

"He's very handsome, too," Isaac said with a smile.

I was shocked when he winked at me before walking out the door. My heart was racing as the door shut behind him and I wasn't sure if it was because Isaac had been flirting with me or because of the truth to his words.

I threw myself into my work, letting budget spreadsheets and government paperwork occupy my mind as I tried to push thoughts of Hudson and Isaac aside. I'd been working for several hours when my concentration was broken by the distant sounds of the kids laughing as they returned from school and I smiled at the sound.

With the growing number of LGBTQA teens that had been turned away by their families and who were either mistreated or completely ignored by a society that should support them, I often wondered if the work I was doing was really making a difference at all or simply putting a Band-Aid on a wound. Then, I'd watch the kids at the center as they overcame the pain they'd been through and found a strength within themselves to carry on and it made me feel empowered. The resiliency they showed despite the adversity they faced was an inspiration to me and provided the motivation that kept me going, even when it seemed like I was fighting a losing battle.

Many of the teens arrived at the center broken and battered; not always physically, but often in spirit. They showed up at our door searching for peace, refuge, and a sense of belonging, and it meant the world to me to hear them sounding carefree and happy, knowing that we had been able to provide them with what they needed. Although, some struggled more than others to break free of the painful past that clung to them, which was why I had felt it necessary to hire a therapist at the new center.

I'd been unable to afford to provide that kind of service at the old center, but with the generous amount of money that Lachlan, Carter, and the rest of their friends and family had donated, I was finally able to do so. Only it didn't seem like I would need to use the money to hire a professional after all. My mind was still reeling with the idea that a man with Hudson's education and experience would be willing to commit that amount of time to my center, completely free of charge. That told me a lot about the type of person Hudson

Westley was.

My thoughts drifted to the man who had gotten under my skin so quickly. From the moment I'd seen Hudson across the room at the grand opening, I felt a rush of adrenaline and a surge of passion unlike anything I'd ever experienced before. The way he looked at me as he'd walked closer had taken my breath away. There had been a hunger in his eyes that I hadn't seen directed at me in years.

Then his eyes shifted and I'd seen the look of surprise and the sudden interest there as well. I'd glanced beside me, having forgotten that I wasn't alone and my eyes widened when I realized that the new focus of Hudson's sultry gaze was none other than Isaac.

I'd been there when Isaac first arrived at Agape House, looking more lost and broken than most of the kids that had ever come there. I knew a little of what he'd been through, but for the most part, he chose not to talk about his past and I'd respected his privacy. I'd watched him as he began to trust people again and over time he had flourished into a happy, kind, and caring young man.

I'd been there when he became an adult and he began working for me, proving to be an intelligent and vital member of my staff. We'd become friends over time, yet kept our professional distance, not spending time together outside of work activities. I knew that he wasn't the same kid that had come to the center seeking help, but I'd always seen him as a friend and colleague, nothing more. That's why, when I looked at him, *really* took the time to look at him and see what it was that had captured Hudson's attention, I was shocked.

How had I never noticed how vibrant blue his eyes were or the freckles that were sprinkled delicately across his nose? Had I ever paid attention to the way his jaw curved or how soft his hair looked? My hand lifted as if to run through it and test its silkiness, but I caught myself and drew my hand into a fist at my side.

What the hell was happening to me? Not only had I reacted strongly to a complete stranger, but now I was noticing things about my coworker that I had no business noticing. Not to mention, both things had happened within mere seconds of each other.

I somehow made it through the weighty introduction to Hudson, staring at my hand in disbelief when he shook it and a tremor of electricity traveled up the length of my arm. In that moment, I felt aroused and excited and more alive than I could remember in years. Then, just as quickly, those feelings turned to guilt and sadness and I felt the hollow ache that was my constant companion. My chest suddenly became tight and I felt like I couldn't breathe so I made an excuse about needing to talk to the mayor and got out of there as quickly as I could without attracting too much attention.

There were people milling about everywhere and I pasted a smile on my face as I brushed past them and made a beeline for the stairwell. I climbed the stairs quickly, opening the door at the top and stepping out on the building's rooftop. I'd first gone up there during my walk-through of the building as a potential site for the new center and had immediately fallen in love with it.

Since we'd made the move to the new building, I'd taken to going up there whenever I needed an escape. I spent my entire day trying to meet the demands of everyone around me and once in a while, I just needed a few moments to myself. I had never needed it more than I did right then. The tightness in my chest slowly began to ease and I made my way over to the half wall that ran the perimeter of the building and sat down, leaning my back against the higher corner pieces.

I wasn't sure how long I sat there until a sound from the sidewalk below caught my attention and I looked down. With the added security lights Morgan Greene had installed around the new center, I was able to make out the lone figure as he rushed out of the front door. My body hummed with an unexplained familiarity and I knew that I was watching Hudson as he leaned against the wall as if he were trying to catch his breath.

Unable to look away, I'd continued to watch him as he stood and began walking towards the parking lot and climbed into his SUV. It wasn't until his tail lights had completely disappeared that I was able to release the breath that I hadn't even been aware I'd been holding.

I'd remained on the roof awhile longer, completely bewildered by the events of the night. When I'd been standing in front of Hudson and Isaac, I'd wanted nothing more than to escape and for things to go back to the way they were supposed to be. I should have felt relieved to see him go. So, then why did it feel as if I'd missed out on something important?

Eventually, I'd made my way back down to the party and forced a smile on my face as I showed the various politicians and media personnel around the new center. I'd done my best to stay away from Isaac the rest of that evening and had in fact been avoiding him at work ever since, but I knew I couldn't ignore him forever. I owed it to the center's teens to put my own feelings aside, no matter how bizarre they might have been, and focus on what was best for them.

That was why I'd sought Isaac out and asked him to meet with me to go over the ideas I had for the community service project. I'd felt guilty when he asked if he'd done something wrong which had caused me to avoid him, and, I realized I'd been acting like an immature asshole. Isaac was my friend and we'd worked together for years. I just needed to find the simple, easygoing friendship we usually shared and ignore the stirring in my gut that had started to occur whenever he focused his attention on me.

Unfortunately, while that had sounded good in my head, it was actually much harder to put into practice once Isaac followed me into my office. All I could think about was how we were all alone in there, how good he smelled and the fact that I wanted to taste his full bottom lip that pushed out into an adorable pout. *What the hell is wrong with me?* I rarely took notice of that sort of thing anymore, especially not with someone I worked closely with every day.

Shaking my head to clear it, I'd pushed my inappropriate thoughts aside and refocused my attention on the project. It wasn't hard to get caught up in the plan though once Isaac showed his enthusiasm, and before I knew it, we were bouncing ideas off each other and making lists of how we were going to make them into reality. The experience reminded me of how well Isaac and I had always worked together and I felt myself relaxing and a genuine smile spreading across my face.

We'd shared a smile when Allison had told us that someone was there for the therapist position and it seemed as if everything was finally getting back on track. That was until the person stepped into my office and I found myself staring into the warm brown eyes of the man who had sent my world spiraling out of control in the first place.

I'd listened as he'd explained that he was a therapist and I was stunned when he stated that he wanted to work at the center free of charge. My head spun at the idea of what this would mean for the kids; the ways that this could help them get further along in their journey towards the happy and fulfilling lives they all deserved.

I'd sifted through the stack of diplomas, references and awards he had in his file and I had to admit that I was very impressed. Dr. Hudson Westley was obviously much more than a handsome face. He was also highly educated and revered by his colleagues and friends. When I'd seen the glowing recommendations written by Lachlan and Rylie, my mind had been made up.

Then Hudson had made the comment about wanting both Isaac and me to know that he was single and I'd seen the same look of interest in his eyes that I saw when we first met. I watched as he and Isaac exchanged a look and the heat between them was palpable. My cock began to stir as I envisioned the two of them kissing, which then switched to an image of me sandwiched between the two of them as they kissed their way down the length of my neck, hands and mouths everywhere, all at once.

Startled by the direction my thoughts had taken, I jumped to my feet and thrust my hand out for Hudson to shake, welcoming him to the staff. I knew my words and actions had been abrupt, but I needed to end the meeting and get them out of my office. Hudson had slid his large hand around my own and I'd felt the same sharp surge of electricity that I'd felt the last time we'd touched and I pulled back, cursing my body and my thoughts for betraying me. How could I be feeling these things and why were my reactions the same for both of the men standing in front of me?

I'd tried my best to dive back into my work and had been somewhat successful until the sound of the kids had distracted me. After that, it had been a lost cause. No matter how hard I tried to shut them out, my thoughts always returned to Isaac and Hudson and those damn images of the three of us together that refused to give me peace.

I rubbed at my tired eyes and glanced at my watch, surprised to see how late it had gotten. As I'd been sitting there, lost in my thoughts, the hours had slowly drifted away. With a sigh, I shut off my computer and pushed my chair from my desk. My back ached from sitting hunched over my desk for too long and I decided that a run was what I needed to ease the tension in my body and to clear my head.

Grabbing my car keys and the beat-up leather briefcase that went everywhere with me, I made my way down the hallway, relieved when I saw the light off in Isaac's office which told me that he'd already left for the evening. I found myself wondering where he lived, what his home looked like and if it was as warm and cheerful as the man who lived there.

I drove to my house quickly and changed into my running gear then set off out the door, trying to ignore the empty look of the place with its stark white walls and minimal furniture and noting the difference between my place and what I had envisioned Isaac's home to look like.

I ran for nearly an hour, letting everything else go as I concentrated on the steady thumping of my feet as they hit the pavement. I'd always loved running and found it very therapeutic when my mind got too full of stuff. Feeling more centered, I returned home and took a quick shower, scrubbing the sweat from my body and letting the hot water relax my tired muscles.

I finished my shower and began toweling off as I tried to remember if I had anything in my kitchen to eat, but then a yawn hit me and I decided I didn't have the energy to mess with cooking. I brushed my teeth then walked to my room and pulled the covers back from the bed. I climbed between the sheets without bothering to put anything on and reached for my phone, putting it on the charger and setting the alarm for six a.m.

Then, I reached for the framed photo I kept next to my bed and pulled it towards me. I settled against the pillows as my finger traced the figure in the picture. I said a few words, as I did every night, and then laid the photo next to me on the pillow and turned on my side to face it as I drifted off to sleep.

CHAPTER
Four

Isaac

I STARED OUT THE WINDOW, MY FAVORITE SONG PLAYING through my earbuds, as I rode the train to work. My mind began to wander and I wasn't surprised at all with where it ended up. It was the same place my thoughts always went these days—Matt and Hudson.

My mind had been swirling ever since Hudson had shown up at the center, looking to volunteer. I was confident that his working there would be a good thing for the kids, but I'd wondered what it would mean for Matt and me. Hudson had boldly stated that he wanted us both to know he was single, but what did that mean? He'd shown interest in both of us, but did he want to date each of us before choosing which one he liked best?

I wasn't sure how I felt about that. On one hand, I was very flattered that he would show any interest in me at all. After all, Hudson was a gorgeous, intelligent, and successful doctor; what could someone like me possibly have to offer him? On the other hand, I didn't particularly like the idea of him and Matt going off together. The question was, was it because I wanted Hudson for myself or because of my feelings for Matt? The whole thing was very confusing and I never seemed to be able to come up with an answer.

Hudson had been working at the center for a couple of weeks and already he was having a positive impact on those around him. The kids were wary of him when we first introduced him to the group and told them that he was there to offer counseling. Most of them shied away from adults in general, but particularly those who wanted to pry into their pasts. I understood their reluctance to talk about it. Sometimes it was just easier to push the painful things that had happened out of your mind and try to move on.

I'd found myself observing Hudson as he interacted with the kids and I'd been amazed at his gentle, laid-back attitude. Instead of scheduling times to meet with each teen, he'd simply hung a dry-erase calendar on his office door, giving them the choice of when or if they wanted to talk with him.

Hudson seemed happy enough just hanging out with them, offering to help with their homework and playing basketball with them in the center's gymnasium. He joked around with them and I found myself smiling when I'd hear his boisterous laugh ringing out. It didn't take long before the kids were teasing him back and I noticed as names slowly began to appear on his calendar.

The kids weren't the only ones being affected by Hudson's presence though. I'd caught Matt staring at the handsome man on several occasions when he didn't know I was watching. At first his looks were as wary as the kids' and I knew that he was watching how things unfolded, making sure he'd made the right decision for the teens in his care. As he saw them opening up to Hudson, the look in Matt's eyes began to change to one of appreciation.

Sometimes though, I would catch a glimpse of something more, something that looked a lot like longing. I'd caught Matt staring at me a few times as well and I would feel a strange stirring in my chest when that happened. He always turned away quickly though, leaving me to wonder what he'd been thinking.

I found myself acting differently too on the days when I knew Hudson would be working at the center. I always enjoyed my job, but those particular days, I felt myself smiling more and anxiously watching the clock. I liked the fact that Hudson always took the time to stop by my office and say hello and ask how my day was. He flirted with me occasionally, but I never managed more than a few mumbled words as I felt my face heat up. I'd never had anyone show an interest in me before and I was quickly becoming addicted to the way he would look at me as if I were the only person in the room.

The train came to a stop and I looked out the window, my forehead wrinkling when I saw it had begun to rain. The forecast hadn't shown any rain and I blamed our local meteorologist for my lack of an umbrella. I stood, pulling my earbuds out and tucked them and my phone into my pocket then lifted the hood of my jacket over my head trying to protect myself as much as possible. I walked as quickly as I could to the center, but the rain came down in thick sheets and I was soaking wet by the time I reached the front door.

"Rough morning?" Allison asked, giving me a sympathetic look.

"It was fine until I got off the train. I didn't know it was supposed to rain," I explained as water dripped from my hair. I was sure I looked like a drowned rat.

"Why don't you go get a change of clothes from the free store? Get into something dry and I'll bring you your coffee and the breakfast Gladys left for you." I managed to thank her as a shiver wracked my body, then walked down the hallway to where the free store was located.

The store had been Kathy Greene's idea. She'd contacted many of the local churches and schools, asking them to set up boxes at their locations where people could donate new or gently used clothing and various toiletries. The response had been tremendous and donations continued to pour in more quickly than we could give them away. Many of the kids at the center arrived with only the clothes on their backs and so they'd been thrilled when the store opened and they could pick out clothing for themselves.

I sorted through the piles of clothes and finally found a pair of socks, jeans, and a shirt I thought would fit me then grabbed a small bath towel and headed back to my office. I was thankful to have dry clothes to put on, but I wouldn't take anything away from the kids so I made a mental note to wash and return the clothes to the store the next day.

I shut my office door behind me and pulled my wet clothes off. Standing in just my boxer briefs, my teeth began to chatter and I quickly toweled the worst of the water from my hair then rubbed the towel vigorously over my body, hoping the friction would warm it. I'd just picked up the shirt when I heard the door open behind me and I cursed when I realized I'd forgotten to lock it. I turned around, ready to apologize to Allison for putting her in an embarrassing situation, but the words died on my lips as I saw it wasn't her in the doorway.

Matt's mouth hung open as he stood there, staring at me and he reached out and gripped the frame of the door with his hand. I felt frozen in place as his eyes traveled over my body, and I swear, I felt it as surely as if he'd reached out and touched me with his hands. I shivered again, but that time it had nothing to do with my being cold. In fact, I suddenly felt warm all over and I lowered the shirt in front of my groin when my cock began to stir. Matt's eyes narrowed as they caught the movement and I was mortified that he'd noticed the physical reaction I was having to him.

"I got…I got caught in the rain. I was just changing," I stammered.

"I'll, uh, leave you to it," Matt mumbled. His eyes swept over me once more and his tongue darted out, wetting his lips before he finally stepped back, shutting the door behind him.

I sagged against my desk and laid my palm against my chest, feeling my heart beat wildly beneath my rib cage. *What the hell just happened?* I recognized the look of desire on his face, but I never thought Matt would direct that kind of heated look my way.

I tamped down my excitement as much as possible, reminding myself that Matt had always seen me as a friend and nothing more. There was no point in getting my hopes up. The more my heart rate slowed the more I was able to convince myself that I'd imagined the whole thing. I quickly got dressed, sighing when I slipped the dry pair of socks on over my cold toes and placed my shoes next to the heater to dry.

Allison brought me my coffee and breakfast and I thanked her, although I knew I wouldn't touch it. My stomach was too tied up in knots to handle food at the moment. I was tempted to go find Matt and ask him why he'd stopped by my office to begin with, but I was afraid he'd be able to see my desire too clearly on my face. I didn't want to make things any more awkward between us, so I sat at my desk and dove into my work instead.

Sometime later, there was a knock on my door which made me jump and I glanced up as it swung open. Hudson stood there, his large frame taking up most of the doorway and I glanced at the time on my computer, surprised to see how late it was. I'd worked straight through the entire day, not even stopping for lunch or dinner and my stomach let out an embarrassing rumble in protest. Hudson's deep laugh had me glancing back at him.

"Are you hungry?" he asked. His question was simple enough, but the way he was looking at me had me thinking he was talking about more than just food. I felt my skin heat up under his watchful gaze, but I didn't look away and I saw his lips turn up, obviously pleased.

"Uh, yeah, I guess so. I was so busy, I must've lost track of time," I told him.

"Well, I'm finished for the day and was going to grab a bite to eat somewhere. Would you care to join me?" Hudson must have seen the surprise on my face. "It's just food, Isaac. I'd like to get to know you better," he said sincerely.

"You would? I mean…sure," I squeaked out. My face felt like it was on fire and I half expected him to change his mind, but he just smiled at me. I was thrilled to spend more time with him and looked forward to getting to know him better as well.

He waited while I shut my computer down and straightened my desk and then I stood and made my way over to him. My pulse began to race when instead of backing out into the hallway as I'd expected, he took a step into my office. He moved close enough that I could feel the heat of his body emanating through the thin material of his dress shirt and the scent of his cologne, something woodsy with a hint of spice, filled my senses and made my head spin. He stared down at me and I had to tilt my head back to look at him, losing myself in his soulful brown eyes. The rich timber of his voice resonated through me when he spoke.

"You might want to get some shoes on, seeing as most restaurants require them." It took me a moment for his words to catch up, but then my eyes grew wide and I felt a puff of minty air hit my lips as he laughed.

"Oh yeah, I suppose so," I said with a nervous laugh of my own. Something about Hudson always seemed to leave me feeling off balance, but surprisingly, it wasn't an unpleasant feeling at all.

I grabbed my shoes, which luckily had dried from the rain that morning and slipped them on before hitting the light switch on my way out the door. Hudson was waiting for me in the hallway and he looked at me curiously.

"What do you think about inviting Matt to come with us?" he asked.

"Sure! The more the merrier," I answered. Hudson laughed at that and I smiled back at him, not quite understanding what was so funny.

We walked to the end of the hall where Matt's door was standing open. His head was bent as he signed some papers. He looked up when Hudson knocked on his door, but he didn't say a word as his eyes darted back and forth between the two of us, curiously.

"We decided to go out and get something to eat and we wondered if you'd care to join us," Hudson explained.

"You two are going out together?" Matt asked, his eyes narrowing slightly.

"Yes, but we'd like it if you came too," I assured him. His eyes met mine and I struggled to read the various emotions I saw there before he hid them once again. He was way too good at that and it was starting to frustrate me.

"Thank you for asking, but I still have a lot of work to do before I can get out of here," Matt replied.

"Is there anything I can help with so you can get done sooner?" I offered.

"No, thank you, Isaac. You guys go and have a good time." I wanted to argue, but I could hear the finality in his words and I saw the rigid set to his jaw. Hudson watched Matt quietly for a few seconds, a curious expression on his face, but then he nodded.

"Maybe next time, then," he said.

Matt didn't answer, but he continued to watch us as we turned to leave. I glanced one last time over my shoulder and felt my heart squeeze in my chest when I saw Matt looking at us with a mixture of sadness and resignation. I almost turned back, but he looked down, directing his attention back on his work.

"Don't worry. We'll keep working on him," Hudson whispered as we made our way down the quiet hallway. I looked up at him questioningly, but he just smiled and placed his hand on the small of my back as he led me out the front door and across the parking lot to his car.

I felt a little unsure when I saw the large black SUV, but I climbed in when he opened the door for me. I glanced around, taking in the creamy leather seats and the sleek interior as I waited for Hudson to make his way around to the driver's side. I suddenly felt completely out of my league and I wondered what in the world I was doing there.

"You ready?" Hudson asked as he slid into his seat and I wanted to ask him what exactly I should be ready for. His warm eyes met mine and when he smiled, I suddenly realized that I didn't care.

"Yeah, I'm ready," I whispered. I didn't know what Hudson wanted with me or why, but I was going to enjoy finding out.

CHAPTER
Five

Hudson

I SMILED OVER AT ISAAC SITTING IN THE PASSENGER SEAT. THE lights of the dash showed off the soft curve of his jaw and the full bottom lip that lifted when he smiled back at me. His wide blue eyes were framed with long lashes that brushed his cheeks whenever he blinked. *God, he is spectacular.*

I felt my cock twitch in my pants and I had to fight the urge to reach for him and drag him to me so I could feel his lips pressed to mine. I'd spent many nights dreaming of that mouth and all the things I wanted to do to it, but I would have to be careful. The last thing I wanted to do was push him too far or scare him off.

"How does a big, juicy burger sound?" I asked as I pulled out of the parking lot and onto the road.

"That sounds perfect," he answered happily.

It didn't take long to get to the restaurant and I pulled into an open spot and parked my SUV. Isaac's brows furrowed as he peered out the window at the building and his shoulders suddenly looked tense.

"Is something wrong? Do you not like this place?" I asked him.

"No, it's not that. I've never been here before, but I'm sure it's good," he said. He turned his head to face me and I hated the nervous look in his eyes. I didn't even stop to think before I reached over and covered his hands which were folded in his lap. Both of his hands fit neatly in one of mine and I was surprised at how protective of him that made me feel. Isaac's eyes shot down to our joined hands and stayed there as he continued.

"I just wasn't expecting a place like this and I'm not sure that I can afford it," he admitted shyly. I squeezed his hands gently and he looked up at me.

"It was my idea to ask you to dinner so I fully intended on it being my treat, but we can go somewhere else if it makes you uncomfortable," I assured him.

I didn't really care where we ate as long as I got to spend time with the young man beside me. The more time I spent with Isaac, the more I liked what I saw and I wanted to continue getting to know him. He stared at me for several seconds and then nodded his head once.

"No, this place is fine. Thank you." A small smile graced his lips and I hoped that by the end of the night, I would know what those lips tasted like. I reached for the handle on my door and opened it, letting the cool night air clear my head before I could do anything stupid.

We made our way into the restaurant and were quickly shown to a table. Isaac picked up the menu and began studying it while I took the opportunity to study him. He was dressed in a bright blue polo shirt which matched his eyes perfectly. The longer hair on top of his head flopped down over his forehead in a sexy way. My eyes traveled over his face, the small nose dotted with freckles and the delicate cheekbones that most supermodels would kill for, to his full lips which had turned up into a crooked grin as I watched. My eyes darted to his and I felt my face growing hot as I realized I'd been caught staring.

"Hudson, do you know what you want?" I wanted to tell him that yes, I definitely knew what I wanted and it had nothing to do with the choices on the menu, but then I heard a small giggle and I turned my head to find our waitress staring down at me. *How long have they been trying to get my attention?*

"Oh, yes! I'll have the bacon cheeseburger with everything, fries, and a Coke," I said, handing my menu to the waitress then looked at Isaac as he ordered the same. The waitress took his menu and walked away.

"Tell me about yourself, Isaac," I urged. He seemed a little uneasy as he shrugged his shoulders.

"There's really not a lot to tell. What would you like to know?" he asked.

"Let's start with something simple. Do you like working at Agape House?" I already knew that he did, but I could tell he was nervous and I wanted to put him at ease by talking about something he enjoyed. It worked too because his face lit up and I could hear the happiness in his voice as he described his work at the center. It was obvious that he loved interacting with the teens and helping them create a better life than the one they'd been given.

"It's an amazing place," I agreed. "What made you want to work there?" He paused as the waitress came back and set our drinks in front of us. After she walked away again, he answered and his words took on a more guarded tone.

"I used to be one of the teens that lived at the center," he told me. The same protective feeling I'd experienced in the car came over me again, but much stronger that time, and I had to fight to school my features so he wouldn't see my distress. I knew that there was only one reason he would've ended up living at the center and that was if something bad had happened to him. The thought of anyone causing him pain, either physically or emotionally, had my gut churning, but I could tell by the way his jaw was clenched that it was not a subject he wanted to talk about.

"When did you start working there?" I saw his shoulders relax when he realized I wasn't going to push.

"I'd been living there about a year and had just graduated. I'd been making myself sick with worry about where I would go and how I would live once I turned eighteen. I had no job prospects, nothing higher than a high school diploma and soon I wouldn't even have an address to put on applications. I knew Matt wouldn't just turn me out on the street, but I felt guilty taking a spot since he would lose his government funding for me as soon as I aged out of the system." Isaac's mouth lifted in a small smile and he got a faraway look in his eyes.

"One day, Matt came to me and offered me a job working the front desk. He said with my organizational skills and my friendly attitude that I was the perfect person for the job. He even insisted that I stay at the center until I could afford a place of my own. I'd spent months feeling as if my world were about to fall apart and in one moment, Matt had fixed everything." Isaac's eyes met mine and in his gaze, I could see all of the admiration he had for the other man.

"You care about Matt a lot." It was a statement, not a question because the answer was written clearly across his face.

"Of course, I do. He's my friend and he's helped me in ways that I could never repay," Isaac told me. I knew that he was being sincere, but I could also tell there was more to it than just that. I let it go though because our food arrived just then.

"Oh my God! This is so good," Isaac moaned as he took the first bite of his burger and my eyes flew to his face. He took another bite and I watched in fascination as his eyes practically rolled to the back of his head and I couldn't help but wonder if that's what he would look and sound like during sex.

"I'm glad you're enjoying that," I said. My voice sounding strained to my own ears.

"It's delicious," Isaac said. His tongue darted out, catching the bit of mayonnaise that had been lingering at the corner of his mouth and I was glad I was sitting as my dick became rock-hard. Did he have any idea what he was doing to me? The innocent smile he gave me as he dipped a fry in some ketchup told me that he hadn't done it on purpose.

"Aren't you going to eat?" he asked. I huffed out a laugh and shook my head as I picked up my burger. Isaac intentionally being seductive would be dangerous to my self-control. Isaac being seductive without even realizing it, was downright lethal.

We talked some more as we ate, getting to know each other and I found myself really enjoying Isaac's company. He was intelligent and quick-witted and before I knew it, a whole hour had passed. I paid the bill and then we headed back out to the parking lot.

"Thank you. That was the best burger I've ever had," Isaac said as we climbed in the car.

"You're welcome. I'm glad you agreed to come with me. I liked getting to know you better," I told him.

"I liked that too," he answered with a shy smile.

We were quiet most of the way to his place other than when he'd speak up to give me directions. I spent that time trying to figure out what I wanted to say to him. How could I explain what I wanted without scaring him off? I still hadn't decided when I pulled up alongside the curb outside his apartment. I put the car in park, but left the engine running and turned to face him, the soft lights of the dash illuminating his face.

"I had fun tonight and I'd really like to do it again," I told him. He smiled happily so I continued, cautiously. "Maybe next time we can convince Matt to join us," I suggested. Isaac's smile dimmed just a bit and I was sure he'd reached the wrong conclusion.

"Oh, sure. That would be fun. Matt needs to get out with friends more. I worry that he works too hard," he rattled. He reached for the door handle and I could tell he was about to make his escape so I reached over and grabbed his hand. His eyes shot to mine, startled.

"I don't want to hang out just as friends. I'm attracted to you and I'm attracted to Matt as well," I told him, laying it all out on the line. I watched him closely for a reaction and wasn't surprised when I saw first shock and then confusion flitting across his face.

"So, you want to date us both at the same time until you decide which one you like best?" he asked.

"No, that's not quite what I want," I answered.

"I don't understand. What is it you want exactly, Hudson?" His voice was full of confusion so I took both of his hands in mine and began rubbing soothing circles over them with my thumbs.

"Remember the night we met?" I waited until he nodded his head yes. "What did you feel that night?"

"I don't know what you mean," he responded warily.

"Come on, Isaac. I know you felt it, too. What did you feel when you and I looked at each other then, or the first time we touched. What are you feeling right now?" I pressed. His eyelids lowered as he stared in my eyes and I knew he was experiencing the same thing I was.

"Like electricity is shooting through my veins," he answered, his voice taking on a husky quality.

"Exactly. It's an inexplicable chemistry that I've never experienced with anyone else...except Matt," I stated. Isaac swallowed and his mouth dropped open like he wanted to say something, but no words came out.

"I've seen the way you look at Matt when you think no one is watching and I recognize the longing in your eyes. You want him, don't you?" Isaac tried to look away, but I reached up and gripped his chin gently with my thumb and index finger, forcing him to keep eye contact.

"Yes," he finally admitted. "But..." I could see all the things he wanted to say, but couldn't find the words for.

"But you want me, too," I supplied knowingly. My heart soared when he nodded his head, confirming my suspicions. "It's okay, Isaac. I feel the exact same way and believe me, it took me by surprise too."

"Then why do you seem so calm about it?" he demanded. "And what do you mean it's okay? How could it possibly be okay that we like each other when we want Matt too?"

"This is uncharted territory for me too, but I recognized what was happening and have had more time to think about it. Besides, I'm more familiar with this kind of thing. A patient of mine was involved in a similar situation and I always found the dynamics of their triad intriguing," I told him.

"I have no idea what you're talking about. What situation and what is a triad?" Isaac nearly screeched. I had to fight not to let him see my amusement at the panicked look on his face.

"A triad is when three people find themselves attracted to each other and they decide to have a relationship. Some people also refer to it as a throuple or ménage relationship." I let go of his chin and lowered my hand back to his as I let my words sink in. I could tell the moment they did because his eyes widened.

"You mean, you want to date both of us together instead of individually?" he reiterated slowly.

"I've thought a lot about it and I like both of you equally, although, I've gotten to know you better, but I'm going to work on getting Matt to open up more. He's a tough nut to crack," I mused. "So, to answer your question, I'm not suggesting we jump into a relationship or anything, but this kind of overwhelming chemistry doesn't come along every day, at least not for me. I think we owe it to ourselves to figure out where it could lead," I explained. He stared at me for several long moments and I found myself holding my breath.

"There are a couple of flaws to your thinking," Isaac finally said. I was so relieved that he hadn't already run screaming from the car that I was sure I could handle whatever he was about to say.

"Tell me," I coaxed.

"I'm pretty sure Matt is attracted to you, but he's never seen me as more than a friend. Believe me, I've had a crush on him for years and he's never shown any sign that he felt the same way about me," he said.

"I've seen the way he looks at you, Isaac. He tracks your every move as you do things around the center," I informed him. Isaac's eyes nearly popped out of his head.

"He does?" he asked incredulously.

"Yes, he does," I chuckled.

"Okay, but that still leaves the other problem," he said in a serious tone.

"And what is that?" I asked.

"In all the years I've known Matt, I've never seen him date. In fact, I've never seen him even show an interest in anyone until you came along," he stated. I pursed my lips as I looked at him, taking his words into consideration.

"What do you want, Isaac?" I asked him, my tone and question both serious.

"I'd like to spend more time with you and, of course, I would love it if Matt showed an interest in me," he answered shyly, still looking as if he thought that was impossible.

"I want more time with you, too," I told him, reaching up to run my finger over the edge of his jaw. His skin was smooth, with just the barest hint of stubble along his jawline.

His smile was immediate and it made my heart race. Without any further thought, I slid my hand around the back of Isaac's neck and pulled him towards me, covering his lips with my own. I slid my hand up into his hair, finding it just as soft and silky as I had imagined, and I swallowed his gasp when my tongue dipped inside his mouth to taste him. His tongue sought out mine, timidly at first, but soon we were caught up in a kiss so passionate that my head began to spin. I pulled back when my lungs began to burn with the need for air and I smiled when Isaac let out a whimper of frustration.

"Don't worry. I plan on doing a lot more of that, but for now, I think we need to slow things down. I've thrown a lot at you. You need to take some time and really think about everything we've talked about," I told him gently.

"You're right," he said with a nod, but I moaned when he reached down to adjust himself. My mouth watered at the thought of his hard cock and I almost told him to forget everything I'd just said, but then he continued. "I do need some time to think, although I usually go with my gut in most circumstances."

Everything in me wanted to push and find out what his gut was telling him about the situation we were in, but I owed it to him to give him time to form a decision on his own without any added pressure from me. As much as I wanted him and Matt, I was just going to have to be patient.

"Isaac, wait," I said as he reached for the door handle. His head turned and he looked at me expectantly. "I just wanted to be very clear about something so there's no confusion. Regardless of Matt's decision, I still would like to continue seeing you."

"You would?" The surprise in his voice made my heart hurt. Did he really not know how incredible he was? I didn't know him all that well yet, but already, I knew that any man would be lucky to be able to date him.

"I would," I whispered as I cupped the side of his face and leaned towards him for another kiss. This one was softer, gentler, but I hoped it proved to him how sincere I was.

Isaac was smiling as he pulled away and opened the door. I watched as he got out and climbed the steps to his apartment, making it safely inside. As I started to drive away, I caught my reflection in the rearview mirror and I wasn't surprised to find a wide smile across my face. I seemed to be doing that a lot lately, ever since I'd met those two men. I was fairly certain what Isaac's decision would be. The question was, how were we going to convince the very guarded Matt to give us a chance?

CHAPTER
Six

Matt

I READ OVER THE EMAIL THAT HAD BEEN SENT TO ME FOR THE fourth time, but I still wasn't able to comprehend what it entailed. I leaned my elbows against my desk and rubbed at my eyes. They felt itchy and my head had begun to pound which were both products of a long night with little to no sleep.

I'd gone home shortly after Isaac and Hudson had left Agape House, hoping to get a good night's sleep. Instead, I'd spent hours tossing and turning, my head filled with images of what the two of them might be doing. Where had they gone to eat? What had they talked about? Was it a date? Had they kissed? Those questions and more ran on an endless loop through my head, ensuring that I had a long and restless night.

I knew I had no one but myself to blame for the questions I had.

If only I'd taken them up on their invitation to join them, I would know exactly what had happened and I wouldn't have been left wondering. But I hadn't gone, I'd held back just as I always did. I let out a long sigh and pushed my chair away from my desk, checking the time on my watch. It was getting late and as much as I would've liked to call it a day, I convinced myself to stay and get a little more work done instead. First, I needed a cup of coffee though.

I walked out of my office and down the hallway towards the kitchen, but my footsteps slowed when I heard a familiar voice coming from Isaac's office. The door was ajar and I peered around the corner, holding my breath as I saw Hudson throw his head back, laughing at something Isaac had just said. His laugh was deep and rang out across the room and I found myself smiling at the sound of it.

Feeling weird about spying on my friends, I turned to leave when suddenly the mood between them changed. I felt it as surely as if I'd been standing between them and I found myself unable to move as the air became thick with sexual tension. Hudson placed his large hands on either side of Isaac's waist as he whispered something that I couldn't make out and I watched as Isaac's hands landed on Hudson's chest, his fingers curling in on the well-developed pectoral muscles.

Hudson smiled down at Isaac and then he lowered his head and let his tongue trace the younger man's bottom lip. My face felt flushed and my skin stretched too tight as I observed the two of them together. The differences in their height and stature just served to make their passionate embrace even hotter. Hudson towered over Isaac's slight frame, but instead of appearing overbearing, his posture seemed protective of the smaller man, which had me feeling relieved and turned on all at the same time.

Their kiss became more heated and I followed Hudson's movements as his hands reached down to cup Isaac's pert ass. Isaac's soft whimper had my eyes darting back up to their faces and my heart nearly stopped when I found Hudson's eyes locked on me. His eyes wandered down over me and I knew the moment he saw the obvious bulge in my pants because his eyes widened slightly. Not breaking their kiss, he lifted his right hand from Isaac's waist and crooked his index finger at me in a come-hither motion. I knew exactly what kind of invitation he was extending and God help me, I wanted to accept.

That jarring thought was what finally got me to move, but instead of moving towards the two men, I turned on my heel and ran down the hallway. Excitement and guilt battled for space inside my head as I made my way to the stairwell and raced up the steps, not stopping until I reached the top. I flung the door open and stumbled out onto the roof of the building, gasping for air. I bent down and placed my hands on my knees as I willed my heart to quit racing.

After a few moments, I stood and made my way over to the half wall that ran the perimeter of the roof and sat along its edge. I looked up at the night sky, the stars glittering in the distance when I felt a gentle breeze across my face. I closed my eyes and swallowed hard as I tried to make sense of all the emotions that were running through me.

My pulse picked up speed as I pictured the scene I had just witnessed. I'd been surprised at first that I'd wanted to take Hudson up on his invitation, but more surprising was how natural the idea seemed to me the more I thought about it. I'd never considered being with two men at once, but lately that's all I'd been able to think about and somehow, it made sense when I thought about being with those two men in particular.

Watching the two of them, I'd felt excited and more *alive* than I'd felt in years. Sure, I'd had occasional hookups, but those were more about the physical act of getting off than forming any real attachment to another person. There were no emotions involved in those situations. I already knew that there was no way I would be able to do anything with the two men downstairs and keep myself completely unattached. They were good men, friends of mine. Besides that, we worked together. I was already more emotionally involved with them than I usually allowed myself to be and that was part of why I'd run. The other part was the guilt I'd been feeling ever since I'd found myself attracted to the two men.

My thoughts turned to Sean, as they always did, and I felt the aching loneliness that often-accompanied thoughts of him. Sean had been my first real friend, my first love, hell, he'd been my first everything. Losing him had been the single hardest thing I'd ever been through. In my head, I knew he wouldn't want me to be lonely, but it was my heart that struggled with the guilt of moving on, of letting go. Just the thought had the backs of my eyes burning and I reached up, rubbing my hands over them.

Another breeze blew over me, sweeping my hair back off my forehead and drying my eyes. With it came a sense of peace and I breathed in deeply, letting it calm my frayed nerves. The truth of the matter was that I was lonely. I'd been lonely for so long that somewhere along the way, it had become my new normal and I'd clung to it, as if the loneliness itself were my companion.

I was envious of people like Caleb and Carter Greene who had found their soulmates and were living the life that I'd dreamed of having at one time. Sean had taken that dream with him though and so I'd opened Agape House, throwing myself into my work and never letting anyone get too close.

The feelings that Hudson and Isaac had evoked in me scared me at first. It had been so long since I'd really felt anything at all that it had come as a shock to find myself wanting not just one, but two men. It was a reminder that as much as I loved my job and the kids I cared for, it wasn't enough to hold the loneliness at bay.

When I'd sent Isaac and Hudson off the night before without me, I'd been torn between wishing I'd gone with them and hoping that the two of them would hit it off so I'd be free to move past whatever strange thoughts I'd been having and get back to my usual routine. Seeing them wrapped in each other's arms in Isaac's office, I'd thought that I was going to get the second option, but then Hudson had crooked his finger at me, changing everything.

I'd understood in an instant what that gesture meant and it had terrified me because of how badly I'd wanted to say yes. So, I'd run. *Would it have been that bad to say yes, though?* I knew that most people wouldn't understand and some would have problems with three men getting involved with each other, but none of that bothered me. Most of the people I interacted with on a daily basis were very open-minded. Even if they weren't, I knew that would be their problem, not mine.

Hudson and Isaac were both incredibly kind and handsome and my only concern was whether or not I was ready. I knew I needed more in my life than just work, I *wanted* more than that, but was I strong enough to put my heart out there and take a chance again? *"How will you know if you don't try?"*

I sighed as I stood up, my body feeling drained from the tidal wave of emotions and the lack of sleep the night before. I made my way back down the steps, deciding to forego the coffee and go home instead. I slowed my pace as I neared Isaac's office, wondering what I might find in there, but the light was off and there was no sign of him. My shoulders sagged and I tried to tell myself I was relieved, but the heaviness in my heart told me that it was disappointment I was feeling.

I grabbed my keys and my leather briefcase and then I headed back down the hallway, calling out my goodbyes to a couple of the kids on my way out the door. I pulled out of the parking lot and turned in the direction of home, but as I drove down the familiar roads, I thought about what waited for me there; nothing but a frozen dinner and my TV for company. Suddenly home was the last place I wanted to be.

Making a quick decision, I turned the car around and began heading in the opposite direction. My palms were slick with sweat and my heart was beating furiously as I neared my destination. It shouldn't be a big deal to go out, especially when I'd been invited numerous times, but I rarely went anywhere besides work and home and I felt a little anxious about going to a new place. I needed to try though, I reminded myself. It was time to start making some changes and what easier way to start than with dinner and some familiar faces?

I'd heard how popular the place was, but I was surprised at how many cars were in the lot and I nearly turned the car around and left. My grip on the steering wheel had my knuckles turning white and I had to take a few deep, cleansing breaths before I was able to convince myself to step out of the car. I opened the front door and my eyes scanned the restaurant. Nearly every table was full and I realized somewhat embarrassedly that I should've probably called ahead for a reservation.

I turned to leave, proud of myself for at least trying when I was stopped by someone calling my name. I looked over my shoulder and saw Giovanni Romero making his way between the crowded tables, a giant grin on his face. Giovanni and his husband, Caleb, owned the restaurant I was standing in and both had played a very important role in getting the new Agape House up and running.

Caleb's family had been longtime volunteers at the center and over the years had become friends of mine. They'd asked me several times to stop in and have dinner, but I'd always assumed they were asking just to be polite. Seeing Giovanni's surprise and happiness at my being there made me feel badly that I'd waited so long to take them up on the offer.

"Matt! I'm so glad you're here," he exclaimed, shaking my hand.

"Umm, thanks, but I was just getting ready to leave," I told him, gesturing over my shoulder with my thumb.

"Leave? Why?" Giovanni's face fell as he looked at me.

"I didn't realize...I don't have a reservation," I rushed to explain, stumbling over my words. I watched as his face broke out into a big smile.

"You don't need a reservation, Matt. Friends and family never need a reservation. Come on," he said. I started to object, but he was already walking away, giving me no choice but to follow him.

"Caleb will be so excited that you're here." He smiled at me as we reached a swinging door at the back of the restaurant and pushed it open. I stepped into the kitchen and my senses were immediately assaulted with the wonderful aroma of oregano and garlic cooking in melted butter. Caleb was standing in front of a huge stove and looked up as we walked in, smiling adoringly at his husband before he turned his attention to me.

"Matt!" he said happily. He walked towards me, using the towel slung over his shoulder to wipe his hands before pulling me into a hug. "It's about time you came in. What can I get you to eat?"

"Oh, um. I'm not really picky," I said as Caleb ushered me to a small table in the corner of the kitchen.

"Okay, Curtis will make you our specialty then," he said, nodding to the young chef who grinned back at Caleb and then set to work. "Gio, will you get the wine, please?"

Giovanni nodded and moved around his husband and I noticed as his hand grazed Caleb's waist as if he just couldn't help himself. The two of them shared a tender look and I had to look away as I felt my heart grip painfully in my chest. Caleb must have caught the look on my face because as soon as Giovanni strode out of the room in search of wine he sat down across from me, a look of concern evident on his handsome face.

"Are you alright, Matt?" he asked softly.

I stared into his warm green eyes. I knew Caleb to be a kind and caring person, giving his time and talents freely to the kids at the center and always lending an ear to those who needed a friend. I had spent years keeping myself closed off from everyone so I was surprised by just how much I wanted to open up to him, to finally share some of my story with another person.

And so, I did.

Caleb sat quietly, his eyes never leaving mine as I told him everything. I started at the beginning and didn't leave anything out. Giovanni joined us and held his husband's hand, showing his silent support. My food was delivered in front of me, but still, I never stopped talking. It was as if the floodgates had opened and I needed to purge myself of everything I'd been through. The only thing I didn't mention was Isaac and Hudson and the feelings I'd been experiencing when they were near.

With each word that poured out of me, I felt the tightness in my chest loosening until finally, when I was finished, I slumped back into my chair, feeling exhausted, but also as if I could truly breathe for the first time in years.

Caleb's eyes were swimming with unshed tears and held so much compassion as he stood up, made his way around the table, and wrapped me in a fierce hug. I was startled at first and I looked over Caleb's shoulder, meeting Giovanni's gaze, but he was smiling back at me. I reached up with shaky hands, patting Caleb on the back awkwardly.

"Thank you for telling us all of that," Caleb whispered in my ear and then he drew back, taking my hands in his and looking directly at me. "I'm so sorry for the pain you've been through, Matt, and I'm especially sorry that you've held it in for this long."

"I'm sorry, I'm not really sure why that came out all of a sudden. That was certainly not my reason for coming here," I explained, feeling a bit embarrassed that I had just unloaded that much personal information on my friends.

"Please, don't apologize. We're your friends, both of us," Caleb said, glancing over his shoulder at his husband and I watched as Giovanni nodded his agreement. "And we want to be here for you. There's no reason to go through life all on your own when there are people that want to care about you," he said. I knew he was talking about our friendship, but I also found it quite fitting for Isaac and Hudson as well. I was tired of being a spectator in my own life, so why was I holding back? Was it wrong to want to grab a little bit of happiness for myself?

"You're absolutely right," I told Caleb. "Thank you both for listening and for dinner too, it was delicious," I told them as I stood to leave.

"I'm just glad you finally stopped by. We're going to expect to see your face around here more often, alright?" Giovanni said. He threw an arm around his husband's shoulder and stuck his hand out towards me. I shook it and then Caleb came forward, wrapping his arms around my waist and giving me a firm hug. I hugged him back, feeling less awkward that time, and he was smiling as he stepped back.

"Now that you're out and about more, I hope to see you at the party Saturday night," he said.

"What party?" I asked.

"The going away party for Carter's Creed. They're heading out on tour so we're having a big party to send them off." I could see the pride and a touch of sadness as Caleb talked about his brother's band. I knew as a twin, it must be especially difficult to be apart from each other for long periods of time.

"I'll do my best," I answered. His eyebrow lifted knowingly and I laughed. "No, I mean it. I'll try to be there." Satisfied with my answer, Caleb smiled and I turned and headed out the door, feeling much lighter than I had in a long time. As I made my way out to my car, I made a mental note to stop in once in a while and check on him while his brother was away. After all, that's what friends do, I thought with a smile.

CHAPTER
Seven

Isaac

MY PHONE CHIMED, ALERTING ME TO A NEW TEXT MESSAGE and I smiled when I picked it up and saw who it was.

HUDSON: I'm looking forward to tonight. It's been too long since I saw you.

ME: You just saw me yesterday.

HUDSON: Exactly! That's too long.

ME: It is for me too. I'll see you tonight.

HUDSON: I'll be counting the hours.

My smile widened with his response. It still took me by surprise that a man like Hudson would be even remotely interested in me. I didn't understand what he could possibly see in me, but I'd promised myself that I would try to relax and enjoy it for however long it lasted.

We hadn't gone out anymore since that first night and we barely had time to talk when he came into the center because more and more kids were scheduling private counseling sessions with him, which was a wonderful thing. He did take the time to stop by my office when he was there though to say hello and see how I was doing and we'd started texting each other throughout the day and every night before bed.

We were slowly getting to know each other, but neither of us were in a rush to take things further, as if by some unspoken agreement, we'd both decided we should wait to see what Matt would do. That is, if we ever got the chance to ask him about it. I was afraid to push Matt and had cautioned Hudson that doing so could result in him retreating back into his shell. Hudson, on the other hand, was convinced that Matt needed a little push to help him move on from whatever was holding him back. After what happened in my office, I was starting to think Hudson was right.

I'd been working that day when Hudson showed up at my door. We'd talked for a few minutes and Hudson was laughing at something I'd said when his mood suddenly shifted. He'd whispered to me that Matt was watching us from the doorway and before I knew what was happening, he'd taken my mouth in a smoldering kiss that left me weak in the knees.

It was only the second time he had kissed me and it was even better than I'd remembered. Maybe it was the passion behind his kiss, or maybe it was the knowledge that Matt was watching, but either way, I had to hold onto him just to keep myself from falling. Hudson held nothing back with that kiss and I knew that if we were to ever take things further, my body would go up in flames. When the kiss ended, I was disappointed to learn that Matt had gone, but Hudson told me he'd seen excitement in the man's eyes when he'd crooked his finger at him, inviting him to join us.

I suppose I should've been a little more nervous at the thought of dating two men, but I wasn't. In fact, the thought thrilled me. I had never dated anyone before so maybe that's why I was able to seriously consider Hudson's proposal. I had no preconceived notions of what a relationship should be like, so having two people care about me instead of just one seemed that much better.

Although, I was pretty sure the main reason I wasn't nervous about it was because of who the two men were in particular. I had felt safe and cared for by Matt ever since I'd met him. I trusted him and I knew he was a good person. Hudson was proving to be just as kind and trustworthy and in the two brief times he'd held me in his strong arms, I'd felt like nothing in the world could ever harm me again.

It doesn't hurt that they're both mouth-wateringly sexy either, I thought with a smile. The sound of someone clearing their throat pulled me from my thoughts and I looked up, coming face to face with one of the men I'd just been fantasizing about.

"Hey! What has you smiling so much?" Matt asked.

"Oh, just thinking about something," I answered vaguely, grateful that he couldn't read my mind.

"I had to run a few errands and I stopped by that little deli you like and got us some sandwiches, if you're hungry." He looked almost shy as he held the small white bag up in his hand. I smiled, touched by the thoughtful gesture.

"Thank you. I'm starving actually," I told him, moving papers aside and clearing a spot on my desk for the food.

"Good. I hope I remembered correctly. I got you the ham and swiss on wheat with spicy mustard," he told me as he pulled out a sandwich wrapped neatly in wax paper.

"That's perfect," I said.

I tried to hide my surprise at the fact that he had been paying enough attention to know what I liked, but I was sure he could hear it in my voice. I noticed his hands were shaking as he dug through the bag, producing a drink and a bag of chips and I wondered what had him so flustered. He'd never behaved that way around me before. He opened his mouth like he was going to say something, but then, as if he'd changed his mind, he closed his mouth, picked up the bag containing his lunch, and started to walk out the door.

"Matt?" I called out. He whipped back around so fast it was almost comical if not for the wild look in his eyes. "Would you like to stay and eat with me?" There was a moment of indecision on his face as he weighed his options and I was sure he was going to say no.

"Yes, I'd love to." I let out the breath I'd been holding and he smiled as if he were pleased with himself.

Matt walked back over and started unpacking his own food, then pulled a chair closer to my desk so he could sit. He was dressed in gray slacks that showed off his nice firm butt and I swallowed hard as he rolled the sleeves of his blue button-up shirt to his elbows, revealing smooth, olive-toned skin covered in a dusting of dark hair. I never realized that forearms were such a turn-on for me, but just seeing them had me picturing them on either side of my head as he braced himself above me.

"Isaac?" My eyes darted to Matt's face and I saw the look of concern in his eyes.

"Um, sorry. I guess I zoned out for a minute," I said sheepishly.

"That's okay. I just asked how your day had been."

"Busy, but good," I answered. I went on to explain about the girl who had shown up at the center that morning needing a place to stay after the aunt she'd been living with kicked her out. "I showed her around and got her set up in a room. She seems like a good kid. I think she'll fit in here just fine."

"That's great. I hope we're able to help her," Matt said. "So, did you have fun with Hudson?" I started to choke on my bite of sandwich at the fast change of subject and had to grab my drink to wash it down. I looked up at Matt who was wearing a devilish smirk.

"Excuse me?" I finally managed to get out.

"I meant did you have fun when the two of you went to dinner?" he clarified.

"I did," I answered honestly. The gleam in his eye told me that Matt had been trying to get a reaction out of me so I decided it was only fair if I got one out of him. "He's very charming and fun to be around…Oh, and he's an incredible kisser."

I picked up a chip and popped it in my mouth nonchalantly. It was quiet for a few seconds while I waited for Matt's response and I wondered if he'd be angry or shocked. I peeked through my lashes and my mouth went dry at the hungry look in his eyes.

"Is he now?" Matt's usually deep voice had lowered another octave and the sound sent a ripple of goose bumps over my skin. I was pleased with his reaction and it gave me the courage I needed to push him a little further. Hudson had issued his own invitation and it couldn't hurt to let Matt know where I stood on the topic.

"You know, I'm still disappointed that you didn't go to dinner with us that night. I think the three of us could have had a very good time together." My heart was thundering in my chest, but somehow, I managed to hold his stare and I noticed the way his eyes darkened right before he answered me.

"Maybe I will, next time." The inflection in his voice coupled with the way he was looking at me had me very hopeful that we were talking about the same thing. "Isaac…" Matt began, but his words were cut off by the ringing of my office phone.

"Sorry," I muttered, frustrated at the interruption. "Yes, Allison?" I said quickly, speaking into the phone. I listened as she explained the reason for the call. "Okay, I'll be right there." I looked into Matt's beautiful gray eyes, sorry to have to cut our lunch short when it had begun to get very interesting, but I had no choice.

"Another teen just showed up, this time a boy and he's got visible bruises," I explained. Matt's entire demeanor changed as he switched into business mode.

"I'll come with you. We may need to get Seth in here to take a look," he said, referring to the center's on-call doctor. I nodded my agreement as I stood from my desk, tossing the remains of our lunch into the garbage.

"Thanks again for lunch," I told him.

"You're welcome. We should do this more often. I like spending time with you," he responded. He'd said it casually, but it still caused a fluttering in my stomach.

"I like that too," I told him as I followed him to the door and then a thought popped into my head. "Matt, are you going to the sendoff party for Carter's Creed?" He turned around to face me, his hand on the doorknob.

"I was considering it, but I hadn't made up my mind yet," he said.

"I hope you do. I'll be there…and so will Hudson." I let that information linger in the air as he stared directly at me. His gaze ran over my face as if searching for something and I wondered if he were looking for an excuse to turn me down. Finally, he spoke.

"I might just have to do that, then," Matt said simply then he swung the door open and stepped out of my office. I felt a smile curving my lips and I resisted the urge to pump my fist in the air as I followed him down the long hallway to the front desk. It wasn't the definite confirmation I'd been hoping for, but it was closer to a yes than Matt usually gave and I decided I'd take it and hope for the best.

The next several hours were spent talking with the police and children's services as well as having Seth come in to take a look, determining that the boy did in fact suffer from several abrasions and small burn marks which looked suspiciously like they came from the tip of a cigarette.

The boy was reluctant to tell us what had happened, but once he was fed a decent meal and given time to shower and change into new clothes, he seemed more at ease. Eventually, he told the authorities enough that they were able to launch an investigation into the boy's parents as well as begin the proper legal paperwork to ensure that he could remain at the center until a foster home became available.

With nothing left for me to do, I decided to go home and begin getting ready for the party that night. I rarely went out and when I did, it was usually just to a movie by myself, not to a club. I didn't have any friends outside of the staff and volunteers at the center. There was no way I'd ever be able to bring myself to go to a club alone, so most nights I spent curled up at home with a good book.

That night, however, I could feel the excitement thrumming through my veins as I showered and got dressed. I wasn't convinced that Matt would show up at the club, but I couldn't help but be hopeful. The fact that he had brought me lunch and wanted to spend time with me was huge and the way he had looked at me was even better. The whole experience had left me wishing for things that I had long since given up on where Matt was concerned.

I enjoyed getting to know Hudson and if that's all I ever had, he was more than enough to make me happy, but the thought of having both him and Matt, left my mouth dry and my cock growing stiff. I pressed the heel of my hand against the hardness in my pants as I willed myself to calm down so I could leave the apartment.

I checked myself in the mirror one last time. I'd allowed myself one small splurge and I'd bought a new pair of dark blue jeans and a black, silky dress shirt that I thought looked nice on me, even if it was a bit tight. I just hoped Hudson liked it and Matt, if he was there, too. I leaned towards the mirror, trying to smooth down my hair, but I gave up after the third try when it refused to stay tamed.

Satisfied that I looked decent enough to go to the party, I grabbed my wallet and stuffed it and my phone in my pocket before heading out the door. I'd made up my mind to go into the night with no expectations and to just enjoy myself no matter what happened. As long as I remembered to do that then I was sure it would be an amazing night, regardless of who showed up.

CHAPTER
Eight

Hudson

"Are you all done?" I asked, watching as he popped the last bite of chicken in his mouth.

"Yep. Can I have some ice cream now?" Nicholas asked.

"Hmmm. That depends," I told him, scratching my chin like I was giving the matter serious thought.

"On what?" He quirked his head at me.

"On how fast you get your bath and pajamas on. You know you have to be in bed before your mom gets home," I reminded him. "Do you think you can get all of that done quick enough to still have time for ice cream?" He grinned at me, the front two teeth missing from his happy smile. His brown eyes were bright and trusting and I felt my heart trip over itself as I gazed back at him.

"I know I can, Uncle Hudson," he said so solemnly that I had to fight back a laugh.

"Okay then. How about I start your bathwater while you pick out your pajamas?" I suggested.

"Okay!" he exclaimed, jumping out of his chair and running out of the kitchen. I sat there for a moment, enjoying the sounds of his little feet as he raced down the hallway to his bedroom. He was singing to himself as he went and it was such a happy, carefree sound that I felt myself smiling.

My mother had taken off shortly after I was born, leaving my grandmother to raise my older sister and me on her own. I knew it couldn't have been easy for Nonna to take on a five-year-old girl and her newborn brother, but she'd been determined to hold her family together and to keep us from going into the foster care system.

At sixty-five years old, Nonna should've been able to relax and enjoy her golden years, but instead she took on a job working in the laundry room of the local hospital to make ends meet. While we barely scraped by at times, she never complained. She'd taught us to love God and to help others whenever we could and she did it all by the examples she set forth in her own life. In all my years with her, I never heard her say a cross word about another person, choosing instead to look for the good in everyone.

Our family might have been small, but my sister, Aysha, and I were extremely close and Nonna made sure we never doubted how much we were wanted and loved. That's why it had been such a difficult decision for me to go to Los Angeles for college. As much as I wanted to set out on my own and see a new part of the world, I felt like after all the sacrifices she'd made for me, I owed it to Nonna to stay and take care of her.

She wouldn't hear of it though, insisting that the biggest gift I could give to her would be to accept the full-ride scholarship I'd received and go to college to become a doctor like I'd always dreamed. So, with Aysha's assurance that she would watch over our grandmother, I left.

It was an experience that I was grateful to have, making many friends and enjoying being a young man out on my own for the first time. Nonna and Aysha were both there to cheer me on when I graduated at the top of my class, and celebrated with me when I got an internship with a well-known group of therapists.

A couple of years later, Aysha got married and had a little boy. I was working as a therapist at a private clinic in L.A. and it seemed that everything was going well for us. Then, in the blink of an eye, everything changed. I will never forget the phone call in the middle of the night, informing me that the woman who had been like a mother to me, my nonna, had passed away. I'd been filled with guilt and regret for not having been with her when it happened, but Aysha told me that I had nothing to feel badly about and that Nonna had always been so proud of me for becoming a man that helped people.

I'd returned home for the funeral and it was during that time that Aysha found out that her husband had been cheating on her. Heartbroken and a single mother to a young boy, I could see her scrambling to figure out where to go next. That's when I decided it was time for me to come home for good. I quit my job and moved back to Chicago two weeks after we laid Nonna to rest. I may not have been there when she passed, but I was determined to help hold together the family that she had worked so hard to protect.

Aysha and Nicholas moved into Nonna's house and she got hired as an office manager at a dental office. I took on several clients privately while I was working on getting my own practice up and running.

Being back in Chicago and near my sister and nephew had filled me with a sense of belonging and purpose that I hadn't realized had been missing in my life up until then. Aysha had spent so much of her teenage years cooking me dinner, checking my homework, and driving me to and from football practices when Nonna had to work. I knew she had to miss going out with her friends, but she never once complained.

I finally had the chance to give back a little of what she'd always given to me and I was glad I could be there for her when she needed me. Not to mention how much I enjoyed spending time with the sweet little boy that had just left the room. Still smiling, I headed towards the bathroom and began filling the tub with warm water. I gathered a clean towel and washcloth out of the linen closet and then walked down to Nicholas's room to check on him. I found him standing in front of the open drawer of his dresser, with his hands on his hips.

"Your bathwater is almost ready, little man. Did you pick out which pajamas you want tonight?"

"I don't know," he said, his face scrunching up in concentration.

"Well, what are our choices?" I asked. Ever since he'd started kindergarten that year, he'd insisted on doing things for himself and so I tried to respect his independence.

"Batman and Ninja Turtles," he told me, pointing to each of the sets of pajamas that were folded neatly in the drawer.

"That is a tough decision. Which one is your favorite?" He looked at me with such a helpless expression that I ran my hand over the top of his head, hoping to soothe him. "I know, that's a tough decision, too. You know, Batman was my favorite when I was your age."

"He was?" Nicholas asked, smiling up at me.

"Oh yeah. He had a cool costume and an even cooler car and he always fought the bad guys and won," I told him.

"He is cool," he agreed, pulling the Batman pajamas out of the drawer and shutting it. "I'll wear these tonight since they're your favorite and you're my favorite uncle."

"Thanks, little man." I grinned down at him. It didn't matter that I was his only uncle, the fact that I was his favorite *anything* made me feel warm all over. I didn't think I could love him any more if he was my own son.

I helped him get a bath and dressed in his pajamas and then

settled him down with a bowl of ice cream while I cleaned up the kitchen. When he was finished, he picked out a book and then climbed into his bed and snuggled underneath the covers. I sat down next to him and he curled into my side as I read him a bedtime story.

He was asleep before I reached the last page and I climbed out of the bed, careful not to wake him and switched on his nightlight. I turned back when I reached the door, taking one last look at him. He looked so peaceful as he lay there dreaming and it made my heart feel full. Nicholas was an incredible kid and I would do anything in my power to make sure his childhood was as carefree and joyful as possible. I flipped off the light switch and shut his door, leaving it open a crack in case he needed me before I went to the kitchen and washed out the bowl he'd used for ice cream.

"Hey there!" Aysha said, startling me as she walked up behind me. "How was your night?" She began digging through the fridge, looking for something to eat.

"I made dinner. Sit down and I'll warm it up," I told her, moving towards the microwave.

"Oh my God, you are the best, Hudson," she praised as she grabbed a bottle of water from the fridge and sat down at the table, kicking her shoes off and propping her feet up on the chair next to her with a sigh.

I leaned my hip against the counter, crossing my arms and stud-ied my sister as I waited for her food to be ready. She was a beautiful woman, but the weary slump of her shoulders and the small frown line that had formed between her eyes showed evidence of the strain she'd been under during the past couple of years and I renewed the promise I'd made to myself to do anything I could to alleviate that stress.

"My night was great," I said, finally answering her question. "Nicholas is such a sweetheart," I said with a smile and her face lit up at the mention of her son.

"He is, isn't he? Thanks so much for watching him. I know you probably have a million other things you'd rather be doing on a Saturday evening," she said. The microwave dinged and I pulled the piping hot plate out, setting it in front of her then I sat across from her, keeping her company as she ate.

"You know how much I love spending time with him any chance I get," I assured her.

"I know, but you're a handsome man in the prime of your life. You should be going out and having fun," she scolded.

"Don't worry about me, I'm doing just fine." She shot me a doubtful look. "I'm serious. In fact, I'm going to a party tonight," I informed her.

"That's great! Are you taking a date?" I laughed as she waggled her brows at me. I felt a fluttering in my stomach as I pictured Isaac and Matt. I wasn't about to tell my sister about the two men though. It wasn't that I was afraid she'd disapprove. As a matter of fact, Aysha had been nothing but supportive of me since I first told her I thought I was gay when I was thirteen years old. She and Nonna had both assured me that the only thing that mattered was that I found someone who made me happy and who treated me right. The reason I didn't mention the two men to her was simple. I needed to figure out what was happening for myself first, and I wasn't even sure at that point if anything *would* happen.

"No, I'm not taking a date," I assured her, not bothering to explain that I was meeting Isaac at the party. Her expression was so disappointed that I laughed again as I looked at my watch. "I better get going or I'm going to be late."

"Okay, have a great time," she said as I stood and placed my glass of water in the sink.

"Call me if you need anything." I walked back over to my sister and leaned down, kissing the top of her head. "I'll pick you guys up around noon tomorrow, if that's alright. Maybe we can grab lunch before the movie."

"That sounds wonderful. Can we please go to a restaurant that doesn't give away prizes in the meal?" I laughed when she clasped her hands in front of her and gave me a hopeful look.

"Sure, maybe we'll even go somewhere with plates and real silverware," I joked.

"My hero," she teased, batting her long lashes at me. I could still hear her laughing as I walked out and it put a smile on my face.

I hurried home and took a quick shower then rummaged through my closet, picking out a dark pair of jeans and gray V-neck sweater. I topped off the look with a pair of biker boots and grabbed my black leather jacket as I headed out the door.

Traffic was lighter than usual so it didn't take me very long to get to the club. I'd met with Rylie, who was the drummer of the band and a close friend of mine, earlier in the week for a counseling session and he'd invited me to the party. He'd told me that his husband, Lachlan, had rented out the entire club for the evening and had security in place so that no paparazzi or overzealous fans could make it into the private party.

Still, I was surprised by the sheer number of screaming fans and photographers lined up outside the building, hoping to get a peek at their favorite rock band. I pulled up alongside a stern-looking guard who took my name and scanned the list of names he'd been given. Once he saw I was on the approved list, he let me inside the parking area where another guard waited to escort me from my car into the club. The whole thing seemed so bizarre to me, but I supposed it was the way of life for the rock stars inside.

The guard left me at the door and I took a moment to let my eyes wander around the club. There were easily over a hundred people there, all friends and family members of the band. I recognized a few faces from the grand opening of Agape House and some I had met when they came in to volunteer. I scanned the crowd for Matt and Isaac, but didn't see either of them. I turned when someone shouted out my name and I grinned widely when I saw Micah Hamilton approaching me along with his husband, Landon Greene.

I'd been introduced to Micah when I was still living in L.A. and began counseling Lachlan after his brother, Spencer, was killed by insurgents who had taken both Spencer and Micah hostage. Micah had been the one to break the news to Lachlan and they became very close friends. Micah insisted on meeting the person who was counseling Lachlan through his grief and he and I had quickly become friends as well.

"Hey, man, it's good to see you," Micah said, grabbing me up into a fierce hug.

"You too," I told him. I returned the hug, but was surprised by the gesture. In all the years I'd known him, Micah had always been a little standoffish and more than a little unapproachable. The new side to him could only be explained by the handsome man who stood beside him, with a friendly smile on his face. I'd only met Landon once before, but I'd immediately liked him and could see how just his nearness seemed to soothe the rough edges of his ex-military husband. It made me happy to see Micah finally looking so happy.

"Come on, we've got a table. Some of us have already had a few drinks so you might want to catch up," Micah said, nodding his head in his husband's direction with a grin.

"Hey! I saw that," Landon huffed indignantly. "I haven't had that many."

"Oh really, so your grabbing me right in front of your sister was normal behavior for you?" Micah teased.

"I can't help myself," Landon insisted, wrapping his arms around Micah's waist. "I'm drunk on you." He waggled his brows at Micah who threw his head back with a laugh. It was undoubtedly one of the cheesiest lines I'd ever heard, but it obviously worked because Micah pulled his husband in for a quick yet heated kiss.

I followed them around the crowd of people on the dance floor, the bass playing loudly through the speakers and thumping out a steady rhythm in my chest. They led me to a large round table full of people and I smiled when I saw Isaac there. He smiled back shyly, his blue eyes sparkling in the flashing lights of the club. He looked completely edible in a black shirt that showed off his tight little body and I wished I could steal him away into some dark, secluded corner so I could peel it off him. Circling around the table, I sat in the empty chair beside Isaac and he turned towards me, his smile widening.

"Hi!" he said. I watched, mesmerized, as the tip of his tongue darted out to wet his plump, pink lips. There were a lot of people who worked hard to perfect the art of seduction, but with Isaac, he didn't even have to try. Being sexy just came to him as naturally as breathing.

"Hey! How are you?" I reached over and took his hand in mine. Isaac's eyes darted down to our hands and then around the table before landing back on me. "Is this okay?" I could sense his tension and didn't want to make him uncomfortable.

"Yeah, of course. It just took me by surprise. I wasn't sure if you'd want anyone to know we were seeing each other yet," he told me, shrugging his shoulders. I narrowed my eyes at him and leaned in so I could whisper in his ear. If he'd thought I was going to treat him like a dirty secret, then I wanted to clear that up right away.

"I'm the luckiest man in the world to get to be with you and I want everyone in this club to know that you're here with me," I informed him, leaving no room for doubt. I watched the movement of his throat as he swallowed and all the blood rushed to my cock, filling it and making it uncomfortably hard inside my jeans. He turned his head to face me and he must have seen the need in my eyes because he visibly shuddered. The tension between us was palpable and I was seconds from taking his mouth in a passionate kiss.

Luckily, the music switched to a different song, reminding me that we weren't alone and Isaac drew in a deep breath as I pulled away from him. I looked across the table, and immediately caught Lachlan's eye. He looked down pointedly at Isaac's and my clasped hands and then looked back at my face, raising his brows questioningly. I gave him a single, discreet nod and he grinned at me, obviously pleased. I rolled my eyes good-naturedly. Ever since Lachlan had met and fallen in love with Rylie, he'd been after me to go out and meet someone, so I knew the sudden turn of events had made him very happy.

I looked around the table at several familiar faces, including Landon's twin brothers, Caleb and Carter, who I'd met at the youth center as well as their cousin, Morgan Greene, who'd been responsible for building the new Agape House and his fiancé, Akio. The two had apparently become engaged the night of the grand opening and as far as I could tell, they couldn't keep their hands or eyes off each other.

The twins' husbands, Giovanni and Ryan, came up to the table just then, carrying a stack of shot glasses which they spread out on the surface and began filling with the bottle of tequila they'd brought with them from the bar as they declared it was time for a toast.

Landon plopped down in the seat next to me and he handed me two shot glasses. I passed one to Isaac and held the other as I waited for the rest to get handed out. Without intending to, my eyes sought out Rylie. The drummer had worked very hard to overcome his addictions and continued to meet with me on a regular basis. I knew how far he'd come and how determined he was to never go back to the life he'd been living before, but I still felt the need to check in with him. He met my gaze with a self-assured smile and held his glass of ginger ale up to me in a salute then winked at me and gave me a cocky grin.

I rolled my eyes, but smiled back at him, glad that he seemed to be doing okay despite being surrounded by alcohol. Lachlan leaned over and whispered something in Rylie's ear which made Rylie smile even wider. I should've known Lachlan would've made sure his husband was alright with being in that type of atmosphere before planning a party there. Realizing I wasn't going to be needed as a therapist for the evening, I decided it was time to relax and have some fun.

I held my glass up along with everyone else as we toasted to safe travels, great adventures, and rock and roll. Isaac and I tapped our glasses together and then I tossed back the smooth liquid, enjoying the warm feeling it caused in the pit of my stomach. I'd just set my glass back on the table and was admiring the beautiful flush the alcohol brought to Isaac's cheeks when I felt a delicious current run through my veins. Turning and searching the crowd, my heart began to thunder in my chest when my eyes landed on the man who had just walked through the door.

CHAPTER
Nine

Matt

MY HEART WAS HAMMERING IN MY CHEST AS I STEPPED into the club. I knew that Carter's Creed had a lot of fans, but I'd never expected the huge crowd of people that had been waiting when I'd pulled into the parking lot. I was tempted to forget the whole thing and just go home, but I'd told Caleb that I would come to the party and I'd promised myself that I was going to try to get out more. Besides, the thought of going back out and facing that crowd was enough to make my stomach turn.

I hadn't been to a club in several years. The flashing lights, cheesy pickup lines from guys hoping to score for the night, and music thumping so loud you had to scream to be heard had always left me with a pounding headache and a feeling of *why the hell did I come here?* I would much rather spend my nights at home, curled up with a good book, but lately I'd started to wonder if I wasn't using that as a way to hide.

"Matt! I'm so glad you're here," Caleb yelled as he ran towards me and threw his arms around me.

I felt myself stiffen at first, I wasn't used to being touched and it startled me. I gave him an awkward pat on the back and he stepped back, smiling at me happily. His green eyes sparkled and I couldn't help but smile back. Caleb was one of those people who was always happy and his exuberant attitude was infectious.

"Sorry I'm late. That crowd was crazy," I told him, using my thumb to point over my shoulder towards the door.

"I know. It's been getting worse lately with the new album coming out and the tour getting ready to kick off. Micah even had to assign a bodyguard for me because fans see me and think I'm Carter." He rolled his eyes at that and I laughed. It had taken me a long time to tell the identical twins apart. Physically they were exactly alike, but once I got to know them better, I could see how different their personalities were. "Don't worry though, none of the fans or paparazzi can get in here tonight. Between Lachlan and Micah, this place is more secure than Fort Knox. Only friends and family are allowed into the party."

I took a second to look around for the first time and I began to relax when I realized he was right. The crowd was much smaller than it would normally be in a trendy nightclub on a Saturday night and I saw several people I knew, including Caleb's parents and his cousin, Morgan, who had been responsible for the design and building of the new center. He was dancing with his fiancé, Akio, and I felt a pang in my chest at the intimate way they were looking at each other.

I felt the loneliness creeping in and it reassured me that I made the right decision in going to the party. I needed to be around people and not just the teens at the center, but people my own age that I could interact with.

"Come on over and sit with us," Caleb said, grabbing my arm

and pulling me along behind him before I could even ask who *us* was.

I found out soon enough as we walked up to a table with several of Caleb's family members who I was friends with along with Lachlan and Rylie. I tried to smile as they greeted me, but I wasn't sure I pulled it off as my eyes latched onto the other two men who were sitting there.

My pulse picked up speed when I saw Hudson and Isaac sitting next to each other and my eyes darted down to where their hands were joined. I waited to feel some sort of jealousy that the two men I wanted for myself were together, but that feeling never came. When I'd been with Sean, I would've wanted to kill anyone that dared to touch him. Sharing him would have never been an option, but for some reason, seeing Hudson and Isaac together seemed completely natural, like it was meant to be that way. There was only one thing missing as far as I was concerned.

Me.

I wanted to be with them and before my brain could even finish that thought, my feet began to move in their direction. They smiled at me as I walked towards them and my eyes darted back and forth between the two. Physically, they were complete opposites. Hudson was tall, dark, broad-shouldered and looked like he could be a professional football player. Isaac was pale, slender yet toned with delicate features which many people mistook for fragility. If they took the time to look closely, however, they'd see the quiet strength he possessed inside.

"Hey, Matt! It's great to see you," Carter called out and I nearly stumbled. My face heated as I suddenly noticed everyone staring at me. I'd been so caught up in Isaac and Hudson, I'd forgotten there was anyone else in the room.

"Hi!" I said, raising my hand in a wave to my friends and they all smiled back at me and someone handed me a drink.

I was surprised when Hudson jumped up from his seat and

grabbed an empty chair from the table behind him, placing it between his and Isaac's. His eyes held mine in a challenge as he waited to see if I'd take it. Glancing around at the other couples I wondered if anyone had noticed, but they were too busy laughing and talking. I was sure to any of them, it would be no big deal to sit next to someone you were attracted to, but for me it was huge. I felt like I was opening a door that I thought had been locked forever.

I sat down and Hudson lowered his large frame into the seat next to me, leaving a trail of fire where his arm grazed mine. I sneaked a glance at him and the intensity with which he was staring back at me nearly stole my breath.

"We were hoping you'd come," he said.

Hudson's words were innocent enough to anyone listening, but coupled with the hungry look he was giving me, I felt a chill race up my spine. I hadn't missed the fact that he'd said "we" either and I turned to look at Isaac whose bright blue eyes were staring back at me. I saw something in his gaze that I'd seen many times, but had tried to ignore. The look was full of heat and longing and my cock jerked in response. I no longer wanted to ignore the fact that I wanted him too. I wanted both of them and there was no use denying it.

"I didn't want to miss this," I answered honestly, knowing my words could be used to describe the party for our friends or being with the two of them. Isaac smiled, drawing my attention to his full bottom lip and I was filled with the overwhelming need to know what he tasted like. A hand on my thigh had me looking back at Hudson who was grinning.

"You both look amazing," he said. I had to agree with him about Isaac, but I glanced down at my own jeans and dark-green shirt in surprise. I supposed all the running I did helped keep me in good enough shape, but I was nowhere near as built as Hudson or as beautiful as Isaac.

"So, do you," I told him, letting my eyes rake over his broad chest which was barely contained underneath the thin material of his sweater. My mind wandered as I pictured myself peeling him out of that sweater and I shifted in my seat to relieve the building pressure in my groin.

"I want to climb him like a tree," I heard mumbled from beside me and I nearly choked as my head whipped around to look at Isaac. His eyes almost bugged out of his head as he realized he'd said that out loud and I couldn't hold in my bark of laughter. Hudson looked at us curiously, but I just shook my head at him, winking at Isaac. He had no reason to feel embarrassed, especially since I'd been thinking the same thing. How could anyone look at Hudson and not want him?

Carter began pouring everyone another round of tequila and I realized I'd never drank the one I'd been given. I rarely drank because I never went out with friends and it just seemed too depressing to drink alone. I tossed mine back along with everyone else then sat back in my chair as the alcohol ran through my veins and loosened the last bit of tension from my body.

I listened to the playful banter between my friends and found myself laughing at the stories. I was having a good time and I realized just how much I'd been missing out on by closing myself off to the rest of the world. I caught Caleb's eye and he smiled at me, the look in his eyes telling me that he understood. I smiled back at him, grateful to have him as a friend.

I was constantly aware of the fact that Hudson's hand remained on my thigh, its warmth burning a hole through the material of my jeans. I liked the possessiveness of the gesture as if he were telling me I was right where I belonged, by his side. He let out a deep, rumbling laugh as Rylie told about the time that he took Hudson for a ride in one of Lachlan's tiny sports cars. I laughed along with them as I pictured the 6'4" man trying to squeeze himself inside the cramped space.

Rylie had told me a little about his struggle with drugs and alcohol and I was glad that Hudson had been able to help him. The two men had obviously become very good friends through the experience.

The other members of the band walked up just then and soon stories were being told about their travels and the trouble they liked to get into while on the road. They teased Landon about having to babysit them, but he responded that being their manager was more like being a zookeeper than a babysitter. Everyone laughed at that, but I noticed Isaac had become quiet. I turned to look at him and saw his attention was on the dance floor. I glanced over at the people who were dancing and having a good time and I wondered if he wanted to join them. The music switched to a new song and I took a deep breath, a little surprised by what I was about to do.

"Would you like to dance?" I asked him. He turned his head quickly, giving me a shocked look.

"Uh, yeah. Sure," he said.

We stood and I caught Hudson's smile as we moved around the table and out onto the dance floor. I found an open spot and turned to face Isaac. It had been ages since I'd been dancing, but it all came back to me as I began to move, and soon, I was lost in the music and the feel of Isaac's body brushing up on mine as he circled around me. He obviously loved to dance and was very good at it. He danced with a fluid grace, his movements sensual and provocative.

Isaac was always friendly and honest, but as he danced, he let go and became freer than I'd ever seen him. The sight was breathtaking and as the music changed to a slower song, I couldn't stop myself from grabbing his hips and pulling him closer to me. His body was surprisingly firm against mine and I groaned when I felt his hard length against my leg. He tried to pull away, obviously embarrassed that I'd felt his desire, but I slid my arms around his waist, bringing him even closer to me.

"You are so sexy and you feel so good against me," I told him. I could tell that my words shocked him, but I saw no reason to take them back because they were true. "Why do you look surprised?"

"I'm just having trouble believing any of this is real," he replied.

"It's very real," I assured him, thrusting my hips against his. I heard his quick gasp when he felt my own aching hardness pressing against him, leaving no doubt about how much I wanted him. I stared down at his beautiful face, the pale freckles over a creamy complexion and the long lashes that framed the innocent eyes looking back at me.

"I've been attracted to you for so long, but I never thought you would see me the same way," Isaac whispered.

Excitement ran through my veins at the desire I saw in his eyes. It had been way too long since anyone had looked at me that way and it woke something up in me that I wasn't sure could be contained, or if I even wanted to. It made me feel good, it made me feel wanted, and it made me feel alive.

"I've had my reasons for holding back, but trust me, Isaac, I see you. I see what an amazing, sexy, and desirable man you are," I assured him.

Going off pure instinct, I bent down and covered his lips with mine. We swallowed each other's groans as fire raced through my veins. Isaac's hands slid up around my neck and I felt his fingers run through my hair as I gave myself over to the kiss. I couldn't believe that this man, my friend, had been waiting there the entire time and I'd almost missed it.

I ended the kiss before I could get too carried away and smiled when he muttered a curse. I licked my lips, savoring the sweet taste of him and then looked over to where Hudson sat watching us, his eyes dark and hooded with desire. Seeing his heated reaction gave me the confidence I needed and I crooked my finger at him, inviting him in the same way he had when I'd caught him and Isaac kissing.

Hudson didn't run away like I had, however. Instead, his lips pulled up in a wolfish grin and he rose from his seat and sauntered towards us. The look in his eyes was predatory and I felt Isaac's body shiver against mine as he looked over his shoulder, watching the man who would make us his prey.

CHAPTER
Ten

Isaac

I FELT LIKE I WAS STUCK IN A DREAM, ONE THAT I NEVER WANTED to wake up from. My head was spinning with the unbelievable knowledge that Matt, the man I had secretly had a crush on for years, actually wanted me too. *And that kiss!* I had spent nearly every night wondering what it would be like to feel his lips on mine, his body pressed against me in a passionate embrace, but the reality was so much better than I could've ever imagined.

Matt's kiss was different from Hudson's, but every bit as toe-curling. Hudson's kisses were all-consuming, like he wanted to feast on me and devour me whole. His kisses left me shaken and weak in the knees. The kiss I shared with Matt was just as passionate, but in a completely different way. Instead of pulling everything he could from me, Matt poured himself into our kiss, filling me with all of the want and need he had inside of him. More than ever, I wondered what it would be like to have both of them at the same time. To allow Hudson to take what he wanted from me while Matt filled me back up.

In the flashing lights of the club, I could see the evidence of our kiss on Matt's swollen, red lips and I wanted to pull him towards me for another, not caring that others might be watching. Matt's attention had been drawn to something behind me and I glanced over my shoulder to see what it was. Goose bumps broke out across my skin when I saw Hudson coming our way and the look on his face told me that he had one goal in mind.

Hudson wanted to lay claim.

I felt flushed and shaky and I wondered how it was possible that I was still standing, much less moving to the music. I moved my hands down to grip Matt's biceps in order to steady myself as Hudson approached. Matt reached one hand up to cup my chin, turning my head so I was looking back at him.

"Are you okay, Isaac?" he asked gently.

I wasn't sure I could speak just then so I simply nodded. Matt searched my face, looking for any sign that I wasn't telling the truth, but he must've believed me because he bent down to brush his lips against mine once more. It was just a whisper of a kiss, but I knew it was his way of reassuring me.

Just then, I felt Hudson's body press up against mine. Our height difference had his denim-covered erection pushing against my lower back and I gasped in surprise. I couldn't see Hudson's face from my position, but the look on Matt's face said it all.

Matt's gray eyes had turned dark and smoky as they looked at the man behind me and I could feel his own erection straining against my belly. Hudson's hands landed on my waist, his fingers digging into my hips in a gentle tug as if he wanted me as close as possible to him. I had no problem with that whatsoever.

Trapped between the two men, my senses were filled with the combined scent of them. It was both citrusy and spicy and completely intoxicating. The heat from each of their bodies had me sweating and I wondered how I hadn't burst into flames already. Matt's hands moved from my waist, giving Hudson more room and I wished I could see where his hands were.

"I think perhaps we should move this to somewhere more private," Hudson suggested. His deep baritone voice rumbled from his chest into my back and traveled throughout my body until I could feel it tingling in my scalp. Matt nodded his agreement and then looked down at me. I could feel Hudson's hot breath against my neck and then his lips pressed against my skin and a shiver wracked my entire body.

"Yes," I whispered hoarsely.

Matt and Hudson stepped away from me then and I was suddenly assaulted with the lights and sounds of the crowded club. I had forgotten that we weren't alone, too caught up in the touch and feel of the two men I was with to worry about what everyone would think about the three of us being together. My eyes darted to the table where our friends sat, but instead of looks of outrage or condemnation, I was met with curiosity, happiness, and acceptance.

Hudson and I followed Matt over to the table where Hudson announced that we were leaving. We took turns saying our goodbyes and wishing the band safe travels. When Hudson went to hug Rylie, I heard Rylie whisper something to Hudson about having lots to talk about at their next session. Hudson whispered something back to him that I couldn't hear, but it made Rylie laugh.

I shouldn't have been surprised that our friends were so accepting of different types of relationships; they were all very open-minded individuals. Still, it was a relief to know that their reactions weren't going to be an issue while the three of us took the time to figure out what exactly was happening between us. Matt stopped us before we reached the front door.

"I came here in a cab. Should I call one before we step back out into the craziness?" His words reminded me of the frenzied fans who were waiting just outside the doors.

"I drove. Are you guys okay with going to my place? I don't live far," Hudson offered.

I looked to Matt, wondering if he would change his mind, but he was already nodding at Hudson, a look of determination written all over his face. I agreed and Hudson turned and spoke to one of the security guards who escorted us outside. The crowd's excitement picked up when they saw us leaving and they fired questions at us, one right after the other, trying to find out anything they could about what their favorite band was doing inside the party. We kept our heads down as the guard had instructed and soon we were climbing into Hudson's SUV.

We made small talk, mostly about the center, as we drove to Hudson's place, but the air around us remained thick with tension. I was surprised when Hudson pulled into the parking garage of a sleek high-rise building in the heart of the city. I shouldn't have been shocked to find that Hudson had money, after all, he was one of the best therapists in the country with many clients who were well known politicians and celebrities, but it was easy to forget because Hudson was just so down to earth.

We followed Hudson to a set of elevators and climbed inside. There was no one else around and Hudson hit the button for the seventeenth floor then turned to us. He looked at me and smiled and I felt some of the tension leave my body. I glanced at Matt and saw him looking at Hudson. He was chewing on the inside of his lip as he stared at him in concentration.

"Have you changed your mind?" Hudson asked him. I held my breath as I waited for Matt's response. I prayed that wasn't the case, but he'd been scared off before and I still didn't know what had been holding Matt back in the first place.

"No, I've just been thinking," Matt answered seriously.

"What about?" Hudson asked, relaxing back against the wall when he saw that Matt wasn't going to bolt.

"The two of you have kissed," Matt said, glancing at both Hudson and me. There was no reason to respond because he already knew the answer to that so we just stared at him, waiting for him to continue.

"You and I have kissed," he stated, turning to look at me. His voice had taken on a husky tone and the look in his eyes grew heated. I licked my lips at the memory of Matt's mouth merging with mine. I wanted to feel that again. I wanted to slide my tongue inside and spend hours exploring all the flavors he had to offer. I was pulled out of my trance when he moved his gaze to Hudson.

"But I haven't gotten to taste you yet," Matt pointed out and I felt a jolt of excitement at the thought of having a front row seat while the two hottest men in the world kissed for the first time. I watched the sexy smirk that formed on Hudson's lips and I nearly came in my jeans.

"I'm right here," he told Matt, holding his arms out to his sides in a come and get me gesture.

I was surprised at first because I'd been expecting Hudson to take charge of the situation like he usually did when he was with me, but it was like he sensed what a big step it was for Matt to even be there with us and wanted him to be the one to make the first move. My chest warmed at the knowledge that this was more than just sex for Hudson. He cared about Matt and wanted to make sure he was okay with his decision.

Matt hesitated at first as if he were still deciding and then he was moving forward and I watched in awe as he reached for Hudson, gripping the front of his shirt and slamming his mouth over the taller man's. Hudson didn't waste any time as his hands began to run up and down Matt's back, eagerly. I knew what it was like to kiss each of them and so I understood the intense pleasure they each were experiencing.

Watching the raw passion between the two sexy men had my cock straining painfully against the zipper of my jeans and I reached down and pressed the palm of my hand against it so I wouldn't embarrass myself before we even made it inside Hudson's home. Fortunately, the elevator stopped just then and the two of them broke apart, chests heaving as they struggled to catch their breath.

Matt grabbed my hand as we exited the elevator, keeping me close to his side. Hudson pulled his keys from his pocket and led us to a door at the end of the hallway. He held the door open for us and I looked around as I walked in. The condo was designed in an open floor plan with real hardwood floors throughout. The living room had a stone fireplace, black leather furniture, and sliding glass doors that led to a balcony which I was sure provided a breathtaking view of the city.

The kitchen was decorated in stainless steel appliances and a marble-topped island contained barstools for sitting. A set of stairs led to a loft which I assumed was where Hudson slept. All in all, Hudson's home was modern, sleek, and sophisticated, just like the man that lived there.

"Would you like anything to drink?" Hudson asked.

"No, thank you," "Water, please," Matt and I answered at the same time.

I perched on the edge of the couch as Hudson walked into the kitchen and Matt took the seat next to me. My mouth suddenly felt dry as the reality of what was about to happen, of what I was *hoping* would happen, began to sink in. My breathing increased with all the emotions warring inside me.

Excitement, happiness, desire, and fear all fought for dominance within me. I didn't fear either of the men, in fact, I'd never felt safer. I wanted to be with them, but it was the fear of the unknown that had me trembling. *What if I make a fool of myself or do something wrong?*

I didn't realize I'd begun fidgeting until Matt covered my hands with his own. I looked up at him and he gave me a small smile. Matt's eyes were gentle and full of understanding. In his eyes, I saw my new lover, but I also saw my friend, the first man who had ever made me feel safe and cared for.

"We don't have to do anything you don't want to do," he promised and I believed him. I knew beyond a shadow of a doubt that if I wasn't ready, I could say so and neither man would get upset or hold it against me.

"No, I want this. I want to be with you; with both of you," I assured him.

He searched my face for a moment and then he reached up, his fingers tracing a line along my jaw. His hand kept moving until it cupped the back of my neck and he pulled me forward. I went willingly and our mouths met in a tantalizing kiss that made me want to strip him bare and explore every inch of him with my tongue.

All those nights spent dreaming about what it would be like to be held by Hudson and Matt, to feel their weight on top of me, their bodies merging with mine. I couldn't believe it was about to come true and I had to remind myself to slow down and savor it in case this was the only chance I ever got.

Matt's tongue dipped inside my mouth and I groaned against him as his flavor burst across my tongue. He started to pull back, but I followed him, raising up on my knees so I could lean over him, taking control of the kiss. Matt's hands grabbed at my waist, but instead of pushing me away, he pulled me closer until I was forced to straddle his lap.

My fingers ran over his jaw, memorizing the texture of the scruff that was there before they traveled higher until they ran through his silky curls. Matt moved his hands to cup my ass, kneading my cheeks in his firm grip. I cried out as he lifted his hips, causing our erections to rub against each other. Our tongues swirled around each other in a synchronized dance and I lost myself in the feel and taste of him.

I jolted in Matt's arms as I felt a second set of lips against the back of my neck, but then I relaxed as Hudson's hands reached around and began slowly unbuttoning my shirt. Matt pushed his groin up against mine adding a delicious pressure against my cock and I whimpered with the need for more. More friction, more kisses, more everything.

It was an odd feeling to want to be in the moment, while at the same time wishing I could watch from afar so I could see everything, take it all in and catalogue it in my memory to be played over and over again for years to come. I couldn't imagine anything ever being better than that moment, but I was wrong. I was so wrong.

CHAPTER
Eleven

Isaac

HUDSON PEELED MY SHIRT OFF AND MATT IMMEDIATELY leaned forward, swiping his tongue up the column of my neck. My head fell back with a groan, landing on Hudson's shoulder. Hudson slid his hands over my chest and down my stomach, the tips of his fingers teasing the waistband of my jeans. Matt's tongue found my nipple and swirled over it, teasing it until it stood at attention before he took it between his wet lips and sucked hard.

I gasped. Having never had anyone play with my nipples before, I had no idea that they were such an erogenous zone for me. I felt like I was discovering new pieces of myself and it was all at the hands of these two men.

"You are so beautiful," Hudson whispered, his warm breath

against my ear causing a ripple of goose bumps to break out over my skin.

I felt drunk on the unbelievable things they were doing to my body. I turned my head in search of him and Hudson found my mouth with his, licking at my lips until I opened to him, allowing him entry. He sucked on my tongue at the same time Matt moved to my ear and began to nibble at the tender flesh beneath my ear.

Hudson's lips left mine and I groaned in frustration until I saw where he was headed next. He cupped the back of Matt's head and tugged him forward. The two of them began to make out over my shoulder and I reached down, cupping my cock roughly through my clothes, trying to resist the urge to come. It wasn't easy when I could see their tongues sweeping inside each other or the way Matt bit down on Hudson's lip, gently pulling on it with his teeth and eliciting a deep groan from Hudson that vibrated against my back.

Hudson's hand came up and held the back of my head as he drew me towards them. The three of us shared a kiss, full of passion and discovery as our tongues explored each other, and I was amazed at how very right it felt to be kissing two men at once. I wasn't sure how much longer I would be able to hold off my orgasm though so I broke away, my chest heaving as I gulped in air.

Hudson reached around my waist for the button of my pants, but Matt put his hand over Hudson's stopping his movements. Matt looked at me and I could see beyond the heavy lust and need in his eyes, the seriousness of whatever was on his mind.

"Isaac, have you ever done this before?" he asked gently.

Hudson stiffened slightly behind me and I felt my face heat with embarrassment. I must have done something to fuck up already. How else would Matt know how completely inexperienced I was? I wanted to curse my lack of knowledge, but at the same time, I was glad that I had waited to share such an intimate moment with the two of them.

Unable to speak around the lump in my throat, I shook my head once. Matt must've seen my distress because his eyes immediately softened and his hands came up to cup my face. The look in his eyes was almost tender as he spoke.

"Don't be embarrassed, you didn't do anything wrong. I just want to be sure that this is really something you want to do," Matt explained.

My eyes burned with the knowledge that even in that moment when it would have been so easy to just lose ourselves in the needs of our bodies, Matt was still watching out for me, making sure I was protected, just as he'd done since the day I met him.

"We can do as little or as much as you're comfortable with," Hudson said behind me and I turned my head so I could look in his eyes.

He stared back at me with a gentle look that left no doubt as to the sincerity of his words. They cared about me as a person and that knowledge was what solidified the decision in my mind. I wanted these two men more than I wanted my next breath and I was tired of waiting.

"I'm absolutely positive," I answered, my voice steady and sure. They shared a look over my shoulder and then Hudson asked me something that made me want to bury my head in Matt's chest.

"Have you ever had anything inside you before? Your fingers or a toy perhaps?" he asked.

It was strange that after everything I'd been planning on doing with them that Hudson's question would seem so unbelievably personal, but I just wasn't used to talking about sex with anyone else, especially not about what I had ever done or not done to myself. Deciding that I should be able to talk to my lovers about that sort of thing, I decided to answer honestly.

"Just my fingers a few times." My face felt like it was on fire and I was sure I resembled a tomato at that point, but I was grateful when neither man laughed at me, not that I'd expected them to.

"Thank you for telling us," Matt said. "We weren't trying to embarrass you, we just needed to know so we could slow things down;

take care of you properly."

A slow burn started low in my belly at the idea of how the two of them would take care of me and my embarrassment was replaced with a renewed desire to share myself with my new lovers. My lovers. I liked the sound of that, liked the sense of ownership and belonging it brought to mind.

"I want to see you both, naked in my bed," Hudson suddenly announced, his voice was rough with desire and it made my cock leak into my underwear.

He stood up behind me and backed up to give me room as I crawled off Matt's lap. I winced as I adjusted myself inside my jeans, but apparently, I wasn't the only one with that particular problem because Matt and Hudson did the same. Hudson held my hand as we climbed the stairs of the loft and I reached behind me for Matt, not wanting to sever the connection between the three of us.

The loft was spacious with a large California king bed and a nightstand on each side. My heart pounded wildly in my chest as I stared at the bed, but it was excitement rather than nerves that had me shaking.

Matt came up behind me and wrapped his hand around my waist until it lay flat on my stomach. I sucked in a sharp breath at the feel of his hard bulge pressing into the curve of my back. I was still having trouble believing that this was all really happening, but the warmth of Matt's hand as his fingers pressed against my bare flesh and the heat that emanated through his clothes, soaking into me all the way to my bones, served as a reminder that the moment was very much real.

Without letting go of my hand, Hudson turned to face us. His gaze zeroed in to where Matt's hands splayed across me, his pinkie finger tracing circles around my belly button. Hudson clenched his jaw as his eyes turned nearly black with raw desire.

"Tell us what you want to happen, Isaac," Hudson rasped. I bit my lip, unsure of how to respond. There were so many thoughts and emotions swirling through me in that moment and I didn't know exactly how to put them into words. Hudson understood though, as he always seemed to. He took a step closer so that the front of his chest brushed against mine and lifted my chin so I was looking up at him. He glanced over my shoulder at Matt for a few seconds and it was as if they were having a private conversation, but I had no idea what it was about and then he looked back at me, his eyes full of gentle understanding.

"How about this, we'll spend tonight getting to know each other and you promise to let us know if things go too far and you want to stop. Deal?" Hudson said. That sounded perfect to me and so I nodded my head.

"Deal. There is one little thing though," I told him.

"What's that?" Matt asked, his breath ghosting across my cheek. I looked over my shoulder at him and then back at Hudson, seeing their similar looks of concern. "You both are wearing entirely too many clothes," I teased, arching my brow at them. They began to laugh and I smiled at my own joke, pleased that I could make them happy.

Matt swatted my butt playfully with his free hand and I saw the way Hudson's eyes lit up. *He likes that.* We took turns helping each other undress, pausing only to kiss and when the last article of clothing had been shed, I stepped back so that I could see my two lovers.

Matt's body was fit and toned and I wondered what he did to stay in such great shape. My eyes drank in the light dusting of hair that coated his chest, narrowing down to a perfect happy trail until it finally ended in a trimmed thatch of hair at the base of his cock. It was thicker than mine, but not quite as long and it curved slightly to the left.

I turned to check out Hudson and my jaw nearly hit the floor. There was no other way to describe Hudson's body other than *magnificent.* I knew he was built, but nothing could've prepared me for the sculpted muscles on display before me. His chest was broad, the muscles rippling with each of his movements, and he had an unbe-lievable eight-pack that I wasn't sure I could ever produce even if I spent every day in the gym for years.

My eyes lowered to the tightly curled hairs that surrounded Hudson's long dick. It jutted out proudly towards me and Matt as if beckoning us to take it in our mouths. And I wanted to. I wanted to drop to my knees and worship him, but I was afraid that I would mess it up in some way. I looked back at their faces and saw that they were observing each other as well as me and I felt my face heat up.

"You're both so beautiful, I can't make up my mind where I want to start first," Hudson said.

"I think *that* is going to require both of us," Matt answered, star-ing pointedly at Hudson's cock with something akin to awe. I reached down and wrapped my hand around my aching dick, giving it a few slow pumps. My mouth watered at the idea of Matt and me working together to bring Hudson pleasure.

My pulse raced as Matt dropped to his knees in front of Hudson. He glanced up at the man towering over him and Hudson reached his hand down, threading his fingers through the soft curls on Matt's head. I held my breath as Matt circled his hand around the base of Hudson's cock and then flattened his tongue to lick a line up Hudson's long shaft.

I watched with rapt attention as the tip of Matt's tongue circled the thick head of Hudson's cut cock and Hudson threw his head back with a loud groan. His fingers tightening in Matt's hair. I didn't even realize I was moving until I felt the plush carpet of the loft on my knees. Matt watched me out of the corner of his eye as he licked a path along the side of Hudson's dick. When he reached the head, he sucked it into his mouth and worked his tongue over the bundle of nerves underneath the cap.

Hudson gave an answering moan and I took note, memorizing everything that my lover responded to; what made him tremble and what made him groan in pleasure. I'd never given head before, but I was a quick learner and I was eager. That had to count for something, I told myself. I leaned forward and ran my tongue along the side of Hudson's cock, enjoying the thick veins and the silky feel of his skin.

When I got to the base, I nuzzled my nose into his pubic hair, breathing in deeply his clean, masculine scent. The combined smell, taste and feel of him made me dizzy with want and then his large hand cupped the back of my neck and pulled me closer, spurring me on and making me feel proud that I had obviously done something right. Matt held Hudson's cock out towards me in invitation and I flicked my tongue over his slit, tasting the salty fluid that beaded along the tip.

I whimpered at the flavor of Hudson on my tongue and I eagerly sucked down the head of his dick, wanting more. I choked as I went too far too fast and his thick cock filled my throat, hitting my gag reflex. My eyes watered as I pulled off quickly and I flushed with shame at my mistake, but Matt was right there, soothing me with his words.

"It's okay, you're doing great. He's a big boy and it's going to take time for both of us to get used to," Matt said, his lips quirking up in a sexy grin. I appreciated that he had included himself in that statement and my heart kicked up a notch at the thought of there being more times in the future in which we'd have time to practice. I hoped Matt meant that because I already knew I wanted there to be more, but I also knew not to get my hopes up. He may have been just talking in the heat of the moment.

My eyes traveled up the tall expanse of smooth, ebony skin until they landed on Hudson's face. He was staring down at me through hooded eyes and his voice was rough when he told me, "Everything you're doing is perfect. You both make me feel so good." I saw the honesty in his eyes and so I knew he hadn't just said that to placate me. I felt proud of myself and I quickly went back to work, trying to draw every bit of pleasure from him that I could.

Matt's tongue flicked over mine as we took turns licking and sucking Hudson, stopping occasionally to kiss. I cried out when I felt Matt's long fingers circle around my cock. He pulled on it a few times and let his thumb smooth over the tip, spreading my pre-cum all around and driving me insane. I was having trouble concentrating on what I was supposed to be doing to Hudson with Matt's hand working over me like that.

All of a sudden, Hudson leaned down, cupped me under the arms and lifted me off the floor and onto the bed in a move that seemed effortless. Matt got to his feet beside Hudson and they both stared down at me. I had to resist the urge to cover myself as I lay there, naked and exposed, under their watchful gazes. The appreciation and carnal lust I saw in their stares made my apprehension fade away, replaced with a feeling of power like I'd never experienced before.

I decided to tease them by running my hands down my stomach and tugging on my cock a few times. Their eyes continued to follow my every movement as they reached for their own leaking cocks. My skin felt like it was on fire and I found myself liking this little bit of exhibitionism.

Hudson growled and grabbed Matt in a fiery kiss that made my toes curl. The men clawed at each other as they kissed and Hudson bent his knees so that their cocks were lined up with each other. His large hand slid between their bodies and wrapped both of their dicks in his tight fist. Pre-cum dribbled out of them like a faucet, slicking their shafts and making Hudson's hand glide quickly up and down. Matt whimpered at what had to be an amazing feeling and I licked my lips at the show they were putting on for me.

No longer satisfied to sit on the sidelines, I climbed onto my hands and knees and crawled to the foot of the bed where they were standing and pushed my head between their two bodies. I could hear their gentle groans as they kissed above me and I began to lap at their combined juices, memorizing the various tastes and textures of my lovers. I was in Heaven.

CHAPTER
Twelve

Matt

HUDSON'S TONGUE SWEPT THROUGH MY MOUTH, URGING me to do the same and I felt long forgotten sensations spark to life once again. The wet heat of Isaac's eager mouth on me made my legs shake and I slid my hands up Hudson's strong arms, clinging to him so I wouldn't fall.

I'd only been with a few other men since Sean, each of which I'd met through a hookup app on my phone. I didn't use the app often, but I kept it there for the times when the loneliness got to be so heavy that I thought I'd drown in it. It was in those moments when I just needed the touch of another person, and it didn't matter who, that I'd find myself giving in and swiping through the app. Those hookups were quick, cold, and done with the sole purpose of getting off.

I could already tell that being with these two men was going to be different. Isaac was all gentle movements and held nothing back as he gave of himself freely. Hudson on the other hand was intensely passionate, taking what he wanted without apology, but giving back just as much in return. The contrast between the two was addictive and I didn't think I'd ever be able to get enough. And that right there was what scared me.

Hudson's mouth made a path across my jawline, kissing and nibbling his way over to my ear. I shivered as he licked along the shell of it and then dipped down to gently suck the tender skin right under my ear.

"I think it should be you," he whispered in my ear. I pulled my head back so I could see his face, but it was hard to concentrate on what he was saying because Isaac's enthusiastic mouth was pushing me closer and closer to the edge.

"What?" I rasped.

"I think you should be the one to take Isaac for the first time." My eyes widened in surprise and I glanced down just as Isaac's head shot up, our cocks leaving his mouth with a wet pop. "That is, if you even want things to go that far. We'll only do what you're comfortable with," Hudson assured the younger man. I studied Isaac's reaction closely, but he didn't look nervous anymore. Instead, his expression was one of curiosity, surprise, and, as he focused his attention on me, longing.

"Is that something you'd like?" Isaac asked me. I couldn't speak as I stared into those sweet, innocent, blue eyes that I had looked at for years but that I felt like I was just getting to know.

What he was offering was huge and not something that I took lightly. I cared about Isaac, he was important to me. Even though I'd never told him about my past, I was closer to him than just about anyone. The fact that he wanted to give so much of himself to me was humbling and I wasn't sure I deserved it. I dropped down to my knees beside the bed and cupped his cheeks in my hands.

"I would love to be with you in that way, but you need to be sure.

You won't ever have a first time again and it should be with someone very special. I can't make you any promises and I won't lie and say that I can, so you need to be sure," I told him.

"I'm ready and I want to be with you; with both of you." Isaac glanced at Hudson and then back at me, staring directly in my eyes as he answered. "I'll be honest and say that I really hope this isn't our only night together, but if it is…if this is the only chance I ever get to feel you and experience what it's like to be this close to you, then I'm not going to let that opportunity pass me by."

I must have taken too long to answer because I heard his whispered, "Please, Matt," and that was all it took. It was as if something clicked inside me and I could no longer hold back. He regarded me warily as I got to my feet, probably expecting me to grab my clothes and leave, but there was nowhere else I wanted to be than in that room with those two men.

"Will you get him ready?" I asked Hudson. He'd been wearing a gentle smile during my exchange with Isaac and it grew until I saw a flash of his white teeth. My breath caught in my throat at the caring look in his eyes.

"I'd love to," he answered. Hudson's fingers squeezed the back of my neck as he bent down for a kiss. The weight of his hand helped calm the quaking inside me and I placed my hand on his smooth chest. His heart beat rapidly against my palm as our kiss deepened and his hand snaked between us to wrap around my length. I sighed into his mouth as he began to pump my cock. It felt unbelievable, but he was far too good at it and after a few seconds, I reached down and grabbed his wrist, halting his movements.

"This will all be over if you touch me one more time," I panted. A puff of air blew across my lips as Hudson chuckled.

"Sorry about that," Hudson said, but when he stepped back, he was wearing a smirk that told me he wasn't sorry in the least about the effect he had on me. Honestly, neither was I.

Hudson moved around the bed to the table and opened the

drawer, pulling out a strip of condoms and a bottle of lube. I glanced down at the bed and nearly swallowed my tongue when I saw Isaac, lounging with one hand behind his head on the pillows, his other hand moving slowly up and down his shaft as he watched me through hooded eyes. The blatant need and longing in his eyes sent my pulse racing.

Hudson's hand brushed over my lower back as he moved to the foot of the bed so he could crawl up between Isaac's thighs. Hudson whispered something to him that made a beautiful smile spread across Isaac's delicate features.

Hudson lowered himself on top of the younger man and began kissing him as his hips rocked back and forth, working their pelvises in a slow grind. Isaac's eyes rolled to the back of his head and he let out a long moan which Hudson swallowed greedily.

I reached between my legs with my free hand and cupped my balls, squeezing them slightly in order to gain control over the orgasm that threatened. I was mesmerized by how breathtaking the two of them were together. Isaac's pale ivory skin was in perfect contrast with Hudson's darker ebony tone as he smoothed his hands up and down Hudson's back, grasping the taut globes of his ass with his fingers.

Hudson began to make his way down Isaac's body, alternating between nipping and licking and making Isaac squirm underneath him. Isaac spread his legs wider, allowing room for Hudson's broad shoulders between his thighs and his hips punched up as Hudson found his target and swallowed Isaac's cock down in one swift move.

Hudson locked his forearm across Isaac's waist, holding him down and showing him no mercy as he worshiped every inch of Isaac's leaking dick. Isaac's head thrashed back and forth on the pillow and he garbled nonsensical words. Hudson's hand searched blindly on the bed, his mouth never letting up on his ministrations. I knelt on the bed quickly, scooping up the bottle of lube and pouring some onto Hudson's outstretched fingers.

My mouth went dry as Hudson raised up to kneel between Isaac's legs, spreading them even further apart and I got my first look at Isaac's pretty pink hole. Hudson's slick finger circled his opening, bringing life to all the nerve endings there before dipping in just to the first knuckle. Isaac made a sound in the back of his throat that was a mixture of a plea and command.

Hudson responded to his need and I watched in awe as his finger disappeared into Isaac's tight channel. Soon enough, he added a second finger and began stretching him, twisting his wrist and coaxing Isaac's muscles to relax and allow him entry.

I glanced up at Isaac's face and saw that he had his eyes closed, his bottom lip turning white where he bit down on it. I knew the enormity of the trust and care he was putting in me by letting me be his first. Memories of my own first time flitted through my mind. Sean and I had had no idea what we were doing, but we were so in love that it was amazing all the same.

I felt a wave of doubt as I wondered if Isaac shouldn't wait for someone who he loved to share the special moment with instead of with me. As if he heard my thoughts, his eyes sprung open and searched around until they locked with mine. He stretched his hand out towards me in invitation and there was no way I could refuse.

Isaac and I may not have been in love, but I cared about him as more than a friend or I wouldn't have been there and I suspected it was the same for Hudson. Isaac had made it clear that this was what he wanted and we would both make sure that this was the kind of experience that someone as wonderful as Isaac deserved.

I bent down and swept my lips over Isaac's, soothing away the marks his teeth had left behind. Isaac's eyes fluttered closed, long lashes brushing his pale cheeks and I stared down at him for a second, taken aback by the sheer beauty of him. I couldn't resist the urge to kiss over the freckles on his nose. His eyes opened, looking surprised by the tender gesture and I froze, wondering if I'd crossed a line.

Isaac cupped a hand around the back of my neck though and lifted his head to kiss me. His lips were soft and lush against mine and I let myself get lost in the sweet taste of him, our tongues mating.

Out of the corner of my eye, I saw Hudson's head moving up and down over Isaac's long cock, his fingers moving in and out of him. He was being careful with him and I could tell he was having to hold a lot of himself back. I knew the exact moment when Hudson's fingers grazed over Isaac's prostate because he nearly flew off the bed.

"Feels amazing, doesn't it?" I whispered. Isaac could only nod his head in answer.

I reached down and placed my hand on the back of Hudson's head, pushing him down to take Isaac all the way in his throat. I watched as he swallowed and Isaac's body shivered against me. After a few seconds, Hudson sat up, licking his lips and winked at me, letting me know that Isaac was ready. We switched positions wordlessly and Hudson stretched out alongside Isaac while I settled myself between his legs.

I lowered my body on top of Isaac's so that we were face to face. "This will hurt some, but I'm going to do my best to keep it to a minimum. I want you to tell me if you need me to stop or slow down though, okay?"

"I will. I trust both of you," Isaac said sweetly.

"We're going to make this so good for you," Hudson promised, echoing my thoughts from before.

I kissed Isaac soundly and then turned my head to kiss Hudson. The tangy saltiness of Isaac's pre-cum lingered on his tongue, mixing with Hudson's own unique flavor and driving me wild. I deepened the kiss, desperate to get every last drop then I rose up on my knees to prepare myself.

Hudson was quicker than me though and he snatched up a condom, ripping it open and then slid it down my cock with steady, sure movements. He grabbed the bottle of lube and poured some in his palm then began to slick my length. A shiver wracked my body at the firm grip he had on my cock and I pushed his hand away, afraid I would embarrass myself if he continued.

I looked to Isaac one more time and was met with a gentle smile. Reassured that this was what he wanted, I lined the head of my cock up with his entry and pressed forward watching as the mushroomed head slipped inside his tight sheath. He gasped and I felt his body go rigid at the sudden pressure inside his body.

I stilled my movements while Hudson talked him through it, telling him how well he was doing and reminding him to relax. He reached down and rubbed his still slick hand over Isaac's flagging erection, bringing it back to life. When I heard Isaac's sigh, I began to rock gently, pushing my way into his snug passage.

I felt sweat trickle down my spine at the strain of holding myself back as I watched Isaac's hole swallow every inch of my cock. I was certain I was about to lose my mind from the pleasure of the heat surrounding my shaft and the way his ass squeezed me so perfectly, but I ground my teeth together to stop myself from thrusting forward and burying myself in his tight channel. I was determined to make Isaac's first time as pleasurable as possible and I refused to hurt him beyond what was necessary.

I moved slowly, watching Isaac's face for any signs of distress as Hudson continued to whisper words of encouragement to him in between kisses. When I was finally in as far as I could go, I held still, waiting for Isaac to give me a signal that he was ready for more.

His eyes were screwed shut and sweat dotted his forehead as he struggled to relax and accept my invasion on his body. He breathed in and out slowly as Hudson's hands wandered over his chest in a soothing manner. After several long moments, Isaac's gorgeous blue eyes opened and he nodded at me.

"I'm ready," he whispered.

Hudson kissed him once more then climbed up the bed, kneeling with his legs on either side of Isaac's head. He grabbed Isaac by the ankles, holding them up in the air and providing me better access. Hudson and I shared a look and then turned our attention to the scorching view of my cock sliding in and out of our lover.

"Oh, God! Matt, it's…" Isaac gasped as his pain quickly switched to ecstasy.

"I know. You feel incredible," I told him.

It was true too. I couldn't remember sex being that satisfying in years. I knew it was because what was happening was more than a simple hookup, but I refused to think too much about it in that moment.

The position Hudson was in left his dick jutting out right over Isaac's head and I watched as Isaac tilted his face up and swiped his tongue over the shaft. Hudson let go of one of Isaac's ankles and took his own cock in hand, feeding it into Isaac's hungry mouth. Isaac fisted his own dick and began to jerk it wildly as he feasted on the swollen cock before him.

My mouth watered at the erotic display and I lowered myself on top of Isaac, my hips thrusting deep and hitting that perfect spot inside that made him cry out, releasing Hudson from his mouth. I took advantage of the situation and swallowed Hudson into my own mouth, loving how his wide girth stretched my throat.

My body was slick with sweat and glided smoothly over Isaac as I thrust into him. His cock which was trapped between us, continued to leak, coating our stomachs with sweet, sticky fluid. My tongue dueled with Isaac's over the head of Hudson's cock and the combination of being inside Isaac while also sucking Hudson had my balls pulling up tight against my body.

I wouldn't last much longer, but I wanted Isaac to get off first so I began to talk. I described everything, from the feel of the vise-like grip his ass had on me to the sight of him swallowing Hudson's cock between his pretty pink lips.

Isaac screamed suddenly as an orgasm ripped through his body and I struggled to hold on as his hole spasmed around me, squeezing me in the most perfect way. White ribbons of cum shot from his dick and landed on his chest as he continued to call out our names.

Hudson lifted up on his knees and began to jerk off quickly, his brown eyes focused on me. It only took a few pumps before he was spilling over onto Isaac's chest, his seed mixing with Isaac's spunk and our combined sweat. The sight was too much for me and I shouted as I finally let loose, filling the condom.

I eased out of Isaac, careful not to hurt him and tossed the condom in the trash can next to the bed before I collapsed beside Isaac, still gasping for air. Hudson moved back down to lie on the other side of Isaac and I noticed he was shaking. Isaac looked back and forth between the two of us and then grinned.

"That was incredible! When can we do it again?" he exclaimed. Hudson and I shared a look of disbelief over top of Isaac's head and then, unable to stop ourselves, started laughing.

"Give us a few minutes, okay? Some of us aren't as young as you and need a little more recovery time," Hudson responded, still smiling.

"I think I'm going to have to pick up some vitamins for you two old men so you can keep up," Isaac teased. Hudson reached out and pinched his nipple, eliciting a squeal from Isaac before he burst into laughter.

My heart fluttered at the easy way they both assumed it would happen again. Darkness tried to creep in around the edges of my mind, but I pushed it away, allowing myself to enjoy being with the two men who'd made me feel so much in such a short amount of time.

I leaned up and captured Isaac's mouth with my own, swallowing his laughter and turning it into a groan. I reached for Hudson and he came willingly and the three of us shared a blistering kiss as we fed the flames of desire between us once more.

CHAPTER
Thirteen

Hudson

I LOOKED IN THE REARVIEW MIRROR AS I TURNED ONTO MY
sister's street and caught the smile that hadn't left my face
all morning. I knew the chemistry between Matt, Isaac, and
myself was off the charts, but I hadn't expected to feel so completely
connected to both of them.

It had just seemed right to me that Matt be the one to take Isaac
first. They'd known each other longer and while they had only been
friends up to that point, they had established a level of trust that I
was just beginning to develop with each man. Still, I was surprised
that I hadn't felt left out at all.

I'd been prepared when I'd made the suggestion to Matt, for me
to end up on the sidelines for much of it, but they'd kept me right
there with them. The looks and touches shared between the three of

us had me feeling as involved as if it were my cock sliding into Isaac's virgin hole. Hopefully, I wouldn't have to wait long for my turn with Isaac, or with Matt for that matter.

There was a burning need in Matt's eyes whenever he looked at me and I wondered if he had wanted me to top him, but I could tell he was still holding back for some reason. Something was keeping him from letting his guard down and so it hadn't been the right time. I refused to push him because when I took Matt for the first time, and I refused to think of that moment in terms of *if* but rather *when*, then I wanted him to get lost in the moment with me, free of whatever restraints had been holding him back.

Seeing the two of them together had been the single most erotic experience of my life. They'd been incredible together and even if I'd done nothing but sit in the corner as a quiet observer, it would have been enough for me. That's how I knew that what was happening between the three of us, what I was beginning to feel for Isaac and Matt, was already so much more than I'd ever shared with anyone else.

After that first round of spine tingling sex, the three of us had climbed into my large shower where we explored each other's bodies with slick, soapy hands. We knew Isaac would be too sore to bottom again so soon, but we were more than happy to get each other off using our hands and mouths.

I'd been disappointed when they decided to leave after that, turning down my offer to drive them home and sharing a cab instead, but I'd understood their need for space. After the intensity of everything that had occurred, I think we all needed time to process what was happening, but I was already looking forward to spending more time with the two of them.

I pulled into Aysha's driveway and laughed as the door swung open and Nicholas came bounding down the front steps, calling out my name. I climbed from the car and my knees hit the ground just as he reached me, throwing himself into my waiting arms.

"Hey, little man. Are you ready to go to the movie?" I asked, kissing his nose. He giggled in my arms and my heart melted a little.

"Yep! Mommy said if I eat all my lunch that I can get popcorn," he announced happily.

"Tell you what. If you do exactly as your mommy says, I'll get you a giant popcorn and candy too," I told him.

"You will?" he asked incredulously.

"I will," I promised before swinging him above my head and sitting him on top of my shoulders.

I carried him inside the house, ducking down low so he wouldn't hit his head on the doorway and making him squeal in delight at being so high up. Aysha came out of her room, slipping a pair of earrings in as she went. She was dressed in a pair of jeans and the red silk blouse that I'd bought her for her birthday. She looked good and I whistled at her in appreciation.

"Wow, Nicholas! Your mommy looks really pretty, doesn't she?" I said, chuckling when Aysha rolled her eyes at me.

"She's pretty," Nicholas parroted.

"Thank you, gentlemen," Aysha said, puckering her lips. I lowered Nicholas so she could give him a kiss and then I hugged her with my available arm, kissing the top of her head.

"Are you ready to go?" I asked.

"Yes, I just need to grab my purse," Aysha said, moving towards the front door where her purse hung on a rack by the door.

"This is my treat and I don't want any arguments, got it?" I told her sternly.

She spun around to face me with narrowed eyes. We'd had this argument many times, but I liked doing fun things for her and Nicholas that they wouldn't normally be able to do for themselves. It made me happy to be able to give a little back to her after everything she'd done for me growing up. Aysha surprised me when instead of fighting me on it she smiled and I immediately went on alert. I knew my sister well and I could tell when she was up to something.

"Fine, you can treat on one condition," she said, a devious grin forming on her face.

"What's that?" I narrowed my eyes, but smirked down at her.

"I want to hear all about last night," she said, wiggling her eyebrows at me. My heart stuttered as visions of my night with Matt and Isaac flashed through my mind. My sister certainly didn't need to know about that.

"What?" I choked.

"Hey, if you're going to party with the rich and famous then I at least want to hear the details," she informed me and my heart rate started to slow back down.

"Okay, I'll tell you all about the party over lunch, but we need to get a move on because I made reservations," I responded playfully, hoping she hadn't noticed my shock from before.

"Reservations? Like at an actual restaurant?" she squealed excitedly, following me out onto the front porch.

I waited as she locked the door and then I carried Nicholas to the car, stopping to grab his booster seat from her car and putting it in my own before strapping him in. Aysha climbed in beside me and looked at me expectantly. I took my time buckling up and starting the car, pretending to ignore her. We may have been close, but we were still siblings and we enjoyed torturing each other from time to time.

"You better start talking right now, mister." I looked over and my eyes widened when I saw her stern mom face on full display. Nicholas had better watch his P's and Q's because I had a feeling nothing was going to get past his mother.

"Fine. I'm taking you to that new French restaurant that you said you wanted to go to." She opened her mouth to say something, but I held my hand up, stopping her. "I already called and they have several items on the menu that Nicholas will like, so you can relax."

I watched as she sank back into her seat, giving me a tender look. "You're a really good man and brother, you know that?" I rolled my eyes at her praise, but she continued. "I mean it, Hudson. I don't know any other man that would do the things you've done for me and Nicholas. We might not have survived the last couple of years if it hadn't been for you," she ended with a whisper. I could see the tears that threatened to spill from her eyes and I rushed to stop them. I hated to see my sister cry, for any reason.

"You would've survived because you're the strongest woman I know, just like Nonna was," I told her, reaching across the armrest to squeeze her hand. "And there are a lot of great men out there. Just because you got a toad the first time doesn't mean your prince isn't still out there."

Aysha laughed as I'd hoped and wiped the moisture from her eyes. "I don't need a prince. I'd settle for a man who can hold down a job and keep his eyes from wandering outside the home."

She said it with a laugh, but I knew how badly it still hurt her that the man who had promised to love her forever had ended up cheating on her. Not only had her ex betrayed their vows and left her to raise their son alone, but he'd stolen her trust as well and I wished I could do something, anything, to make it so she'd never had to go through that.

The restaurant was just as fancy as I'd heard, and Aysha's eyes lit up when she saw the candles and cloth napkins on our table. She helped get Nicholas situated in his chair and then turned to me with a happy grin.

"Thank you so much, Hudson. This place is unbelievable," she gushed.

I looked around at the crystal chandeliers and the intricate wall sconces and I had to agree. The place was really quite impressive. We looked over the menus and then gave our orders to the waiter who did a double take when he noticed my sister. He eyed the three of us and then left to get our drinks. Aysha pulled a small notebook and some crayons out of her purse and laid them in front of Nicholas, who got right to work drawing pictures. She caught my grin and tilted her head at me.

"What are you smiling at?" she asked.

"It makes me happy seeing you with Nicholas. You're a terrific mom, you know," I told her. Aysha's eyes softened as she stared at me.

"Thank you. Sometimes I wonder if I'm doing alright by him, giving him enough love and attention." She shrugged her shoulders then reached over to run her hand over Nicholas's head.

"Look at him, Aysha. He goes to bed every night feeling happy and loved. Don't worry, you're doing everything right. Besides, you practically raised me and I turned out alright, didn't I?" I winked at her and she laughed, the worry gone from her eyes.

"Yes, I'd have to say that you turned out rather remarkable," she admitted.

"Oh my gosh! Did anyone else hear that?" I joked, looking around the room.

"Sorry about your luck. There's no evidence and if anyone asks, I'll deny the whole thing," Aysha informed me.

The waiter came back with our drinks. He was handsome with hazel eyes and thick brown hair. His eyes kept darting back and forth between me and my sister and his forehead wrinkled like he was trying to figure out a puzzle.

"Uncle Hudson, I made this for you!" Nicholas exclaimed, waving his drawing in the air.

"You did that for me? Thank you, little man," I said as I took it from him.

"I'll make you the next one, Mommy," Nicholas promised, looking adoringly at his mother.

I had to fight back a laugh when I saw the waiter's shoulders relax as he finally pieced together what Aysha and my relationship was to each other and he realized we weren't a couple. His smile widened as he handed her a glass of tea and I noticed the way his fingers purposely brushed over hers, smiling as he looked into her eyes. My sister, however, seemed completely oblivious to the attention she was receiving as she helped her son with his cup. I almost felt sorry for the poor guy as he turned and headed back towards the kitchen.

"Please tell me you're not that clueless," I said and Aysha's head popped up, her eyes wide.

"What are you talking about?" she demanded.

"I'm talking about the way our waiter has been staring at you," I stated.

"He was not! You're imagining things," she said, rolling her eyes at me as if the idea of someone flirting with her was ridiculous. The thought hurt me because I knew that's probably how she really felt.

"I didn't imagine him staring at you or the way his eyes lit up when Nicholas called me Uncle and he realized we weren't a couple. I also didn't imagine the way he made sure to touch your hand as he gave you your drink," I replied, laying the facts out and hoping she'd see what was happening as clearly as I did.

Her eyes widened, but then I saw them shutter. "It doesn't matter," she said.

"What do you mean?" I asked, knowing I wasn't going to like her answer.

"I mean nothing would come of it anyway. He probably flirts with everyone to try and get a better tip," she said, waving her hand in the air like the conversation was over.

I hated the cynical tone in her voice because I knew that wasn't my sister. That was her insecurities talking; the insecurities that that cheating bastard, Tommy, had given her. I wasn't a violent person, I believed in talking through your issues, but in that moment, if her ex-husband had been standing in front of me, I would've decked him.

"Now, enough stalling. Tell me about the party you went to," Aysha said.

I clenched my jaw at her obvious attempt at changing the subject. I wanted to argue with her, but then I saw the pleading look in her eyes and I knew it wasn't the right time. I'd brought her there to enjoy herself and have fun and I wouldn't spoil that for her. We would, however, be revisiting the conversation eventually.

I told Aysha about the crowd of fans outside the club and some of the funny stories that had been passed around among my friends. The waiter brought us our food and Aysha mostly kept her head down, but I did see her dart a look at him as he set her plate in front of her. His smile broadened, displaying a row of perfectly straight white teeth and he winked at her boldly. Aysha's gaze dropped back to the table, but I could see a slight grin on her lips as the waiter walked away. I was glad that she had seen the man's reaction for herself, but I kept my face blank as she looked my way.

"I miss dancing. Please, tell me you did some dancing. Let me live vicariously through you," Aysha pleaded dramatically.

My mind immediately flashed to the night before when I'd sat, watching Matt and Isaac out on the dance floor. The way they'd moved together had been natural and fluid as if their bodies were made for each other. The heat between them could be felt from across the room and when they finally kissed, I'd felt like my body was going to go up in flames.

I swallowed hard as I realized I'd been quiet too long and Aysha was staring at me through narrowed eyes, her head tilted to the side as she studied me like a bug under a microscope. It was time to come clean. I'd never been able to hide anything from my sister because she knew me better than anyone else in the world and besides, if things went the way I was hoping they would go with Matt and Isaac, then I would have to tell her about them eventually anyway.

"I did dance just a little," I told her, trying to figure out how to explain my infatuation with two men.

"You've met someone," she said with a growing smile and I shifted in my seat nervously.

"Well, sort of," I said slowly. "The thing is, I've actually met two men." Aysha's face crinkled in confusion and my palms began to sweat.

"Wait, you're seeing two guys at the same time? Do they know about each other?" I could hear the touch of disappointment in her voice and I knew she was comparing it to her own experience with her ex.

"It's not like that," I rushed to explain. "The three of us…we all like each other." Aysha leaned back in her chair and eyed me for a moment as she let my words turn over in her head then she leaned forward, placing her elbows on the table and folding her hands under her chin.

"Okay, tell me about them," she said simply, as a small smile lifted her lips.

I stared at her, stunned by her easy reaction to the news. My sister had always been very open-minded and my biggest supporter, but I'd figured the news that I was getting involved in a ménage would've thrown her just a little.

"You seem to be taking this very easily," I said and Aysha laughed.

"Hudson, you've always done things your own way; moving to L.A., starting your own practice, and it's worked out for you each and every time. I don't see any reason for this to be any different. You're a smart guy with a good head on your shoulders and I know you wouldn't rush into something like this without giving it some serious thought first," she explained.

"You're right. I have thought a lot about what it would be like to be with both of them and it just feels right, you know?" Aysha smiled at me knowingly and I could see the excitement in her eyes.

"Don't get too excited though. It's still very early and I'm not quite sure how they each feel about it yet. We have a lot of things to work out and there are many things we don't know about each other yet," I cautioned her.

"Okay, I get it. I'd still like to hear about them though. I've never seen you look the way you did when you were thinking about them earlier. It has me intrigued about who these men are," she said.

I felt so much love for my sister right then and I relaxed as I spent the rest of our meal telling her everything I knew about Isaac and Matt. She thought they sounded like amazing people and said she couldn't wait to meet them someday. I wanted that too, I just hoped we made it that far. I worried that in the light of day, they may be second-guessing what had happened between us.

Aysha took Nicholas to the bathroom while I paid the bill and I smiled when I saw the waiter's name, and his phone number written on the receipt along with a note. *To the beautiful woman seated at my table, I'd love the opportunity to take you out and get to know you. If you're interested, please give me a call.* I held the receipt out to her as we climbed in the car and she immediately opened her mouth to object, but I cut her off, folding her hand around the thin strip of paper.

"Don't say anything right now. Just promise me that you won't throw it away, okay? Even if you never call him, let it serve as a reminder that there are perfectly nice men out there who find you attractive and want to get to know you. Not every man is a sleaze ball like Tommy," I said, hoping she'd finally start to believe me.

I breathed a sigh of relief as she took the paper and folded it carefully before sliding it into her purse. I leaned over and kissed her cheek. I knew how difficult it would be for her to take that first step towards trusting people again, but she was a wonderful woman and she deserved to be happy. I smiled as I pulled out of the parking lot and started heading towards the movie theater. Maybe it was time for both of us to find some happiness.

CHAPTER
Fourteen

Isaac

I CHECKED THE TIME ON MY WATCH AND THEN LEANED AGAINST the small counter in my kitchen as I drank my coffee. I had a few minutes before I needed to leave to catch the L train into work. I'd spent all day Sunday feeling as if I were in a daze. I worked on autopilot as I cleaned my apartment and did laundry. I tried to relax and read, but my thoughts constantly returned to the night before and I found myself reading the same paragraph over and over without taking any of it in. My body was sore, but every twinge and ache served as a delicious reminder of what had happened between me, Matt, and Hudson.

I'd always wondered what my first time having sex would be like. I'd hoped that it would be with someone who liked me and would do their best to make it good for me, but never in my wildest dreams had I imagined anything as good as my night with those two men.

There'd been an instant chemistry between the three of us from the first time we met. It had continued to smolder each time we were together, but the night of the party, that slow burn had ignited into a fiery passion that I was surprised hadn't left my body in a pile of ashes.

However, it was so much more than just desire between us. It was also the looks that had been exchanged. The way we all seemed to feel the need to reach for one another, keeping the connection between us. The gentle, caring way they'd taken care of me, making sure my first time was nothing short of amazing. I'd never experienced anything like it before and I craved more.

I'd always been kind of a loner, keeping to myself both at school and at home, but with good reason. I'd only ever had one person I was really close to, but even he hadn't known all my secrets. Although I think he suspected, especially there at the end. I pushed the thoughts away, not allowing myself to go down that dark path.

Once I'd started living at Agape House, I'd learned to accept help from others, to trust in other people. For the first time in my life, I'd begun to let my guard down. Once I began working there and I was in the position of helping others, I'd opened up even more, spending time with the kids and making friends with the other staff members and volunteers. I'd slowly begun to realize that I wasn't the introvert I'd always thought I'd been. Given the right environment, I was actually quite outgoing and friendly.

Still, with all my newfound friends, I'd never felt fully connected with any of them. Even Matt who knew me better than anyone else at the center was held at arm's length. Although I'm not sure if that was more on my part or his. Probably a combination of the two. The other night had changed all that though. I'd seen deeper inside Matt than ever before and it had given me the confidence to hand over more of myself.

At the center of it all was Hudson, whose open honesty had kept the three of us tethered, binding us in a way that made me feel safer and stronger. When I was lying there, Matt inside me and Hudson hovering above my head, I'd felt safer than I ever had in my life. It was as if when I was with those two men, nothing and no one could touch me. I'd never felt that level of security, ever. I knew that after that first taste of it, I'd never be able to let that feeling go.

I just hoped my two lovers had felt the same. I had no experience when it came to those kinds of things. For all I knew, sex was always that powerful and what had seemed earth-shattering to me, had been normal for them. I sighed as I poured the last of my coffee into the sink and rinsed out my cup. I guess there was only one way to find out, I needed to get to work so I could see them.

"Isaac! Hey, man, we're just about to start a game. You in?" someone called out as I walked in the door of Agape House.

I looked up and saw Troy standing near the front desk, a basketball tucked under his arm. Troy had shown up at the center nearly six months before, battered and bruised from a father who refused to have a gay son. The bruises had all healed and after many sessions with Hudson, he had finally started to show his true self. Beneath the quiet, scared kid who had arrived at our door, was a fun-loving, outgoing, adventurous young man.

"Don't you need to catch the bus soon?" I asked, checking the time on my watch.

"No school. It's a teacher in-service day," he answered. I chuckled at the broad smile that spread across his face, remembering how excited I used to get when there was no school.

"Okay! Let me just put my stuff up and check in with Matt, then I'll play," I told him. I started down the hallway towards my office, but stopped in my tracks when Allison spoke up from her desk.

"Matt's not here yet. He wasn't at breakfast and I haven't heard from him," she said.

My stomach twisted in a knot. I couldn't remember Matt ever being late. He was always the first one to arrive at the center, often before the kids woke up. He'd told me once that it was because it was quiet and he was able to get some of his work done so he could spend more time with the kids before they had to go to school. I always thought it was sweet that he wanted to make sure he had breakfast with them and saw how they were doing before they left for the day. The fact that he hadn't done so that morning, especially since there was no school, had me feeling concerned. I hoped he wasn't sick.

"I'll check my messages, see if he called," I told Allison.

I told Troy I'd be right back and then I walked down the hallway, frowning at Matt's dark office. I stepped into my office and put my messenger bag in my bottom desk drawer then hung my jacket on the coat hook on the back of the door. I sat down at my desk and saw the light flashing on my office phone, alerting me to three new messages. I pushed the button quickly so I could listen to them, hoping one of them was from Matt.

My shoulders sagged with disappointment when none of the voices were his. I pulled my cell phone out of my pocket just to be sure I hadn't missed a message or call, but there was nothing. I hoped he wasn't sick, but then I brushed the thought aside. If he weren't feeling well, he would've called either me or Allison already to reschedule his appointments. Maybe he just had car trouble or an early appointment he forgot to mention.

I rolled my eyes. It wasn't like it was late in the day, just late for Matt. The man had a life outside of the center, I reminded myself. He gave so much of himself and if he wanted to take the morning off, that was his prerogative.

Feeling better, I grabbed the T-shirt and shorts I kept in my cabinet and changed into them so I wouldn't get my work clothes all sweaty, then I hurried down the hall to shoot some hoops with Troy and his friends. It felt good to let loose and have some fun with the kids. They kept me laughing with their antics throughout the entire game and soon enough, the tension began to seep from my body, replaced with warm, limber muscles and the exhilaration that came with my blood rushing through my veins.

The game ended and there was a lot of friendly razzing from the winners. I was happy to see that no one got their feelings hurt and seemed to understand that the teasing was done in good-natured fun. They were a great group of kids and I liked that they all got along and had fun together. I ran to my office and grabbed my good clothes then I went to the employee bathroom and used the shower there to clean myself. I got dressed and grabbed a water and an apple from the kitchen then headed to the front of the building.

"Hey, Allison! Have you seen Matt yet?" I asked.

"No and he still hasn't called either. This isn't like him at all. Do you think we should be worried?" The look on her face told me how concerned she was and I had to admit, I was really starting to get worried. Matt never missed work and if he needed to take a day off, he would've called to let us know. Something wasn't right. I could feel it in my bones.

"I'm going to try and get ahold of him. I'm sure everything's fine," I assured her, trying to convince myself that it was true.

I walked quickly to my office and checked both phones, but there were still no messages from Matt. Everything from the flu to a car accident raced through my mind as possible reasons for him to miss work without calling.

Then another possibility occurred to me and a feeling of unease rippled through me. What if Matt had gone home Saturday night and decided that being with me and Hudson had been a mistake? What if I'd done something wrong and he decided I wasn't good enough? I was glad that I'd waited to be with the two of them, but a part of me cursed my inexperience. He'd seemed like he enjoyed it, but Matt was a good guy, could he have been pretending to avoid hurting my feelings?

I quickly dialed his number, holding my breath as it rang. Once, twice, three times before finally going to voicemail. I tapped my fingers on my desk nervously and without giving it any thought, I called Hudson.

As it began to ring, I remembered that he was probably with a patient and that I shouldn't interrupt. I went to hang up, but then he answered and just the sound of his voice calmed me and I was able to take a deep breath.

"I was just thinking about you," Hudson said.

"You were?" I couldn't hide the surprise in my voice. I still had trouble believing that a man like Hudson would be interested in me. Hudson chuckled into the phone and the sound made goose bumps break out all over my body.

"I think you'd be surprised how much of my day is spent thinking about you and Matt," he informed me.

"I think about both of you all the time too," I admitted quietly. I was pretty sure I could hear him smiling through the phone and I felt the beginnings of a smile forming on my face as well.

"So, it's not that I'm not thrilled to hear from you, because I am very glad you called, Isaac," he assured me. "But is everything alright?"

"I'm not sure," I answered.

"What's wrong, baby?" he asked and my eyes itched when I heard the endearment.

"I don't know. Matt never showed up for work today and he's not answering his phone. I thought maybe he just had an appointment and was running late, but he never called. It's just not like him at all. Matt hasn't missed a day of work since I've been here and I'm starting to get really worried," I said in a rush.

I heard what sounded like a door opening and then muffled voices as if Hudson had covered up the phone with his hand as he spoke with someone. A second later he was back.

"I'm coming to pick you up. I should be there in about ten minutes. Do you know where Matt lives?" he asked. I felt bad for taking Hudson away from his work, but I was also relieved to know that he would be there soon and would help me figure out what was going on.

"I've never been there, but I know his address. I'll watch for you," I told him.

"Try not to worry, Isaac. I'll be there soon and we'll go see him together and make sure he's alright." Hudson sounded so sure and it helped calm my frayed nerves.

I grabbed my phone and my jacket off the back of the door, rushing down the hall to tell Allison we were going to check on Matt. She seemed relieved that we were handling it and asked me to let her know once we found him. I promised I would and then I went outside to wait for Hudson. It didn't take long before I saw his black SUV pulling into the parking lot and I hurried to climb into the passenger seat.

"Thank you for doing this. I'm so sorry to bother you, but I was worried and I didn't know who else to call," I explained as soon as I shut the door. Hudson turned to face me and his eyes held so much kindness that I felt myself melting.

"Don't apologize for reaching out to me, ever. I'm glad you called me, I want to be here for you whenever you need me," he said and I could hear the sincerity in his voice. My breath hitched as he leaned in and kissed me. It was gentle, sweet and full of promises.

"Thank you," I whispered. I'd never had anyone I could rely on except Matt, but even with him, I hadn't felt comfortable calling him unless it was work related, until recently. I was hoping that Saturday night had been a turning point in our relationship, but now I wasn't so sure.

"Come on, let's go see what's going on with our guy."

Hudson grabbed my hand and held it as he drove away from the center. My body flushed warm all over at the thought of Matt being *our guy*. I wanted both of them to be mine so badly and I wanted to be theirs. I just hoped Matt hadn't already closed the door on the idea without giving us a proper chance.

CHAPTER
Fifteen

Matt

M Y HEAD FELT LIKE IT WAS ABOUT TO SPLIT IN TWO AS I stepped in the shower. I stood there and let the hot water beat down on my shoulders, hoping it would relieve some of the knots that had formed there. I rarely drank, so to go off on a bender like I had was taking a serious toll on my body.

I washed myself carefully, my movements slow so as not to upset my fragile stomach. I'd already spent the evening losing a lot of the alcohol I'd consumed and while I doubted there was anything left, my stomach still cramped uneasily every now and then. It was stupid to drink that much, I knew that, but it had started as something to help take the edge off and quickly escalated into the need to feel completely numb.

Isaac and I had held hands as we shared a cab ride home from

Hudson's place and I gave him a quick kiss before he climbed out of the car and walked up the steps to his apartment. I'd had an amazing night with the two men and I'd been surprised at how natural it seemed to be, having sex with both of them at the same time. I'd expected it to be a little awkward at first as we figured out who would do what, while making sure everyone was included. Instead, we'd moved together as if we'd done it a thousand times before, while at the same time exploring and learning each other's bodies.

Isaac had been so open and honest, holding nothing back as he'd given himself to us for the first time. Hudson had taken control over my body, kissing and tasting me, silently begging for me to let go. I'd wanted to give myself over to him, to let him consume me until there was nothing left to do but feel the power of his body next to mine. I'd held back, not quite ready to take that leap, but Hudson had seemed satisfied with whatever I was willing to give.

After Isaac had been dropped off, I'd sat in the darkened back seat of the cab, alone with my thoughts. I'd enjoyed myself and my body was already craving more of the two men. More than that, I genuinely liked spending time with them. They were funny and intelligent and I was happier just being around them. I smiled, thinking to myself that perhaps I could invite them over to my place for dinner one night, spend more time getting to know each other and maybe see where this thing would lead us.

With that thought, guilt reared its ugly head and slammed into me with a viciousness I hadn't been prepared for. I felt like the wind had been knocked out of me and I struggled to catch my breath. The cabbie gave me a strange look as I tossed a wad of cash at him, but I ignored it and stumbled up the sidewalk and into my house.

I slammed the door behind me and collapsed against it, sliding down until I was seated on the floor. I drew my knees up to my chest and wrapped my arms around my legs, resting my forehead against my knees. I was shaking all over and a cold sweat had broken out across my body. I closed my eyes and just focused on my breathing, wishing I could get back even a little bit of the happiness I'd felt before. It was no use, though.

Eventually, I'd climbed to my feet and made my way to the kitchen, remembering that I had a couple bottles of whiskey in the pantry that someone had given me for Christmas the year before. I opened one quickly and took a drink, not even bothering to pour it in a glass. After all, it wasn't like I had anyone to share it with. The thought made me laugh even though I had no idea why. The sound echoed in the empty kitchen, and I could hear the high-pitched hysteria in it.

I took several more swallows, enjoying the smooth burn that traveled down my throat and the warmth that spread through my limbs. It wasn't enough to ward off the cold that had settled into my bones though; that would've been too much to ask.

Taking the bottle with me, I made my way down the hall to my room. I sat on the bed and set the bottle on the nightstand, then picked up the framed picture that I always kept beside me as I slept. My hands shook as I lifted it up to my face and for the first time ever, I found it difficult to look at the face staring back at me from beneath the glass.

I'd been with other men before and never felt this level of guilt, so why was it so different this time? A small voice in the back of my mind whispered that it was because being with Hudson and Isaac had meant so much more than any of those other encounters.

Tears filled my eyes, blurring my vision as I knew the voice was right. Even after just one night in their arms, I knew that there was more to the three of us than a simple fling. There were feelings there that I hadn't even begun to explore. I hadn't allowed myself to because of moments like this. Moments when the guilt loomed over me like a tidal wave about to crush the life right out of me.

Rage boiled up inside of me and I swiped at my tears angrily. We'd had so many plans, made so many promises, but Sean hadn't been able to hold up his end of them. None of our dreams had come true and I'd been left all by myself, trying to find a way to move forward when my heart had been ripped out of my chest.

Would it be so wrong for me to move on? To find someone to share my life with so I wouldn't have to be so lonely all the fucking time? I glared back down at the face in the photo and the anger drained out of me just as quickly as it'd come in. Neither one of us had wanted it to end, but sometimes the universe has other plans and one person moves on while the other is left behind. I just wished it didn't have to hurt so badly.

I swiped the bottle from the table and took another drink, then cradled it against my chest as I curled up on top of my comforter, wrapping myself into a ball. A part of me wanted to call Hudson and Isaac and beg them to come over. I knew that the two of them would be able to chase the darkness away, but the other part of me felt like that would mean I was moving on, forgetting, and I couldn't allow that to happen. I swallowed another long drink and let the guilt and the sadness carry me away.

Sunday had been much the same. I'd woken up in the clothes I'd come home in, the scent of Hudson and Isaac still lingering in the material and on my skin and I'd raced to the bathroom to throw up. I'd spent the rest of the day drinking, trying to forget everything that had happened between me, Isaac, and Hudson as well as pushing away painful memories of the past.

I'd spent Sunday evening regretting my choice to drink and feeling sicker than I ever had in my entire life. It was noon by the time I woke up on Monday and I groaned as the light from the window hit my eyes, causing a sharp, stabbing pain to shoot through my skull. I knew I should call Allison and tell her I was taking the day off so she wouldn't worry, but I needed aspirin and a shower first.

I climbed out of the shower and dried myself off, running the towel over the wet curls on my head before wrapping it around my waist. I stood in front of the shower and grimaced at my reflection. My skin looked sallow and there were dark circles around my eyes. I reached for my toothbrush, desperately needing to rid myself of the vile flavor that the alcohol had left behind.

Minty fresh and feeling halfway human again, I made my way to the bedroom and pulled on a comfy pair of sweats and an old T-shirt. I was just heading into the kitchen to make some toast when there was a knock on my door. I glanced at it in surprise. No one ever came to see me. I opened the door, expecting to have to get rid of a salesman, but my jaw dropped open when I saw Hudson and Isaac standing on my front porch instead.

"What are you two doing here?" I asked.

"We were worried when you didn't show up for work. You never miss work. And you didn't call anyone or pick up when I tried to call. Of course, the two of us are going to show up and make sure you're alright," Isaac nearly shouted. He'd pushed his way inside during his rant and I had no choice but to back up and let them in. I'd never seen him look that mad, but I could see how shaken he was and I immediately felt guilty for having scared him.

"I'm sorry. It was selfish and thoughtless not to call and let everyone know I was alright," I admitted quietly.

My eyes darted over to Hudson who'd been quiet so far and I found him staring at me. His head was tilted to the side and there was a look of deep concern on his face. I looked down at my feet, unable to hold his gaze. He was a perceptive man, he dug into people's minds for a living and I was afraid he'd be able to see too much if I looked at him right then. I was vulnerable at the moment, the memories and emotions still too fresh, too close to the surface.

"I'm just glad you're okay. You are okay, aren't you?" Isaac asked, running his eyes all over me to be sure. He looked worried as his gaze reached my face again and I shifted uncomfortably on my feet. I'm sure he was startled by my appearance and I was thankful that I had at least taken a shower and brushed my teeth, but there was no way of hiding my red-rimmed, puffy eyes.

"Yes, of course. I'm fine," I answered, making sure not to look at either of them directly, for fear they'd see I was lying. There wasn't anything right about the way I'd reacted after sleeping with the two of them. The guilt and the loneliness had been going on for too long and it wasn't healthy. I was aware of that, but I didn't know how to stop it or make it go away.

"I'm sorry. Would you like to come in and have a seat? Would either of you like anything to eat or drink?" I offered in a rush as a sudden bout of nerves coursed through me.

Hudson stepped towards me and I felt myself tense, but then he reached out and ran his fingers along my cheek and up through my hair. The move was gentle and comforting and I felt myself instinctively leaning into his touch. I looked up into his soft brown eyes and could see the compassion there. I was sure then that he could sense the pain I was in, even though he didn't know the cause.

I swallowed hard. It would be so easy to just let go and open up to them, but I was worried that once they found out what a mess I was they'd decide I wasn't worth the trouble. Hudson leaned down and brushed his lips over mine.

"How long has it been since you've had anything to eat?" There was no judgement in Hudson's voice, only concern, and I felt myself frowning as I struggled to recall the last meal I'd had. "That's what I thought. Where's your kitchen?" he asked.

I pointed to the doorway behind me and then watched as Hudson brushed past me and walked right into my kitchen as if he'd been to my house a thousand times before. Isaac stepped up to me then and took my hands in his. My eyes darted to our hands and then to his face. His smile was gentle and reassuring and I was suddenly so grateful to have both of them there.

I was embarrassed at the tears that filled my eyes, but I knew that they both had stopped what they were doing and left work in the middle of the day to come check on me. It had been so fucking long since anyone had cared about me. Sure, I had friends at the center who cared, but things with Hudson and Isaac were different and I'd be lying if I didn't admit it.

Isaac's eyes softened when he saw the well of emotion on my face and he leaned up on his toes and wrapped his arms around my neck. My hands went to his waist, instinctively, and a shiver raced down my spine as he whispered in my ear.

"It's okay. We're here now and whatever is going on, it will be okay. You're not alone."

Those last three words had my knees buckling beneath me and I felt Isaac's arms tighten around me, lending me his strength. My arms wrapped around his waist and I buried my face into his neck as we held each other. There was no way he could possibly know how much I wanted that to be true. I was so tired of being alone.

After a few moments, I pulled back and looked at him. His blue eyes stared back at me with so much adoration that I felt like a fool for having not noticed it before. I bent my head down, kissing him gently and smiled when I heard him sigh.

"Come on, let's go see what Hudson is up to in your kitchen," Isaac said, grinning up at me. I smiled back at him because it was impossible not to and he grabbed my hand once again before pulling me towards the kitchen. As we walked in, Hudson shut the door of my refrigerator and turned to us with a frown.

"I couldn't find anything but frozen meals," he said.

"That's what I eat most nights. Not much point in cooking when it's just me," I said with a shrug. Hudson's eyes narrowed, but he didn't respond to that.

"Okay, I'll order something and have it delivered. What are you hungry for?" he asked.

"My stomach's not all that happy with me right now," I said with a grimace. "I was just going to make some toast when you guys showed up."

"Copious amounts of alcohol will do that to you," he said, arching an eyebrow at me. My eyes dropped to the floor. I was ashamed at my behavior, but it would be pointless to try and deny it. The look in his eyes told me he already knew.

"You need grease to cure your hangover, plus lots of water because you're probably dehydrated," Hudson said as he pulled his phone out of his pocket.

He set to work ordering burgers and fries with chocolate shakes for each of us and Isaac went to my cabinets, opening each one until he found the glasses then he pulled one out and filled it with water from the sink. He handed me the glass and I sat down at the kitchen table to drink it. The two of them came over and sat down across from me.

"We're going to get you fed and feeling better and then we're going to talk," Hudson informed me in a voice that brooked no argument.

I sagged in my chair as I felt the weight of everything I'd been holding in pressing down on me. The anger and hurt, the sadness and guilt from my past, along with my confusion over my feelings for the two men sitting there had suddenly become too much. Instead of getting defensive and arguing with him, I simply nodded. I wanted to share my story with them. I was ready.

CHAPTER
Sixteen

Matt

THE CONVERSATION WAS KEPT LIGHT AS WE ATE AND I HAD A feeling they were doing it on purpose. I think they sensed that what I had to tell them was going to be difficult for me and so they were giving me a bit of a reprieve. I appreciated the gesture as it gave me time to figure out exactly what all I would tell them. In the end, I decided that I wouldn't hold anything back. No matter how difficult it was to revisit the past, I owed it to them as well as myself to get it out in the open.

Both my head and my stomach felt much better after the greasy meal and Isaac made sure to refill my water glass whenever he saw it empty. When we were finished, we moved into the living room where it was more comfortable. I sat down on the couch, leaving the two armchairs across from me for Hudson and Isaac. I leaned forward with my elbows on my knees as I tried to think of where to start.

"Did I do something wrong?" Isaac asked and my head shot up in surprise. "I know I'm not as experienced as you two, and I know I probably messed things up, but is that why you stayed away?"

"No, not at all," I assured him. I hated the worried look on his face and I was horrified that he would think my staying away from work had anything to do with his sexual performance. "You were perfect, both of you were absolutely perfect…and that was part of the problem." Both men wore matching confused expressions on their faces and I took a deep breath, letting it out slowly.

"I was in love once. His name was Sean and we met when I was fifteen years old. My family had just moved because of my dad's job and I was miserable and grouchy about having to leave my friends behind and start all over at a new high school. It was the beginning of summer break and I must've been getting on my mom's nerves because she suggested that I go outside and take a walk or go for a bike ride. I don't think she really cared as long as I got out of her hair for a while." I chuckled at that, knowing what a pain I'd been to live with back then.

"Anyway, I went outside and sat down on the back steps and began tossing my baseball up in the air." I smiled as I let myself get lost in the memory.

"Hey! You want to play catch?" A voice called out from nearby.

I looked up and saw a pair of green eyes and a shock of red hair peering at me from over the privacy fence that ran between ours and the neighbor's property. I couldn't see anything else because the rest of him was hidden behind the wooden slats, but I could tell he was young, probably around my age. I was bored and could use someone to toss back and forth with so I said sure.

I unlocked the gate so he could come into our yard and then stood there stupidly as I stared at him. He was a little bit taller than me with a wiry frame. His skin was very pale and I wondered if it was because he was a redhead or if he just spent most of his time indoors. He looked like the type that probably spent a lot of time on a computer or playing video games.

Then he smiled at me and my mouth went dry and my heart began to beat wildly in my chest. He was probably what most kids our age would consider a nerd or geek, but to me he was the most remarkable creature I'd ever seen.

I'd started noticing boys when I was about twelve years old and I'd talked to my parents about it, wondering why all of my friends seemed to like girls and I didn't. They asked me if I knew what being gay meant and I told them I'd heard it used before and I didn't think it was a very good thing from what I'd heard.

They'd frowned at each other and then explained to me the truth of what being gay meant and that there was nothing wrong with a person being whoever they were born to be. Because of my parents, I'd never given another thought to being gay and was just content with who I was.

I stood there, trying to not make it obvious how attractive I thought he was, but he'd left me completely tongue tied so I looked at the ground instead. His hand shot out and he snatched the ball away from me. My head shot up and he winked at me as if he knew what I'd been thinking.

"Come on, let's play some ball before my mom catches me out here." I watched as he walked away from me, further into our yard. It took a second, but I was eventually able to get my legs to work and I jogged over to catch up.

We tossed the ball back and forth in a steady rhythm and he asked me for my name and where I had moved from. He told me his name was Sean and that he'd seen me out in the yard a few times and had been waiting for an opportunity to come over and say hi. I was shocked to learn that he'd been watching me and it made a tingle go up my spine, but in a good way. A very good way.

Sean was really easy to talk to and I found myself laughing with him a lot. We had many things in common, including music, video games, and books. I was disappointed to find out that while we were the same age, he was home schooled and wouldn't be attending the public school with me.

"I'm trying to convince my parents to let me go, but I don't know if they'll go for it," he said.

"Why would they say no if they know you'd rather go there?" I asked.

"Because I get sick a lot." Sean stared at the ball in his hand for a few seconds and then looked up at me as if he were deciding whether to tell me something or not. "I used to have leukemia," he finally blurted out.

I'd heard the word before and I was pretty sure it was a type of cancer, but beyond that I didn't know anything about it. My stomach knotted and I wanted to tell him I was sorry, to ask him if he was alright, but he was watching my face closely and I knew that how I reacted would make the difference in whether he stayed or went back to his own house. I liked him and I was in desperate need of a new friend so I kept my face blank when I spoke.

"You said used to, right?" I asked.

"Yeah, I've been in remission almost a year now," he answered cautiously.

I shrugged my shoulders and then held my hand out. "They should let you go to school. Maybe we'd even end up in the same classes," I said casually.

I held my breath, praying I'd said the right thing. Sean stared at me for what felt like ages and then the most beautiful smile spread across his face, lighting it up and it felt like Christmas and my birthday all in one. He tossed the ball to me and we resumed our game back and forth as we laughed and joked and got to know each other.

Sean went back inside when he heard his mom calling him, after explaining that she worried about him way too much and preferred it when he stayed inside where she could see him. He rolled his eyes and laughed, but I could tell it bothered him. I would've gone crazy if I could never go anywhere or do anything. Maybe his mom would let me come over to their house sometimes, that way Sean and I could still hang out.

I went back into my house and told my parents all about my new friend. I wasn't even sure they got a word in during dinner, but they looked happy to see me finally smiling again. Their happiness turned to concern though when I told them about Sean being sick, but I assured them that he was in remission, because Sean had made that sound like a good thing. They frowned when I told them about Sean wanting to go to school and I saw them exchange a look. My parents did that a lot, communicating with each other with just a look. They said it was because they were in love, I just thought it was weird.

As soon as I got to my room, I logged onto my computer and searched leukemia, hoping to learn everything I could so I wouldn't say something stupid in front of Sean. I was surprised at how many different types of leukemia there were though as well as things called stages and treatment options and big medical terms that I couldn't even begin to pronounce. Frustrated, I shut down my computer and went to bed.

The next day, my mom baked a cake and asked me to carry it as we walked over to Sean's house. She told me she wanted to introduce herself and get off to a good start with the neighbors, but I knew she was up to something. I didn't get to ask her more about it though because the door swung open and Sean's mother was standing there with Sean smiling at me over her shoulder.

Sean's mom invited us in to have some cake and she and my mom seemed to hit it off. Sean took me to his room to show me his video game collection while our moms had coffee. By the time we left their house, Sean's mother had invited me to come over whenever I wanted and had told my mom that she would talk things over with her husband. They'd hugged each other and then my mom and I walked back to our house.

"What was all that about when she said she'd talk to Sean's dad?" I asked.

"Oh, I just talked to her a little about how it would be nice if the two of you could go to the same school. She said she'd talk it over with her husband," Mom answered nonchalantly. I stopped in the middle of *the sidewalk and she turned back when she realized I was no longer beside her.*

"Are you serious?" I asked, getting excited.

"Don't get your hopes up too much, I don't want you to be disappointed. They may still say no. I can't imagine how difficult it is to let your child out of your sight after everything they've been through."

I heard what she was saying, but all I could concentrate on was the fact that there was a chance, a possibility that Sean and I could spend the school year together. I grabbed my mom in a bear hug, not caring that we were standing out where anyone could drive by and see. At that moment, I wasn't a fifteen-year-old boy trying to be cool, I was a fifteen-year-old with a mom who could work miracles.

I looked up and saw Hudson and Isaac each smiling as they listened intently to my story. My heart actually felt lighter as I talked about Sean, even better than when I had told Caleb and Giovanni. Of course, I'd given them a much more condensed version. With Hudson and Isaac, I found myself wanting to tell them everything.

"Sean and I saw each other nearly every day after that. The only time we missed was when he had to go to a doctor appointment, but each one of those ended in good news and finally, by the start of the school year, his parents had agreed to let him attend the public high school with me." I smiled at the two men across from me.

"We were inseparable. We walked to school together since neither of us could drive and had almost all the same classes. Sean's mom had decided over the summer that it was okay for him to hang out at my house so after school we did our homework together, alternating houses. He was my first real friend and I was his. We were very close and shared everything with each other, but I never had the nerve to ask him if he liked girls or boys, and he never really talked about either one." I glanced up and saw Isaac and Hudson still listening.

"One night a couple years after we met, we were doing homework in my room. I was reading out loud from my history book and I looked up when I noticed Sean had stopped taking notes. He was staring at me with an odd expression on his face and then he leaned forward and kissed me." I closed my eyes as I remembered the sweetness of that very first kiss.

"First kisses are the best," Isaac said. I opened my eyes and saw him turning to look at Hudson with a dreamy expression on his face. I was glad that Hudson and I had both been able to share firsts with Isaac. Hudson smiled back at him, a soft look in his eyes and then he turned to me.

"What happened next?" he asked.

"Oh, I kissed him back. I'd been wanting to do it for two years and it was like Sean had opened a floodgate." Hudson and Isaac laughed at that and I joined in. It felt good to laugh at the memories and I had them to thank for that.

"After that, it was pretty clear that we both liked boys and particularly each other. We agreed to be exclusive, which wasn't very hard considering neither one of us went anywhere without the other. We were each other's first everything and I loved him with my whole heart, so when he asked me to marry him on graduation day, I said yes." I heard Isaac's soft gasp and I looked up at him.

"You and Sean were married?" he asked.

I shrugged my shoulders. "Unfortunately, same-sex marriage wasn't legalized in Illinois until several years later, but we had a private ceremony and exchanged rings. We made vows to each other before God and our families regardless of what the state said. So yes, we were married in all the ways that mattered," I explained. Isaac smiled at me.

"After we got married we found a small apartment off campus and started taking classes at the college. Sean decided to major in law. He told me he wanted to do something that would make a difference for the LGBTQA community. He figured if he majored in law, maybe he could help change some of the laws like the one that kept people from marrying whoever they chose. I majored in education because I wanted to work with kids." I smiled, thinking how I had still ended up doing that even if it wasn't in a classroom.

"Towards the middle of our second year of college, Sean got sick. We thought it was just the flu, but after a while he just wasn't getting better. The doctor ran a series of tests and I held Sean's hand as he told us that the cancer was back. I remember feeling like I was staring down a tunnel at the doctor as he explained that the cancer had remained undetected for a long time and by the time it had presented itself in what we had thought was the flu, it was already at stage four."

My chest felt tight as I remembered the hopeless feeling of seeing the man I loved dying and knowing there was absolutely nothing I could do to stop it. I'd tried though, I'd begged and pleaded for God to take it away, to give it to me instead, but neither of those things happened. I rubbed at my chest to ease the ache and Hudson and Isaac moved to sit on either side of me on the couch.

"Do you want to stop?" Hudson asked and I heard the catch in his voice. I looked at him and then Isaac who had tears streaming down his cheeks and I shook my head.

"I need to do this. I need to tell you," I told them. Isaac grabbed one of my hands and held it in his lap. Hudson wrapped an arm around my shoulder and laid his other hand on my leg. I took a deep breath, drawing strength from their closeness.

"Sean did everything the doctors told him to do. He knew all the dreams we had for our future; vacations, kids, buying our first house. He fought like hell to hold on, but eventually the cancer was just too much and I held his hand as he took his last breath. It was almost exactly six years to the day that we met."

I gasped as the tears I'd been trying so hard to hold back came crashing forward and I doubled over from the pain of reliving the day I'd lost my husband. Hudson and Isaac wrapped their arms around me, whispering soothing words in my ears and letting me get it all out. Eventually, my sobs quieted, but they continued to hold me until I raised my head.

"Thank you," I whispered hoarsely.

"Thank you for sharing that with us," Hudson said.

"Is that why you started Agape House? Because Sean had wanted to make a difference in the LGBTQA community?" Isaac asked.

"Sean's parents came to me shortly after he died and they told me that I had made their son happier than they could've ever hoped for. They said that they'd been so afraid of losing him after the first round of cancer that they'd held on too tight, nearly suffocating him. They told me that because of me, Sean had truly lived a full life. They gave me the remainder of the money they had set aside for Sean's education, saying that they knew I would do something good with it, something to honor their son.

"I combined Sean's dreams with my dream of working with kids and I started Agape House. Every teen that we're able to help at the center, has Sean to thank," I said proudly.

"Including me," Isaac whispered. I turned to look at him and saw fresh tears running down his face. I reached out and wiped them away with my thumb.

"Including you," I whispered back and a slow smile spread across my face.

"Why did you get drunk?" Hudson asked and my head whipped around at him, surprised by the sudden change in topic. He looked almost sad as he asked me, "Did I push you to do something you weren't ready for?"

"No, that wasn't it at all," I said, shaking my head. "I've been with other men since I lost Sean," I admitted quietly. "Not many and only when I felt like I would suffocate from the loneliness." Isaac's hand tightened in mine and I squeezed his fingers gently.

"So, what made this time different?" Hudson asked.

"Because you guys are different," I told them honestly, then I took a deep breath and let it out slowly. "I've spent the last several years going to work and then coming home, day after day and for the most part that was enough. I was fulfilled by my job and I spent all day surrounded by people. When the loneliness got to be too much,

I'd hook up with someone, but I realized I wasn't living, I was only existing, and that wasn't fair to Sean. That wasn't what he would want for me, but I didn't know how to change it.

"Then we had the grand opening and I met you," I said to Hudson. I turned to Isaac. "And felt like I was meeting you for the first time. I couldn't believe the way I reacted to the two of you. The zing of electricity and the way my heart pounded in my chest; I hadn't felt like that since…"

"Sean." Hudson finished for me. I nodded, unable to say it out loud.

"I felt like I'd betrayed him in some way so I tried to stay away from both of you other than work, but it was harder than I thought it'd be. The loneliness seemed to get even worse when I saw you two getting closer. I wanted so badly to join you when you went to dinner that first night and again when I saw you kissing in Isaac's office, but I stopped myself.

"Then I talked with Caleb. I told him a little bit about Sean and he convinced me that I needed to get out more. He made me promise that I'd at least try. I knew he was right so I agreed. That's why I went to the club. Plus, I knew you two would be there and I wanted to see what this thing between us was."

"But you weren't ready?" Isaac asked.

"No, I was ready. I loved everything we did that night. I liked being with both of you, touching you, tasting you both, being inside you," I said while looking at Isaac. I watched as pink tinged his cheeks and thought to myself once again that he was so beautiful.

"I enjoyed all of it and I was fine until I was alone in the back of the cab and I realized I was really happy for the first time in years. That's when the guilt hit me. It was almost as if by being with the two of you, I was forgetting Sean and everything we had shared together. By the time I got home, I couldn't breathe and I just wanted something to numb the pain. I knew I was drinking way too much, but it felt good to not hurt for a while so I just kept drinking."

Hudson looked at me tenderly. "It sounds like Sean was an incredible man," he said.

"He was, he was the best," I agreed.

"What you two shared sounds amazing. There's no way you'll ever be able to forget him or what he meant to you, and you shouldn't," Isaac chimed in. I stared into his kind eyes. Hearing him say it out loud, I felt ridiculous because Isaac was right. There was no way I could ever forget Sean and the love we'd shared.

"Let me ask you something, Matt," Hudson said. His eyes were gentle, but serious. "Do you care about me and Isaac?"

"Yes, of course I do," I answered quickly.

"Did you ever think you'd care about two men at once?" I wasn't sure where he was headed with his questions, but I shook my head no. "If your heart has room for you to care about both of us at the same time, then what makes you think there isn't room for three?" I couldn't answer. I felt like such a fool for thinking that it was an either-or situation. Just because I cared about the two men sitting next to me didn't mean I had to stop loving Sean.

"If Sean were here right now, what do you think he'd tell you to do?" Hudson asked softly.

I was quiet for several moments as I gave his question serious thought. I closed my eyes and pictured Sean's face, the way he used to smile at me and the sound of his laugh. Before he'd gotten sick, he was so full of life. He was always excited to try new things and the first one to suggest something adventurous. It was almost as if he'd known he was on borrowed time and wanted to make the most of his life while he could. He would be devastated to learn that I'd quit living the day I lost him. I opened my eyes because I had my answer.

"He'd want me to be happy. He'd want me to enjoy life to its fullest and grab as much happiness as I possibly could," I answered.

"What would make you happy?" Isaac asked beside me. I felt a sense of peace as I looked at him and then at Hudson.

"Being with the two of you."

CHAPTER
Seventeen

Hudson

I HADN'T EVEN REALIZED HOW NERVOUS I'D BEEN UNTIL MATT admitted that Isaac and I made him happy, and suddenly, I felt like I could breathe again. I'd known Matt had something that was keeping him from opening up to us. Even when we'd slept together, as wonderful as it was, I knew he'd been holding a part of himself back. It weighed heavily on my mind, but I couldn't push him or force him to talk until he was ready. I wasn't his therapist and I didn't want to be.

I wanted to be more.

I wanted to be the man that Matt and Isaac *chose* to come to with their secrets and their worries. Not because they were paying me to listen, but because they trusted me to be there for them and take care of them. I felt protective of the two of them, but I also wanted them to provide shelter for me when I needed it. I wanted a relationship.

When I'd woken that morning, I still wasn't sure if that were possible, but after Matt had told us everything, I was more hopeful than ever. I'd been shocked to learn he'd been married before, but the love and devotion he still carried for his first love, proved what a remarkable man Matt truly was. He cared deeply about others and when he gave someone his heart, he gave it fully and forever.

I'd grown up without either of my parents, and while Nonna and Aysha had made sure I'd felt loved, there had always been a part of me that had wondered why my parents hadn't. I'd had boyfriends I'd cared about and who had cared about me, but I'd never had someone treat me like I was their whole world. As I listened to Matt talk about Sean, I realized they'd had that, and while I was happy for them, I also wanted it for myself.

I looked into Matt's gray eyes with his mop of curls on top of his head and then past him to Isaac with his bright blue eyes and freckles across his nose and my heart stuttered. I wasn't sure where this thing between us was headed, but I was more determined than ever to find out. As far as I was concerned, they were *my* guys and until they told me otherwise, I was going to treat them that way.

Matt laid his head on my shoulder and sighed. "Thank you both for coming to check on me. It feels good to have someone care and it felt good to finally talk about Sean. To tell you all about him and what he meant to me." I ran my fingers through his hair and Isaac laid his head on Matt's shoulder, their hands folded together in Isaac's lap.

"Thank you for finally telling us. All I ever wanted to do was be there for you in whatever way you needed me," Isaac whispered.

"I know and I appreciate that, I just wasn't ready before," Matt told him.

"I think that's because we were waiting for Hudson to get here," Isaac said as if it were the most natural explanation in the world. My breath caught in my throat as Matt moved his head so he could look at me. His gray eyes roamed over my face and then he broke into the sweetest smile that did crazy things to my heart.

"I think you're right, Isaac," Matt whispered. I bent my head down and my lips met Matt's in a gentle kiss. When he moved back, the storms that were normally present in his gaze had cleared. Matt looked like he had finally found peace.

He yawned then and I could tell that reliving his past had taken a lot out of him. He was emotionally drained, not to mention the physical toll his drunken bender had taken on his body. He needed to sleep and hopefully when he woke, he'd be able to move forward with a clear head and a peaceful heart.

"We should go, let you get some sleep," I suggested, but Matt looked startled.

"No, please! I don't want you to go. I mean, unless you have things you need to do. I know you both left work early to come here so I understand if you need to get back," he said.

"I cleared my entire day and there's nowhere else I want to be," I told him. Matt smiled at me and leaned up for another kiss.

"I think my boss will understand if I don't make it back today." Isaac's joke broke the heaviness which I'm sure was his intention and we all laughed. It felt good, but I could see the exhaustion in Matt's eyes.

"We'll stay as long as you get some rest," I promised Matt.

"Sleep sounds good actually," he agreed, standing up and stretching. He turned around and looked at us. "Would you both lie down with me, at least until I fall asleep? I'm sorry, I just don't want to be alone right now. I've had enough of that to last me a lifetime."

"Don't ever apologize for telling us what you need," I said, already getting to my feet.

I slid my hand into Matt's and then turned to look at Isaac, surprised to see him with his phone out, texting someone. He finished and then shut his phone off and looked up at us.

"I was just letting Allison know that we were taking the rest of the day off," he explained and then cleared his throat. "I told her you had a terrible migraine and that's why you weren't able to call earlier."

"Thank you. I'm sorry you had to lie," Matt said sheepishly.

Isaac climbed off the couch and wrapped his arms around Matt's waist. "Don't you know by now that there's really not much I wouldn't do for you. Either one of you," he said, peering around Matt to see me. I winked at him, feeling exactly the same way.

"Come on, let's get you to bed," I said and we followed Matt down the hall to his room.

His bedroom was neat and uncluttered. The bed was smaller than mine, but I was sure we'd all fit, especially since I wanted them both as close to me as possible. Matt sat down on the bed with a sigh and I saw his eyes go to the picture on the table next to him.

My eyes zoomed in on the handsome red-haired man in the picture. He was wearing a suit and his green eyes sparkled as they stared at the man beside him in a matching suit. It was easy to see that the two were crazy about each other. Matt was younger in the photo, but that wasn't what stood out to me the most. No, it was the look on Matt's face, the one that said he was young and in love, with his whole life before him and not a care in the world.

Matt may have gotten a little older, but I had never seen him smile like that or look so carefree before. I wanted to change all that. I wanted to see Matt smile that way again and I was willing to do whatever it took to make that happen. I looked over at him and saw him staring at me, having obviously caught me looking at the picture. He swallowed thickly and then turned the picture face down on the table.

"You don't need to do that," I said as I stepped forward and set the picture back up then I knelt down beside the bed so I could look Matt in the eyes. "We know how important Sean is to you. He'll always hold a portion of your heart that no one else will touch and that's okay," I assured him.

Matt seemed unsure, but then Isaac climbed onto the bed and scooted until he was behind him, draping himself over Matt's shoulders. He kissed Matt on the side of his neck and then whispered to him, loud enough that I could hear. "We don't want to erase the story you had with Sean. We want to be your next chapter."

I stared in awe of the young man who always seemed to know just the right thing to say and do. My heart felt so fucking full and I wondered what I'd ever done to deserve the chance to be with two such amazing men.

Matt turned his head and captured Isaac's lips in a long, slow kiss. "I want that too," he whispered.

We undressed down to our underwear and then climbed under the sheets. It was a tight fit at first, but then Matt scooted closer to me and I put my arm around him so he could rest his head on it. I crooked my elbow and ran my fingers through his soft curls while Isaac curled his body around Matt's side and laid his head on Matt's chest. It felt comfortable and it felt right and I couldn't imagine anywhere else in the world I'd rather be.

The room was quiet, and soon, I could hear the steady rhythm of Matt's breathing as he drifted off to sleep. Isaac soon followed, leaving me to sort through my thoughts. As the sun set behind the curtains and darkness took over the room, I started to close my eyes. Right before I fell asleep, I admitted to myself what I'd known was coming all along, I had fallen in love with Matt and Isaac.

I wasn't sure what time it was when I woke, but it was definitely still night because the moon was streaming in through the curtains. I had woken to a noise, like a low groan and I kept still, seeing if I'd hear it again. It came again a few seconds later and I could tell immediately that it was coming from Isaac. I turned my head in his direction to see if he was having a bad dream and that's when I saw movement at the foot of the bed. I started to sit up so I could turn on the light, but a hand snaked up through the split in my boxers and curled around my cock, effectively halting my movements.

I could see his curls in the moonlight as he crawled up my body, kissing and licking a path along the way. I was rock-hard by the time

Matt reached my chest and I grabbed him, hauling him up the rest of the way and swept my tongue in his mouth, desperate for the taste of him.

"Are you sure? Because I need you to be sure. I don't want you holding anything back this time," I growled in between kisses. Matt paused for just a moment and then his tongue swept over my lips.

"I'm sure," he whispered. My eyes darted over to Isaac and I saw him fisting his cock slowly up and down as he stared at us. It was too dark to make out his expression, but I could feel the heat as he watched us.

"Why don't you take care of our boy over there," I told Matt and then I flipped him around so that he was facing the other direction.

I heard the sound of Isaac's groan and then the wet sound of sucking as Matt pleasured him. The combined sounds of my men getting off ignited a fire in me and I reached for Matt's swollen cock. He raised up on his knees and I took him in my mouth, licking the tip and moaning as I was rewarded with a burst of salty sweet pre-cum. I lapped at it eagerly and then swallowed him down to the back of my throat.

Matt's groan sounded muffled around Isaac's cock and I doubled my efforts. I finally felt like we were all three on the same page and I promised myself that I was going to make it a night they'd never forget.

CHAPTER
Eighteen

Hudson

I SUCKED MATT'S COCK FOR SEVERAL MINUTES, RELISHING THE sounds of Isaac's moans of delight as Matt licked and sucked him. I licked a path up Matt's shaft and over his balls, tonguing them and sucking them into my mouth. His balls were smooth and I loved the taste and the smell of him, a mixture of soap and man.

I leaned my head up and used my hands to spread Matt's cheeks apart and then I flattened my tongue and licked up his seam and over his tight little hole. He cried out above me and nearly jumped off the bed, but I laid a hand on his back and pressed down until he calmed. When he'd settled back down, I continued.

My tongue flicked over Matt's entrance, swirling around and around until he was shaking and then I plunged the tip deep inside him, tasting him and begging him with my mouth to allow me inside. My tongue acted like a cock thrusting in and out of his hole and, slowly, I felt him begin to loosen. Matt rocked back and forth and my chest became sticky with his juices as his dick continued to leak all over me.

Matt panted heavily as I slid a finger inside him. He was tighter than I'd thought he'd be, but then he said he'd only hooked up with other men occasionally so I supposed that was to be expected. Somewhere, in my lust-filled daze, I became aware of the bed moving as Isaac shifted down it.

"Oh, God!" Matt cried when I added a second finger, licking his rim to keep him wet as I worked him open.

A blinding heat surrounded my cock and I knew right away it was my Isaac. It was amazing to me how I could already tell the differences in their touch, their smell, their sounds. I was getting to know my men, but I wanted to know more. I wanted to learn every single thing about them.

It was hard to concentrate when Isaac was doing such incredible things with his mouth, but I managed to get Matt loosened up enough that I thought he could take me. I tapped him and he lifted off me, kneeling beside me on the bed. Isaac stopped what he was doing and looked up to see what was going on. The moon was brighter then and I could see how swollen his lips were and the way they glistened in the light from his spit and my juices.

"Do you have supplies?" I asked Matt. He hesitated only a second and then he nodded.

"I have some for the times when I would hook up," he explained, almost as if he were embarrassed. He had no reason to be though so I sat up and hooked my hand behind his neck, pulling him forward for a lingering kiss.

"Go get them," I growled and Matt scampered off the bed, responding immediately to the command in my voice. *Interesting. We might have to explore that further. Another time perhaps.*

Isaac went back to sucking my cock and I threaded my fingers through his hair, urging him deeper each time. Through heavy lids, I watched as Matt opened the top drawer of his dresser and pulled out a box of condoms and a bottle of lube and brought them back over to the bed, laying them down on the nightstand. He crawled back onto the bed and stretched out at my side as we watched Isaac's head bob up and down between my legs.

"It's been awhile so go slow, okay?" Matt said suddenly. I heard the slight tremor in his voice that I'm sure he'd tried to hide and I turned my attention away from Isaac and looked at Matt, frowning at him.

"Matt, we don't have to…" I started to say, but he cut me off.

"No! I want to. I want to so badly. I just needed you to know so we could go slow. I mean, you're a big boy so we kind of have to go slow anyway," Matt said, trying to turn it into a joke, but I'd seen the uneasiness in his eyes and I wasn't going to let that go.

"How long, sweetheart?" I asked. I watched Matt's Adam's apple bob up and down as he swallowed.

"Since Sean," he whispered.

My heart pounded wildly in my chest as I realized what that meant. Matt had never bottomed for anyone but his husband, but he was going to for me. He stared back at me, with wide, trusting eyes and nodded his head just once. I was overwhelmed with the love I had for him, but I was afraid it would be too much for him to handle just yet, that he would think it was too soon or I'd scare him away so I pulled him in for a kiss instead.

"Why don't you ride me, that way you can control how deep and how fast we go," I suggested once we broke apart.

Isaac moved to the side of the bed and grabbed the supplies. I smiled at him as he ripped the wrapper off the condom and then tried to slide it on me. I put my hands over his and showed him the proper way.

"Thanks. I guess I'm still learning," he said with a small grin.

"That's fine. Matt and I are more than happy to be your teachers."

I smirked.

Isaac threw his head back with a laugh and the sound caused a fluttering in my chest. I was so fucked when it came to these two men. Isaac picked up the bottle of lube and poured some into his open palm. He worked it over my length, slicking me until I was good and wet then he turned to Matt.

Matt had moved back up to a kneeling position on the bed and his eyes turned a dark, smoky gray, never leaving Isaac as he scooted closer towards him. My cock twitched as I watched the two of them come together. They were different in many ways, yet each of them was so beautiful in their own right. Their lips moved over each other in a passionate kiss and every once in a while, I would see the flicker of a tongue as it delved into the other man's mouth.

Isaac reached his lubricated fingers down and slid them between Matt's legs, circling them around his hole. Matt let out a strangled moan into Isaac's mouth and I knew that Isaac had his fingers inside Matt. Matt began to ride Isaac's wet fingers the way he would soon ride my cock and I thought to myself that it was quite possible that I could come just from watching the two of them, without anyone even touching my dick.

Isaac kissed Matt one last time and smiled proudly at him, obviously pleased with his ability to drive the other man insane. Matt smacked him on the ass and Isaac yelped in surprise. Matt crawled over to me then and tossed one leg over my waist so he was straddling me. There was no trace of the uneasiness I'd seen earlier in his eyes. It had been replaced instead with excitement and desire.

Matt lay down on top of me and kissed me as he slid his shaft alongside mine. He bit my bottom lip gently between his teeth and tugged on it. I liked the new side of Matt I was seeing, the one that was playful and sexy and let us see who he really was.

I planted my feet on the bed and lifted my hips so that our groins rubbed together in a delicious tease and when his tongue slid between my lips, I captured it and began sucking on it. Matt shivered in my arms and I felt his cock dribble onto my stomach.

I stopped my assault on his mouth and let him sit up. He seemed dazed at first, which pleased me immensely and he shook his head as if trying to clear it. Isaac stood at the side of the bed, pumping his dick in his hand, obviously enjoying the show.

It turned me on to know that he'd been watching us as much as it turned me on seeing the two of them together. In fact, there hadn't been anything we'd done that hadn't gotten me hot. Apparently, they just hit all the right buttons for me.

Isaac got on his knees beside the bed and grabbed onto my cock, holding it at the base as Matt lifted himself and lined his hole up with the head of my dick. I put my hands on his waist and he held my gaze as he began to lower himself onto me.

Isaac rubbed Matt's back with his free hand and whispered soothing words to him as he took me inside. When just the tip of my dick was in Matt stopped and breathed through the discomfort as his body fought to adjust to my width.

"Take it slow, sweetheart," I praised.

His eyes opened and held mine as he lowered himself some more, sliding down my length and gripping me in his tight heat. He felt so good wrapped around me.

When he was finally down as far as he could go, Matt breathed out a sigh of relief. "Damn!" he said and I couldn't stop the rumble of laughter that rolled up out of my chest.

Matt gasped as my laughter made my cock jerk inside him and when he looked at me I saw the raw lust in his eyes. He began to rock back and forth on me, testing the feel of me inside him, and I clenched my teeth as I resisted the urge to lift my hips and drive up into him over and over again until we both lost touch with reality.

As Matt began to lift himself, riding up and down on my cock, Isaac described everything he was seeing, his voice coming out breathy and a little husky. "Oh, God! This is so fucking sexy. Matt's hole is so tight, but somehow, he's able to take your fat dick. I bet his cock feels so good, stretching you open, doesn't it, Matt?" He went on and on, feeding the flames with his words until I couldn't take it anymore.

"Get up here!" I nearly shouted and Isaac stood, his hand around his cock and his pupils blown. I could see the effect watching Matt and me fuck was having on him, but I needed him too. Matt looked at me gratefully and I could tell he'd been wanting the same. We both needed our mouths and hands on our guy.

I reached for Isaac and he didn't hesitate. The look in his eyes told me that he was willing and ready for whatever I had planned. "I want you to sit on my face turned towards Matt. I want to eat your ass," I told him bluntly.

Isaac looked momentarily stunned by my request and I had to remind myself to take it easy, sex was still new to him. I should've known to expect the unexpected from Isaac though because he bent down and slammed his mouth onto mine in a kiss that left me reeling then he climbed onto the bed and positioned himself as I'd instructed.

I didn't waste any time, I was too hungry for him to do that. I spread Isaac's cheeks apart with my hands and stared at his hole, so pretty and pink like a little rose bud. My tongue swept over it and I was rewarded by Isaac's sharp gasp. That's what I wanted. Every gasp, every cry, every moan I could wring out from my men; I wanted them all.

Isaac lowered his body as much as he could, opening himself up even more to me and I began eating him, feasting on him as if he were my last meal. The dual sensation of my tongue in Isaac's ass and Matt's tight channel squeezing my cock as he rode up and down soon had me going out of my mind. I wanted to be everywhere, on them and in them all at once. No matter what I did, I couldn't get close enough. I wanted to crawl inside each one of them and take up residence.

Matt's movements slowed, though he kept riding me and I heard his low groan and then, "Oh, Isaac. Your mouth feels so good. That's it, right there." The mental image of what we must look like, me with my face in Isaac's ass and Matt riding me while Isaac has his luscious lips wrapped around Matt's dick, their flawlessly pale and olive skin tones in direct contrast with my own darker skin, was so erotic that I worried I would blow way too soon. I wasn't the only one though.

"Oh, God! You guys are going to make me come," Isaac whimpered. Matt's movements ceased and I felt Isaac tense above me.

"Stop! I don't want you to come yet," Matt said forcefully. Isaac lifted and moved to sit on the bed next to me. His hand squeezed the base of his dick, pushing back his orgasm as he looked at Matt in frustrated confusion.

"I want to be inside you when you come," he explained and Isaac immediately smiled, apparently loving that plan. Matt lifted off of me and we all moved at once, Isaac lying down on his back and coating his entrance with lube while I helped Matt with a condom. Matt slicked himself up and positioned himself between Isaac's legs, then he turned those smoky gray eyes on me as he looked over his shoulder.

"As soon as I get inside him, I want you back in me. I want us all to be together." He held my gaze for several seconds and my breath caught in my throat. There was something in his eyes that had me wondering if he was talking about more than just sex, but Matt turned his head before I could get a clear read on him.

I moved in behind Matt, kissing his neck and nipping at the sensitive spot beneath his ear as he prepared Isaac to take him. I watched Isaac from behind heavy lids and I saw the way he stared back at the two of us, his expression so honest and sincere, just like his personality. Isaac didn't waste time playing games like many men his age and I appreciated that about him. I liked that he told us with his words and showed us with his body exactly what he was thinking and feeling.

I watched as Matt slid inside the younger man and Isaac's eyes rolled back up in his head, a blissful smile gracing his lips as if he finally had everything he'd been dreaming about. I could understand because I felt the same way when I was with the two of them.

Matt glanced at me over his shoulder in a silent command and I nodded; he didn't have to tell me twice. I placed my hand between his shoulder blades and pressed down. He gave me a wicked smile and then he stretched down over Isaac. The two of them began kissing as I lined the head of my cock up with Matt's opening.

Matt groaned as I filled him once more and Isaac's hands ran up and down his back, never stopping their kisses. I lay over Matt's back and stretched my neck, wanting to join them. Isaac lifted his head and we were able to share a passionate yet all too short kiss.

Satisfied, I lifted back up onto my knees and began to rock my hips into Matt. I was mesmerized by the sight of my cock being swallowed up by Matt's perfectly round ass. The reality of seeing it was even better than Isaac had described and I thrust forward, needing to be deep inside him.

"Give it to me, Hudson. Don't hold back," Matt cried out as I plunged into his depths.

Matt's words were the green light I'd been waiting for and I shoved my cock in deep. I was relentless in my movements, but Matt's excited moans told me that he was loving every single second of it. Each thrust of my hips caused a ripple effect through the three of us as my cock was propelled into Matt's tight hole which drove him deeper into Isaac.

We moved as one fluid entity, striving to reach the same goal. Sweat dripped off my forehead and landed between Matt's shoulder blades and I bent down to lick it, the combination of our flavors bursting on my tongue.

My balls drew up tight and I felt the familiar burning at the base of my spine that told me my orgasm was imminent, but I never halted my movements. I knew I was about to have the best orgasm of my life and I wanted both of them to go over the edge with me.

Matt's breathing faltered and Isaac's moans got louder and then I heard Isaac scream our names. Seconds later, Matt's ass clamped down on my cock as his own orgasm crashed over him. Two more thrusts and my body went rigid as the most powerful orgasm I'd ever had barreled over me, stealing my breath from my lungs and making me wonder if I'd survive.

We collapsed onto the bed in a tangled mess of limbs, wrapping ourselves around one another and gasping for air. Matt's bedroom reeked of sex and sweat and man and I gulped down lungful after lungful of the heady aroma, wondering if there was any better smell on the planet.

Eventually we got up and took a shower together which wasn't easy since Matt's shower was much smaller than mine, but we didn't care as we just moved in even closer. Afterward, we worked together to change the sheets and then fell into an exhausted sleep. It was the most intense night I'd ever had and I was going to fight like hell to make sure there were more just like it, even if I had to fight the two men in bed with me to make it happen.

CHAPTER
Nineteen

Isaac

"THOSE WERE THE BEST BLUEBERRY PANCAKES I'VE EVER had. Thanks for saving me some, Gladys. You always take such great care of me," I said, kissing her on the cheek. She blushed, but I could tell my words had pleased her.

"You deserve to feel special, Isaac. You're a good boy, always have been." Gladys probably said that to all the kids that came through the center, but she'd always made me feel special regardless and I loved her for it. She gazed at me tenderly for just a moment, but someone walked in the kitchen just then and she turned away.

I left the kitchen and walked towards my office, Gladys's words still ringing in my ears. She thought I was a good person and had told me that over and over since I'd first arrived at the center broken and lost, just a shell of my former self. I couldn't help but wonder if she'd still feel the same way if she learned the truth about why I had needed Agape House to begin with.

I didn't like to think about that time in my life because I still felt so much anger and guilt and pain over what had happened. It was easier to just push it aside and focus on all the good things that had happened in my life since then.

Maybe it was because Matt had opened up about his past and I saw the toll that carrying around those secrets for years had taken on him. Maybe it was the way he seemed happier since then, almost as if by telling us he had been set free of his burdens. Whatever the reason, my past had been playing on my mind a lot lately and I was finding it more and more difficult to lock it away.

There were a few times, especially when the three of us were curled around each other after a long night of sex, when I'd wondered if I'd feel better like Matt had, if I just told them everything. But I stopped myself every time, afraid that I'd see shame or disappointment in their eyes.

Gladys said I deserved to feel special. Given what had happened, I would have to disagree. Regardless of whether I felt I deserved it or not, Matt and Hudson made me feel special every time I was with them. I walked into my office and sat down at my desk, smiling as I thought about the two men in my life.

It had been over a month since Matt had told us about Sean and the three of us had become inseparable. We had dinner together almost every night, usually at either Hudson's or Matt's place since mine was too small for entertaining. After dinner, we'd usually curl up on the couch and talk or watch a movie. We had yet to finish a movie however because somehow, we always seemed to get distracted and ended up having sex before it was over. Not that I was complaining at all.

Afterward, we'd take a shower and climb into bed, legs and arms all intertwined with each other. I'd gotten so used to the sounds of their breathing, their heartbeats against my ear that I found it very difficult to fall asleep on the rare occasions I was alone at home.

It was more than just sex between us though. We had a lot of fun together and genuinely enjoyed each other's company. We had many things in common, but we also had several things that we brought to the relationship that were new to each other. I shared with them some of my favorite gay romance books which neither of them had read and Matt took us to a Chicago Bulls game since basketball was his favorite sport.

Hudson had been appalled to learn that I didn't know how to cook and that Matt was basically living off frozen dinners, so he'd taken it upon himself to teach us how to cook. Hudson was an amazing chef and a great teacher. So far, we'd learned how to make lasagna, beef stew, and just the night before, we'd made homemade chicken and noodles.

Matt and I were very proud of ourselves for our accomplishments and Hudson had rewarded us right there in the kitchen. Blood rushed to my cock as I relived the memory and the way Hudson had dominated the two of us.

I wiped down the counter while Matt washed the dishes we'd used to cook and Hudson dried them. We'd made quite a mess, but with the three of us working on it, the cleanup was quick and easy. Everything seemed to go more smoothly whenever we were all together, I thought.

We liked to do and say things to tease each other and rile one another up. Sort of our own form of foreplay and one that I enjoyed immensely. I loved seeing my lovers' eyes darken with just the brush of my hand over their skin or whispered words of what I wanted to do to them later.

It made me feel desired and even a bit powerful in a way, almost as if I could...No! I brushed that thought aside, sure that neither man would want what I'd been thinking and not willing to rock the boat. I was perfectly happy with how our sex life was, but still, I was curious.

I heard a gasp from behind me and looked over my shoulder, my cock springing to life at the sight that met my eyes. Matt was standing with his hands clutched to the front of the sink, his fingers turning white with his tight grip. Hudson had his body pressed against Matt's back, the bulge in his pants sliding up and down the crack of Matt's ass.

Seeing my two lovers together never failed to get me hard, but my cock became painfully rigid when I noticed the dishtowel that Hudson had wrapped around Matt's throat. His hold on it was firm, yet I could see Matt's chest rising and falling as he began to breathe rapidly from excitement so I knew it wasn't too constricting.

Hudson had told me that he thought Matt might enjoy a little light domination. I wasn't sure what all that entailed, but if the glazed look in Matt's eyes and the desperate sounds of his moans were any indication then Hudson had been right.

Hudson pulled Matt away from the sink and turned their bodies so that they were facing me. He reached around Matt's waist with his free hand and undid his belt. He unbuttoned and lowered the zipper of Matt's jeans next and Matt let out a strangled cry as Hudson's large hand plunged down under the waistband of his underwear and pulled out his cock. My mouth watered at the sight of Matt's cock dripping over Hudson's fingers and I reached down and undid my pants, sighing in relief as I slid my hand in and palmed my own cock.

"Get naked, now," Hudson demanded, looking directly at me. His deep baritone voice resonated through me and made me vibrate like a tuning fork. I reached for the hem of my T-shirt, but his words stopped me. "Slowly!"

Matt tracked my every move, his eyes darkening with lust as I slowly revealed my body to them. Hudson continued to fist Matt's cock, keeping the towel in place around Matt's neck while he whispered in his ear all the filthy things he wanted to do to us. His words had me trembling with need by the time I was finished, having been stripped bare. I stood quietly with my arms at my sides as their eyes roamed up and down my body, but instead of wanting to hide, I was empowered by the undeniable desire I saw in my lovers' eyes.

"You're perfect," Hudson told me and I felt my shoulders straighten with his praise. "Come here, Isaac, and undress our man."

I did his bidding and then eagerly followed Hudson's instructions as he had me get on my knees and suck Matt's weeping cock. I lapped at him hungrily, tasting the salty, sweet cum on his tip and sucking him down, trying to draw more of the delicious flavor from him. I could tell that Matt wanted to thrust his hips and bury his dick down my throat, but when Hudson growled at him that he was not allowed to move, he immediately stilled. It was obvious that Matt loved the control that Hudson was enforcing over him.

"Keep your hands behind your head. You do not have permission to touch him," Hudson instructed.

Matt's jaw clenched and I knew it was killing him not to reach for me. Once he'd opened up to us, we'd discovered that Matt was a very touchy-feely kind of guy and he rarely spent any time with us that he wasn't touching us in some way.

Hudson stepped back and began to undress himself while I continued to suck Matt. I licked a path down his long shaft and sucked one of his balls into my mouth, swirling it with my tongue. Matt moaned above me and I gazed up at him. His head was bent and he was staring down at me with a look that had my heart beating triple speed. I had seen that same look in his eyes a lot over the last month, but I was afraid to get my hopes up about what it might mean.

Hudson moved back up alongside Matt then and I let my eyes feast on the miles of glorious dark skin over rippling muscles. I was filled with pride at how magnificent my two lovers were. I wasn't sure I'd ever understand why they had chosen to be with me, but I was eternally grateful.

My tongue swept around the head of Matt's cock, teasing the bundle of nerves right under the tip, while my hand glided up and down over his shaft. I kept my eyes trained on the two men towering over me and I saw Hudson whisper something in Matt's ear. Matt's eyes widened, but I could tell that whatever Hudson said had excited him because he nodded vigorously.

"Come here, baby," Hudson said as he stretched his hand out and helped me to my feet. "There's something you've been wanting. What is it?" I tilted my head and scrunched my forehead in confusion.

"I'm not sure what you're talking about," I said, but my voice didn't come out as strong as I'd hoped.

My heart began to thump wildly, but I told myself there was no way he could possibly know. It had only ever been a thought in my head. Hudson glanced at Matt and they were both suddenly surrounding me, one on either side with their arms wrapped around me. Hudson captured my chin between his thumb and forefinger and lifted so I was forced to look him in the eyes.

"This will only work between the three of us if we're always honest with each other. That includes telling us when there's something you want or need from us," Hudson told me and my eyes widened.

"You are an equal part of this relationship. Your needs are just as important as ours," Matt chimed in. I started to chew my lip nervously, but Hudson used his thumb to pull it out from between my teeth.

"Tell us, Isaac. I want to hear you say it out loud." Hudson's voice picked up the commanding tone from earlier and I responded immediately.

"I want to try topping," I told them. I held my breath, half expecting to hear them laugh at me for my ridiculous request, but Matt reached for my cheek and turned my head in his direction.

"Will you top me, Isaac?" His gray eyes had turned smoky with arousal and I realized that Matt was actually excited by the idea of me fucking him.

"Ye…" I started to answer, but his mouth slammed over mine before I could get the entire word out. Matt's tongue slipped through my parted lips, rediscovering every inch of my mouth. Hudson nipped my shoulder with his teeth and my body shivered in response.

"Lie down on the table, on your back, Matt," Hudson growled. "I want you to prepare him while I get you ready," he told me.

Hudson ran to the bedroom to get the supplies while Matt hopped onto the kitchen table and lay down, planting his feet on the edge. I stepped between his legs and stared down at him. He looked so beautiful spread out like that, so open and trusting. The thought of being inside Matt, of feeling a part of him that he'd only shared with two other people, was humbling.

"Touch me, Isaac," Matt whispered and my eyes shot to his face. He was staring at me with a tender expression and my heart tripped over itself. I had it so bad for both of these men.

I reached out to him and trailed my hands down over his chest, feeling the soft hairs underneath my palms. His body trembled beneath my touch as my hands glided over his firm stomach and down to the juncture of his thighs. I felt like I was exploring Matt's body for the first time because it felt different. The moment was different because he was letting me inside for the first time. Not just inside his body, but inside his circle of trust, and, hopefully, inside his heart.

"Do you have any idea what it does to me to see the two of you together?" Hudson said and I looked over my shoulder to see him leaning against the island counter, watching us. I hadn't even heard him come in, but I gave him a warm smile. I knew exactly what it felt like to watch my two lovers getting lost in each other. It was so magnificent, I'd often wished I could capture it in a photo that I could carry around with me and pull out whenever I was away from them.

Hudson sauntered towards us, his cock jutting out proudly from his body. My mouth watered at the sight of it and I glanced down at Matt who was also staring at Hudson with rapt attention. He licked his lips and I knew that he too was wishing he could get a taste. Hudson was calling the shots that night though, and he instructed Matt to tell me what he wanted. Matt gave him a grateful look and then turned his attention to me.

"I want you to lick me. I want you to eat my ass and tease me open with your tongue so I can take that long dick of yours." I whimpered as Matt's erotic words caused my cock to grow rock-hard and I wrapped a hand tightly around my shaft to stop myself from coming. I started to get on my knees, but Hudson stopped me.

"Bend at your waist to do as Matt said because while you're doing that, I'll be doing the same to you," he informed me and I felt my body go up in flames.

I bent down and used my hands to open Matt up so I could see. I licked my lips as I stared at his tight pucker then I pressed forward and licked a path through his crease. I hummed in pleasure at the taste and the familiar smell of my lover. I buried my face in Matt's crack and began to devour him, licking and sucking and wetting him enough that I could work my fingers inside.

The entire time, Hudson was doing the same to me. I loved having my ass rimmed and Hudson was an expert at it. The things he did with his lips and his tongue had my toes curling against the hardwood floor until I finally had to shout for him to stop or I was going to come.

Hudson and I quickly slid on condoms and added lube while Matt slicked his hole and then mine. Matt lay back down on the table, sliding until his ass was on the very edge and pulled his knees up to his chest. Hudson kept his hands on my waist, watching over my shoulder as I lined my cock up with Matt's entrance and began to slide in.

"Oh, God! Matt!" I gasped when I felt his tight heat squeezing my cock as he took me inside his body.

"I know, honey. You feel so good," he groaned and then he sighed as I made it in all the way.

Matt and I stared at each other for a couple of seconds, each of us a little overwhelmed by the sensations. Then I moved and every nerve along my cock woke up and started to sing. I couldn't keep myself from rocking back and forth, but Matt seemed fine with that because his eyes rolled up in his head and he moaned loudly.

I reached behind me, blindly searching for Hudson. He had stepped back as I'd begun to thrust, but I wanted him right there with us. I needed to feel him close, to know that he was near in case I started to break apart. He seemed to understand, as he always did, and he moved back in, pressing his chest against my back.

"So beautiful," he whispered in my ear and I silently agreed. I watched my cock as it disappeared into Matt's snug channel and then reappeared, his body gripping me perfectly. Hudson's hands fell on my shoulders and I moaned as his wet cock began to slide up and down through my crease, gliding over my hole and feeding the flames inside me. I needed more though.

"Please, Hudson!" I cried out.

"You know I'll give you whatever you need, baby. All you have to do is ask," Hudson crooned in my ear.

"You! I need you. Please, don't make me wait anymore," I begged. Hudson used his hand to turn my head and he kissed me with so much passion that I was surprised I was still able to stand afterward.

"Promise me you'll always tell us what you need," he demanded.

"I promise," I whispered back.

I slowed my pace as I felt the broad head of Hudson's cock pushing its way inside me. He pressed a hand against my back and I lowered myself on top of Matt. Matt grabbed the sides of my face and covered my lips with his in a bruising kiss.

Hudson had done a good job of preparing me and he was soon past the first ring of muscle and sliding in until his hips were snuggled up next to my ass. He rocked into me which in turn, pushed me into Matt and I thought my head was going to explode. I had never felt anything as incredible as being inside Matt while Hudson was inside me and I was sure that I had found Heaven.

I pushed up from Matt's body as Hudson tightened his hold on my shoulders. I reached behind me and grabbed on to Hudson's thighs, feeling them bunch, and the pull of muscles as he thrust inside me. Hudson set a steady pace and I was thankful to just go along for the ride because I had lost the ability to think at that moment. Matt stared at us through partially closed lids and he reached for his cock, but Hudson barked out an order that Matt was not to touch himself.

"You will not come until I say," Hudson informed him. Matt let out a frustrated cry, but he complied all the same, gripping his knees *tightly instead.*

Hudson's powerful thrusts had me lifting up on my toes. The change in angle must have made me hit Matt's prostate because he shouted my name, giving me a desperate look that told me he was right on the edge. I knew he'd fight it though with everything he had, because he wanted to please Hudson. Matt definitely liked being dominated in the bedroom. In fact, I was pretty sure he craved it, and once again, Hudson had picked up on that without a word being spoken.

I felt the change as Hudson picked up speed and his movements became choppy and I could tell he was nearing the end. I looked at him over my shoulder and saw the sweat pouring down his face and the tight clench of his jaw. He was magnificent.

"Matt, come!" he shouted between clenched teeth.

I turned my head just in time to see Matt squeeze his eyes shut and throw his head back. He screamed my name and I felt him clamp down on my cock. At the same time his cock erupted, sending white ribbons of cum shooting out all over his chest and landing on his chin.

I was amazed because I didn't know guys could even come without some sort of stimulation to their cocks, but Matt had just done it. I didn't have time to think on it though as my own orgasm took me by surprise and I filled the condom with a loud shout. Hudson followed seconds later, his scream muffled as he bit down on my shoulder.

My cock was achingly hard from the memory of that night and I adjusted in my chair, feeling a bit shameful for allowing myself to get so worked up while I was in a center full of kids. I took a few calming breaths, thankful that no one had caught me fantasizing when I was supposed to be working.

I flicked open my planner so I could check over my schedule for the day and sighed. There was no use denying it to myself, I was completely head over heels in love with Hudson and Matt. I just wondered if they'd ever be able to feel the same way about me and would I then lose that love if they found out about my past?

CHAPTER
Twenty

Matt

I FINISHED BUTTONING MY SHIRT AND THEN REACHED FOR THE tie I had hanging on the back of the bathroom door and watched myself in the mirror as I attempted to tie the perfect knot. Satisfied with the results, I pulled on the dark blue jacket that matched my suit and headed out to the living room to watch for Hudson.

He had asked if he could pick up both me and Isaac so we could all arrive at Morgan and Akio's wedding together. It would be the first time our friends had seen us all together since we'd become a triad. We'd seen our friends separately when they stopped by the center to volunteer or when we had dinner at Romero's one night and they seemed thrilled that we were so happy.

It wasn't our friends that were worrying Hudson and I knew it. It was the fact that our showing up together would be making a statement to everyone we cared about that we were in an exclusive relationship. We hadn't spoken directly about it with each other, but we had all agreed that we wanted to keep seeing each other and that we didn't want anyone else.

I was almost positive that a part of Hudson still expected one of us to change our minds and bolt. Or rather, it was me he was worried about ditching them, but that wasn't going to happen. I liked being with the two of them. They made me laugh and enjoy life again and I had even begun to think about the future, one that hopefully would include both of them in some form or another.

The sight of Hudson's SUV turning into my driveway pulled me from my thoughts. I made sure I had everything I needed, including our gift for the happy couple, then I stepped out into the sunshine and locked my door behind me.

I opened the car door to the sound of catcalls and I blushed, even though I was glad that they approved. I climbed into the back seat and leaned forward to get a kiss from each of them, breathing deeply the spicy, clean scent of their aftershaves. They looked spectacular in their own suits and I felt my chest puff up at the thought of walking into the wedding with two incredibly handsome men.

The wedding was being held at Morgan and Akio's home and I smiled when we pulled in and I saw the large white tent and the chairs lined up along the edge of a lake. Carter was on a break from touring, but had offered to stay away during his cousin's wedding so as not to attract any attention that would take away from the couple's special day. Morgan and Akio had insisted on him being there though so they had hired Micah's security team to surround the property. I'd met his team before and they were intimidating. All ex-military and each specialized in various degrees of combat, no one was going to make it into the wedding that didn't have an invitation.

We were some of the last guests to arrive and I saw the tense set to Hudson's jaw as he held the door open for me. I slid out of the back seat and he moved to step away, but I caught his wrist and pulled him towards me. His eyes widened when I leaned up and pressed my lips to his, but then he sighed and kissed me back. He looked a bit dazed when I pulled away.

"What was that for?" he asked with a small grin.

"Because I'm happy to be here with you. With both of you," I told them as Isaac rounded the car and came to stand next to us. Hudson's smile widened and I could see him visibly relax. Isaac smiled at both of us, the sun making his blue eyes look even brighter. It had been ages since I'd felt that happy and I was finally convinced that I was long overdue.

I took them each by the hand as we made our way through the crowd, stopping to say hello to our friends. They all looked at our joined hands and smiled even wider, some of them slapping us on the backs as if they were congratulating us.

We took our seats and a few minutes later, the music started and we stood and watched behind us for the grooms to arrive. Morgan and Akio took turns walking down the aisle between their parents then they turned and faced each other under the awning. The sun had begun to set, but shone beautifully on the lake behind them, making it a perfect backdrop for the couple as they took each other's hands.

We took our seats and listened as the minister spoke about what marriage meant. It meant love and commitment and wanting more for your partner than you could ever want for yourself, she explained. My mind wandered to my wedding to Sean.

We had been so young and so in love. We'd dreamed of a house and children and a long life together. We had no idea that none of those things would come true. Still, even if I'd known then what was about to happen, I would've chosen to marry him. I had loved Sean with my whole heart and when I lost him, it felt like I had died too, but I hadn't. The two men at my side had brought me back to life and I loved them for it. My breath caught in my throat as the thought popped into my head. *Was I really in love with them?*

I glanced at Hudson out of the corner of my eye. He was strong, intelligent, and the definition of kindness and compassion. He understood me in ways that I was just learning to understand myself. I glanced at Isaac then. Sweet, fun-loving Isaac, who accepted me for all my flaws and who could make me feel like I was on top of the world with just one look.

The answer was *yes*. I didn't just care about the two of them as I had thought. I loved them. I was madly, passionately in love with them and I was excited by the discovery. Hudson had been right, of course. My heart had room enough to love both of them and still hold onto the love I had for Sean. I felt a grin spread across my face and Hudson leaned over and whispered in my ear.

"What has you smiling so much," he asked. I looked up at him and saw that he was smiling too. He was happy, simply because I was and if that wasn't love, I didn't know what was.

"I just love…weddings so much," I told him, changing the direction of my words before I could blurt it out. We were there to celebrate our friends' wedding; my declaration of love would just have to wait. Hudson narrowed his eyes at me and I was sure that he had read my thoughts, but if he had, he didn't let on.

"You're not the only one," he whispered, moving his gaze to the other side of me.

I turned to look at Isaac and saw he had his full attention on Morgan and Akio as they exchanged their vows. He wore a dreamy look as we listened to them promise to take care of each other and love each other for the rest of their lives. Morgan added on to his vows, promising to always hold the door open. I wasn't sure what that meant, but apparently it meant something to Akio because he choked back a watery laugh.

Isaac sighed next to me when they answered, "I do" and I wondered if marriage was something Isaac wanted in his life. Was it something Hudson looked forward to as well? We hadn't talked about anything like that yet, it was too early in our relationship, but still, it was something I was curious about. Where exactly did they see our relationship going?

The minister announced that the happy couple was married and Morgan grabbed Akio in a kiss that went on until Landon cleared his throat loudly and everyone began to snicker. They pulled apart, but continued to only look at each other as if they had forgotten anyone else was there.

"You're my husband!" Morgan exclaimed in wonder and Akio bit back a sob, tears of joy streaming down his face.

"Can you believe it? I mean, OMG!" Akio said.

That started a round of laughter among their friends and family who called out in unison, "O-M-F-G!"

Hudson looked confused, so Isaac and I explained to him that when Morgan and Akio had first gotten to know each other, Morgan's mom had let it slip that her son's first name was Oliver. Akio had died laughing as he realized that Morgan's initials spelled out OMG and he teased him mercilessly about it. When they'd become engaged, they'd decided to hyphenate their last names, Forrest and Greene, making him Oliver Morgan Forrest-Green. O-M-F-G.

Hudson stared at us in disbelief for several seconds and then he started laughing, a deep rumbling laugh that I loved. "That might be the funniest thing I've heard in a while," he said. Isaac and I grinned as we shared a look and I knew we were probably thinking the same thing, there was nothing better than making Hudson happy.

We followed everyone under the nearest tent where the reception was being held and saw Caleb waving for us to come join him and Giovanni at their table. Carter and Ryan were sitting there as well and they smiled at us as we sat down.

"I think I'm going to get a drink while we wait for the grooms to get their pictures taken, would you like anything?" Caleb asked his husband.

"I'd love a red wine if you're going up, please," Giovanni told him. Caleb kissed him on the cheek and then scooted his chair back from the table. He caught my eye as he stood and jerked his head in the direction of the bar.

"I think I'm going to go with Caleb. Would either of you like something to drink?" I looked at Hudson and Isaac who both said they just wanted waters. I followed Caleb through the maze of tables which were filled with family and friends of the grooms and stood next to him at the bar. Once we'd placed our orders, Caleb turned to me and smiled.

"Thanks for coming with me. I just wanted a few minutes to check and see how you've been doing," he said.

"Things are going really well," I told him. "We've had a huge in-flux of kids lately, but thanks to all of you guys, we have plenty of space and funding to help them all." Caleb's face scrunched up as he looked at me.

"That's great news. I'm glad you're able to help more kids now, but I meant you specifically. How are *you* doing, Matt?"

"Oh!" I said in surprise. I guess I was still getting used to hav-ing a friend that I could talk to about something other than Agape House. I realized that was my fault though because I had used the center to hide behind for so long that I never really let anyone else get to know me.

"Things are great with me too," I answered. The bartender set our drinks on the counter and then walked off, leaving us to talk.

"It looks like you, Isaac, and Hudson are getting along pret-ty well," Caleb teased, waggling his eyebrows at me. I couldn't help the smile that spread across my face at the mention of the two men's names.

"Very well. They're both incredible guys." I glanced around quickly and then leaned towards him, lowering my voice a little. "I told them about Sean. They know everything that happened."

"I hate that you kept that to yourself for so long. Good, bad, it doesn't matter; everything in life is better when it's shared with someone else," Caleb said gently.

"That's true," I agreed. "It just took me a long time to remember that. I was so caught up in my grief over losing Sean that I lost the ability to let others in."

"I'm glad you told them and I'm assuming they supported you," he said. I nodded my head.

"Hudson and Isaac were wonderful. They listened while I told them everything and then they made me see that just because I allow myself to care about other people, doesn't mean I have to forget about Sean. I've also started seeing a therapist and she's helping me work through everything. I have some ways to go before I'm all better, but with Isaac and Hudson around, I don't feel lonely anymore," I told him. Caleb's green eyes sparkled when he smiled at me.

"I'm so happy for you. You're an amazing guy and you deserve to be happy again," Caleb said, grabbing me in a quick hug. I hugged him back and a wave of emotion swept through me.

"I have you to thank for giving me the nudge I needed to come out of my shell. Thank you for being there when I needed a friend," I told him. His eyes looked a bit watery as he smiled back at me.

"I will always be here for you, Matt. That's what friends are for," he informed me and I could hear the sincerity in his voice.

Caleb was right, that was exactly what friends were for. Friends stood by your side through all the good and bad times, it just took me awhile to realize that and trust in it. I looked around the room at all the friends I had. I was incredibly grateful to have each and every one of them in my life and it was time that I started getting to know them better and letting them get to know me.

We grabbed the drinks and headed back to the table where I took my seat between Hudson and Isaac. Isaac gave me a concerned look so I leaned over and nuzzled my cheek against his as I whispered in his ear.

"Everything's fine. I was just telling Caleb how wonderful you two are." Isaac blushed prettily at that and I gave him a quick kiss because I just couldn't help myself. He smiled at me, his blue eyes lighting up with happiness. I turned and saw Hudson watching us, a smile on his face as well and so I leaned over and kissed him too. I took their hands in mine and placed them in my lap, linking the three of us together.

The grooms walked into the tent a little bit later and everyone stood and cheered. Morgan and Akio looked deliriously happy and all of us were thrilled to get to celebrate their special day with them. Dinner was delicious and we spent the entire time talking and laughing with our friends. Carter and Ryan took turns telling us about some of their more humorous moments on the road and Giovanni and Caleb told us in hilarious detail what it was like for them becoming parents for the first time. After dinner, Landon stood and tapped his knife against his glass to get everyone's attention. We all quieted so we could listen as he toasted the happy couple.

"Akio and Morgan are both very special to me. For those of you who may not know, Akio and I have been best friends for many years. We met when I was working for another entertainment agency. Akio was brought in as a temp for our office manager and we hit it off right away. He reminded me a lot of my little brothers, Caleb and Carter. Just like them, he was feisty, opinionated, and liked to be the center of attention," Landon said, playfully rolling his eyes and drawing a laugh from the crowd, including the men he was referring to.

"But also, like them, he was kind and compassionate and one of the finest individuals I've ever known. I asked him to take a leap of faith and move with me as I started my own agency and he came along for the ride without question. That's how Akio has been with every part of our friendship; standing by my side no matter what and I couldn't have asked for a better person to have as a friend." I glanced over at Akio and saw him wiping tears from his eyes. From the looks of things, he wasn't the only one moved by his best friend's speech.

"Morgan is one of my favorite people in the world, always has been. He's easygoing, hard-working, and loyal. He'd give anyone the shirt off his back, in fact, I've seen him do so; and he's always honest, no matter what. Some of my favorite memories from my childhood include Morgan. He was always thinking up some new adventure we could go on, most of which ended up with either us getting hurt, getting in trouble with our moms, or both." The audience laughed at that, especially when Landon and Morgan's mothers frowned at them, giving them the mom look.

"Sorry, Mom, but it was all worth it," Landon said into the microphone then he turned back to face the newlyweds. "Morgan taught me how to have fun, accept challenges, and to not take life so seriously, and for that, I am eternally grateful. Akio and Morgan, you both deserve all the joy life has to offer and as the two of you begin your life together, I wish you much love, happiness, and many amazing adventures."

We all raised our glasses in a toast and then watched as Morgan and Akio got up to have their first dance as a married couple. They held each other close as they swayed to the music and whispered things that were only meant for the two of them.

When they'd finished their dance, they called all the unmarried men and women to the front where we waited for them to toss their bow ties over their shoulders. Curtis, who worked for Caleb and Giovanni at their restaurant, caught one and then his jaw slackened as Jakob, his boyfriend of over a year, caught the other.

Jakob looked very pleased with the outcome though and he planted a very long, very heated kiss on Curtis's mouth that had everyone cheering and whistling. I had a feeling it wouldn't be very long before we were celebrating their wedding and I couldn't be happier for the young chef. Curtis was a nice guy and I was glad he'd found someone that made him happy as Jakob so clearly did.

We spent the rest of the night dancing, laughing, and visiting with friends. I was exhausted by the time we made it back to

Hudson's place and we quickly undressed and climbed into bed, snuggling up as closely as we could to one another. It had been a beautiful wedding. As I drifted off to sleep, my mind was full of hope for Morgan and Akio, but also for myself and my future with the two men at my side.

CHAPTER
Twenty-One

Hudson

"WHAT CAN I DO, UNCLE HUDSON?" NICHOLAS ASKED hopefully.

"Oh, I have a very important job for you. I need your help making the salad. Would you like to do that?" I asked.

"Yes! I help Mommy make salad all the time. I'm a good helper, aren't I, Mommy?" Nicholas looked to his mother who beamed at him proudly.

"You're the best helper I've ever had. Now, go wash your hands and bring the step stool from your room so you can reach the counter," Aysha told him.

Nicholas stopped long enough to give us each a quick hug and then he ran out of the room to do what he'd been told. My sister and I exchanged grins and then she went back to stirring the potato salad while I finished pressing the hamburger into patties.

"Are you nervous?" she asked.

"Maybe a little. I think I'm more excited than anything else," I answered honestly.

I'd been wanting to introduce Aysha and Nicholas to the two men in my life for quite a while, but between all our work schedules, it had been difficult to find a time when everyone was available. Finally, we'd been able to agree on a date and Aysha offered to have a cookout at her house. I checked my watch for the thousandth time and grinned when I saw that they'd be there in less than a half hour.

Things had been going amazingly well between the three of us. There were a few bumps along the way, as most relationships experience while you learn to adjust to sharing your time and space with someone else. For us, it took a bit more compromise on all our parts because there were three people instead of just two to get used to. We dealt with each issue as it came up though, communicating with each other and being respectful of one another.

We were all pretty good at communicating our needs or concerns. The only exception to that was Isaac's refusal to talk about his past. Matt and I were trying to be patient with him, but we wished he'd open up about whatever had happened so that maybe he could start letting go of it. Isaac claimed that he'd let it go a long time ago and so there was no point in bringing it up, but Matt and I knew better.

There'd been a couple of times when we'd heard his quiet sobs in the middle of the night when he thought we were both asleep. We'd pulled him in between us, shielding him with our own bodies, but he'd said that he'd been having a dream and didn't remember it. Those were the only times Isaac ever lied to us. It hurt, but we had to trust that he would tell us when he was ready. At least I hoped he would. Every day I fell more in love with the two of them and it killed me to think that one of them was hurting and wouldn't tell me about it so I could help.

"Man, you have it bad!" Aysha's teasing voice pulled me from my thoughts and my eyes darted to hers.

"What are you talking about?" I asked.

"I'm talking about the look on your face as soon as you started talking about your boyfriends and the fact that I've been standing here for the last few minutes apparently having a conversation with myself." Aysha stared at me and I felt my face heat.

"Sorry, I didn't mean to ignore you. I guess I got lost in my own thoughts," I said.

"Because you have it bad. Am I right?" She gave me a look that dared me to deny it, but I didn't want to, not with her.

"Yes, you're right, I'm crazy about them," I admitted and her eyes widened, obviously surprised by the fact that she hadn't had to drag the truth out of me.

"Is it serious?" Aysha asked. Her playfulness from before, replaced with a look of concern.

"I can't answer for them, but for me it is. I want to be with them all the time. I think about them when we're apart and wonder what they're doing, I worry about them if I know they're having a difficult day at the center and I want to know every single thing there is to know about them. I also want them to know everything about me, which is why we're having this dinner. You and Nicholas are a huge part of my life and so are Matt and Isaac. It's time the two parts merged." I shrugged my shoulders, not sure how else to explain how much my guys meant to me. I could see the understanding in Aysha's eyes though, and they softened as she looked at me.

"I'm very happy for you. Just be careful, okay? It can be difficult enough to get used to being in a relationship with one person, much less two," she cautioned, but she was grinning at me when she said it.

"Yeah, I know. I'll be careful." I grinned back at her, not all that surprised that we'd been thinking along the same lines since we'd always seemed to do that. A thought occurred to me then and I narrowed my eyes at her.

"Hey! Why aren't you giving me a harder time about all of this?" I asked.

"Did you want me to give you a hard time?" she said with a chuckle.

"Well, no. Of course, not. I just thought you'd be more worried about seeing me in a relationship after…you know," I said, hating the fact that I was bringing up her ex and hoping it wouldn't ruin the mood. Aysha rolled her eyes playfully though which further heightened my curiosity.

"I just decided that you were right, not all men are cheating assholes," she said turning her back to me so she could slide the potato salad in the fridge. My jaw nearly hit the floor. I was shocked, but so happy to finally hear her say that.

"This wouldn't have anything to do with Drew, would it?" I asked carefully. We were entering new territory and I felt like I was dealing with a wild horse, one wrong move and I could spook her. Aysha whipped around to face me, slamming the fridge door shut as she turned.

"What? How do you know anything about Drew?" she demanded, looking flustered.

"His name popped up when he called earlier. I wasn't snooping, you left your phone lying right on the counter where I was working," I said defensively. Aysha looked like she was struggling for a second and then her shoulders slumped.

"Fine, you were honest with me, I guess you deserve the same." I'm sure my eyebrows were up to my hairline. I had fully expected her to brush the call off as something work related or something similar, but apparently, my sister had been keeping secrets.

"Drew is a man I met at the library when I took Nicholas for story hour. We got to talking and found out we had a lot in common. He's a single dad with a girl a year older than Nicholas. He got divorced about three years ago when his wife abandoned him and their young daughter because she decided she'd rather go to California and try her luck at becoming an actress. He's handsome and funny and he owns a chain of grocery stores, so he's hard-working," Aysha said, shrugging her shoulders like she was embarrassed.

"I think it's wonderful that you've met someone," I told her, smiling. She held her hand up before I could go any further.

"Don't get too excited. We've talked on the phone a lot and at the library, but we haven't gone out yet. He's asked several times and I finally agreed to go out to dinner, but it may all fall apart once that happens," she warned.

"Or, it may be amazing," I reminded her. "Just go and see what happens. You might end up having a great time."

"That's the plan," she said, pursing her lips and blowing a breath out through them. I leaned over and kissed her cheek.

"I'm proud of you. It's about time you start thinking about yourself for a change. Let me know whenever you need me to watch Nicholas so you can go out. I could even keep him at my place for the night," I offered. I couldn't hold back my laughter at the shocked look on her face. Aysha picked up the dish towel off the counter and flung it at me.

"I don't even know how to respond to that so I'm going to just go and see what's taking Nicholas so long," she said, shaking her head at me as she turned to walk out. I was still laughing as she left the kitchen, but I realized she hadn't said no.

The doorbell rang a little while later and I nearly knocked over Nicholas's tower of blocks he was building in my rush to answer it. I ignored Aysha's snicker from behind me as I opened the door. Isaac and Matt stood on the porch, looking nervous, but I saw them visibly relax when they saw me and I loved that. I loved that I made them feel safe and protected because that's how I felt when I was with them too.

"Hey! Come on in," I said, holding the door so they could come in and then shutting it behind them. Nicholas came up to me then and wrapped his arms around my leg, eyeing Matt and Isaac warily.

I reached down and scooped him up into my arms and he laid his head on my shoulder.

"Nicholas, this is Isaac and Matt. Remember, I told you that they were coming over to have dinner with us and to meet you and your mommy?" I asked him. Nicholas nodded his head and Isaac and Matt said hello, smiling so he'd know they were friendly.

"It's nice to meet you, Nicholas. Your uncle, Hudson, has told us a lot about you," Isaac told him.

"He has?" Nicholas asked.

"Yep. He told us that you like Batman and Teenage Mutant Ninja Turtles. Is that true?" Matt asked as if he wasn't sure. Nicholas poked his head up off my shoulder and nodded vigorously.

"He told us you like to draw pictures too," Isaac chimed in. I'd only mentioned those things one time, several weeks before and I felt a surge of love as I realized how much they'd paid attention to what I'd said.

"You want to see what I drawed today?" Nicholas asked, scrambling out of my arms and running off to his room before I could correct his grammar. "I'll show you my Batman too," he called over his shoulder. Isaac and Matt stared after him with wide grins.

"He's adorable," Matt said.

"He looks just like Hudson did at that age," Aysha said, coming to stand next to me. "Hello, I'm Aysha. It's so nice to finally meet both of you."

She stretched her hand out towards them and shook each of their hands. They introduced themselves and thanked her for having them over. I knew I had to be wearing the goofiest grin, but I couldn't help it, I finally had all my favorite people in one place and it made me so happy. Nicholas ran back into the room, carting his coloring book, crayons, and three Batman figures with him.

"Oh boy! You've done it now," I joked.

Isaac and Matt squatted down so they'd be eye level with Nicholas and listened intently as he showed them his toys. When he started to get out his crayons and told Matt to sit on the floor with him so they could color, Aysha stepped in and suggested that they go out on the back deck so we could start cooking. I gave her a grateful smile as she helped Nicholas pick up his things and carry them out the back door, giving me a few moments alone with my men.

"Thank you, guys, for showing up and for not running away yet," I joked.

"I think Nicholas is great," Matt said.

"And your sister seems very nice," Isaac added.

I smiled at them appreciatively and then took turns kissing each of them until we were all a bit breathless. They followed me into the kitchen where I handed them a case of beer for the adults and a juice box for Nicholas. I grabbed the plate stacked with hamburgers out of the fridge then headed out to the deck.

Nicholas was in the yard playing with his ball, apparently having gotten sidetracked from coloring. Aysha was sitting at the table and she motioned for Isaac and Matt to join her. I set the hamburgers down and started the grill, keeping my ears open to the conversation going on behind me. Aysha asked them about their work at the center and both men became impassioned as they described what they were doing and how far the center had come in such a short amount of time.

When the burgers were done cooking, we brought the rest of the food out and began digging in. The conversation never stopped and, eventually, Aysha began to tell embarrassing stories about me when I was a kid. Matt and Isaac protested when I covered her mouth with my hand before she could tell them about the skits I used to put on for her and Nonna.

"Oh, come on, we want to hear more," Isaac said, sticking his tongue out at me when I called him a traitor. Aysha slapped my hand away playfully.

"Hudson made the very best Sandy from Grease, that's all I'll say," she said, laughing wildly as Matt and Isaac both started cackling.

"Man, I wish you had recorded that," Matt said around his laughter.

"Wait, did they even have ways of recording back then?" Isaac teased.

"Oooohhh, burn," Aysha said, pointing at me.

"Excuse me, but you're my *older* sister. That joke was a burn to you too," I reminded her smugly.

"Yeah, but that grenade was lobbed at you, so it's still funny," she said with a laugh.

I shook my head and held my hands up in surrender and Matt winked at me from across the table. I smiled back at him, happy that everyone seemed to be having fun, even if some of it was at my expense.

Aysha stood up and patted my head lovingly then she started to clear our dirty dishes. Matt immediately jumped up to help and the two of them carried a stack of dishes into the kitchen with Nicholas trailing behind, asking Matt if he wanted to see his room. Isaac leaned over and kissed me.

"I'm sorry I picked on you. I promise to make it up to you later," he said and my cock began to plump from the look in his eyes.

"Yes, you will. Repeatedly," I growled back. Isaac whimpered, his whole body shuddering and I stood, feeling pleased with myself.

We finished clearing the table and loaded the dishwasher then went back outside to enjoy the cool, evening air. The sun had set and I turned on some quiet music and the decorative patio lights which put off a soft glow. Aysha had stayed inside to give Nicholas a bath and get him ready for bed so it was just me and my guys.

We sat down next to each other on the long bench seat and I leaned back, putting an arm around each of them and pulling them in closer to my side. It was peaceful and I took a deep breath, enjoying the moment.

"It was good to hear Aysha laugh so much. I can tell she really likes you guys," I told them. Matt tilted his head up and kissed the side of my neck which made goose bumps break out all up and down my body.

"I like her too, and Nicholas," he said. I leaned down and brushed my lips over his before kissing him gently.

"You have a great family," Isaac added and I turned to kiss him too.

We were quiet for several minutes as we listened to the music and watched lightning bugs lighting up the backyard, signaling to each other in the hopes of finding a mate. I was blessed to have found mine because that was exactly what I considered the men in my arms to be. They were my soulmates and I couldn't imagine my life without them.

"I love you," I whispered. They both tensed beside me and my chest felt tight so I took a deep breath then stood up and turned to face them.

"I'm sorry to just blurt it out like that. I wasn't trying to shock you or scare you away, but I've felt this way for a long time and I just couldn't hold it in anymore. I am absolutely one hundred percent in love with both of you." I felt dizzy by the time I finished and I wobbled on my feet. Isaac grabbed my hands and eased me back down beside him.

"You love us?" he asked incredulously.

"Yes," I answered, hoping one of them would say something else and put me out of my misery.

"I love you both too. It took a while for me to be sure of what it was because I've never been in love before, but it is and I do. I love you two with all my heart," Isaac announced, a glorious smile lighting up his face. I cupped the back of his neck and pulled him in for a kiss, trying to convey with my lips everything I felt for him, but knowing it couldn't come close.

We were both smiling when we parted, but our smiles dimmed when we turned to look at Matt who was staring up at the stars. He'd been quiet so far and I knew that he was probably the one that would struggle the most with the change in our relationship. I reached for his hand and was relieved when he let me take it. Isaac stood up and climbed in Matt's lap, cupping Matt's face in his hands and forcing him to look at him.

"It's okay, Matt. We understand this is hard for you and that you may never feel the same way, but we love you and we're not going anywhere, right, Hudson?" They both turned their heads and I scooted in closer and wrapped my arms around both of them.

"That's right. I've never loved anyone the way I love you two and I'm not letting go of that no matter what, but that doesn't mean that you can't move at your own pace and do whatever you're comfortable with," I told Matt.

"Thank you," he said then he swallowed hard. "I have been in love before so I know what it is and I know all the signs. Sean stole my heart as a young boy and he's held it all these years. I will always love him."

"It's okay," Isaac said again, but Matt cut him off by placing a finger to his lips.

"I will always love Sean, but the heart really does have the capacity to love many because I love you both more than I ever thought possible," Matt said. I tilted my head for a second, not sure I'd heard him correctly, but then I saw the way he was looking at me and I knew it was true.

We moved in, all three of us sharing a kiss in a way that had become second nature to us. We laughed and whispered things to each other that were only for our ears, caught up in the moment and the euphoria of being in love. I may have been in a small backyard in the middle of Illinois, but right then, I was on top of the world.

CHAPTER
Twenty-Two

Isaac

"ALL I'M SAYING IS THAT IF AYSHA IS GOING TO CONTINUE to see this Drew character then I think we should get to meet him and make sure he's alright. We don't need some jerk coming around Nicholas," Matt stated.

"God, I love you," Hudson told him and I smiled.

It had been a few months since we'd first declared our love, but not a day went by that we didn't say it to each other and my heart still melted every time I heard the words uttered from my lovers' lips. It didn't even matter whether they were saying it to me or to each other because seeing the two of them loving each other affected me the same way. What the two of them felt for each other was just as strong as what I shared with each of them and that was the beauty of our relationship.

It had been a long day and the three of us were relaxing in Matt's office while he finished some paperwork. I was stretched out on the couch with my head in Hudson's lap, luxuriating in the feel of his fingers in my hair and enjoying Matt's protectiveness when it came to Hudson's sister and nephew. I had to agree with him though. Since that first night, we'd spent a lot more time with Aysha and Nicholas, and Matt and I had begun to care about them as if they were our own family. We were thrilled that she was dating again, but we were anxious to meet the guy and see for ourselves if he was good enough to be around them.

A knock sounded at the door and I sat up. Everyone at the center knew we were in a relationship and were happy for us, but we were still careful about PDAs since there were kids around. It was hard at times when all I wanted to do was lay my men out across the nearest desk and have my way with them, but I resisted. *I deserve a fucking medal.*

The door opened and Allison popped her head around it. "I'm sorry to bother you guys, I know you were getting ready to leave soon, but we just had a couple of new kids come in. There may be a bit of an issue with one of them though so I thought I better let you know right away."

"What kind of issue?" I asked.

"He's only eight," she said.

I exchanged concerned looks with the other men and then we followed Allison out the door. The boys were sitting on the couch in the lobby area of the building. There was food on the table in front of them and someone had turned the TV on to Nickelodeon. I gave Allison a small smile of thanks and then I turned my attention to Matt who knelt down in front of them and introduced himself in a quiet, soothing voice.

I'd heard him use that same tone with each new arrival and I knew he did it on purpose to make himself seem less threatening. Matt told me once that most of the kids who came to the center had been hurt in one way or another, often by men and so they would automatically be leery of him. He tried his best to put them at ease and every time I heard it, it made me feel safe just like the first time he'd used it on me.

The two boys were seated closely together, but as they looked up at Hudson, the youngest scooted in closer to the older boy's side. The older boy's eyes never wavered, but his arm curled around the younger boy in a move that was as protective as it was automatic which told me he was used to watching out for the eight-year-old. He also winced when he moved which made me wonder if he was injured and an uneasy feeling began in the pit of my stomach. I was sure that Hudson had seen the boy's pained expression too because he cursed under his breath. Nothing pissed him off more than someone hurting a child.

They looked nothing alike so it was difficult to tell if they were related or not. The older of the two had light brown hair that was long in the front and kept falling down over his green eyes. He swept it back to the side nervously and my breath hitched when I caught a glimpse of a narrow gash on his forehead. It was swollen and just beginning to bruise so I knew that it must've happened recently. I could tell someone had attempted to clean it, but there were still dark smudges of caked blood along the edges and I clenched my jaw.

The younger boy was the complete opposite with jet black hair, crystal blue eyes, and dimples along the sides of his mouth that were visible even without smiling. They both were thinner than they should've been, but I noticed they hadn't touched the food that Allison had laid out. They didn't look dirty so they'd either recently found a place to clean up or they hadn't been out on their own for long.

"Will you tell us your names?" Matt asked. The younger boy started to speak, but the older boy cut him off.

"No names until we know if we can stay here," he said. "If we've got to move on then I don't want you calling the cops and telling them who we are."

"Fair enough. Can you at least tell me how old you are?" Matt asked. The older boy glanced over to the front desk where Allison was on the phone, most likely explaining the situation to CPS.

"I already told the lady that I'm fifteen and my brother's eight." His eyes held a challenge as he stared back at Matt. "Look, I've seen this place on the news when it was being set up. I know it's for LGBTQA kids to have a safe place they can stay. I'm gay, I promise I am, so will you just let us stay?"

Hudson took a few steps forward and both pairs of eyes darted in his direction, nervous and untrusting. He halted his steps and then sat down, right on the floor so he'd be on their level. He was trying to make himself look smaller so they wouldn't be afraid and my heart swelled with love for both of my men and the compassion they were showing.

"There are more things to consider other than the fact that you're gay," Hudson told the boy.

"Like what? You want to know how our mom beats us?" His voice rose as the words started pouring out of him. "She blames us for our dad leaving so she hits us. She likes to drink a lot too which usually sets her off. Last night was the worst though. She'd been drinking all day and I knew it was going to be bad. I tried to calm her down, but nothing would work, it was like she couldn't even hear me. She came after my brother and I knew I had to do whatever it took to protect him or she would end up killing him." His eyes darted around the room, begging us to understand as he continued describing the horrors they'd been through at the hands of their mother.

The more he talked, the more my hands began to shake. I felt sweat trickle down my spine and my chest felt tight, making it difficult to breathe. I closed my eyes, trying to fight back my nausea, but my stomach continued to churn until I was forced to run from the room.

I made it to the bathroom just in time as my body tried to rid itself of not only the food I'd eaten that day, but also the painful memories. I wished it were that simple. I wished I could just throw up and purge myself of everything that had happened that terrible night, but I couldn't. The memories were trapped inside me, burned into my brain.

I flushed the toilet and then went to the sink, rinsing my mouth out and splashing cold water on my face. I got a paper towel and wiped my face, but tears were running down my face faster than I could catch them. I glanced up and caught my reflection in the mirror. My blue eyes looked wild, frantic, and desperate. Exactly the same as *his* had looked on that terrible night as he'd stared at me.

For years, I'd pushed the images of that night to the back of my mind. Each time they tried to creep in, I'd force them back again, telling myself that it wasn't real or that it had happened to someone other than me. The similarity between the boys' story and mine had brought it all back though and this time the memories forced their way in, refusing to be ignored.

I fought. I fought like hell to lock them away one more time, but *his* face flashed in front of my eyes and I heard his voice as he screamed at me. A tremor shook my body and darkness crept in around the edges of my vision. My legs gave out and I fell to the floor, shaking all over as pitch blackness enveloped me.

I felt something cool and wet brush across my forehead and I reached up blindly and tried to brush it away. "Shhh, it's okay, baby. We're here." Hudson. A small smile lifted my lips at the sound of his deep baritone voice.

I felt tired and my body ached, but not the good way it usually did when I was in bed with my lovers. I shifted and wondered immediately why the bed was so hard and cold. I pried my eyes open and found Matt and Hudson leaning over me. Hudson was frowning and Matt had tears in his eyes. It hurt my heart to see him sad so I reached up and wiped his tears away with my thumb. Matt grabbed my hand and pressed his lips to my wrist as he breathed in deeply. He was shaking as if something had scared him and I tried to sit up so I could figure out what was going on.

Hudson helped me into a sitting position and leaned me against the headboard, only it wasn't a headboard, it was a wall and I wasn't in bed, I was sitting on the floor. I glanced around the room and saw that I was in the employee bathroom at work. My forehead wrinkled as I tried to remember how I'd ended up there.

I sucked in a gasp as everything came flooding back to me; the two young boys, what they'd been through, my own past and those blue eyes, so similar to mine, staring straight into my soul as he screamed at me in a voice I barely recognized.

"No, no, no, no," I began to chant as pain swept through me. Hudson grabbed me by the shoulders, speaking to me, but I couldn't hear him over the rush of blood in my ears. I felt like I was about to be washed away by a tidal wave of emotions so I clutched the front of Hudson's shirt in my fists, just trying to hold on. I was having trouble breathing and then suddenly, I felt myself being lifted in the air as Hudson swept one arm under my legs and one behind my back and carried me out the door.

I was barely aware of him walking with me out the front door of the center and tossing his keys to Matt. The car doors slammed and then I was alone with my guys. Hudson held me on his lap with his arms wrapped around me as Matt started the car and began to drive. I sobbed into Hudson's neck, still clinging on to him and his hand came up to run over my hair as he whispered in my ear. Matt reached over as he drove and laid his hand on my leg. I reached down and grabbed onto him, uniting us all together and letting myself feed off their strength.

My sobs turned into softer cries, interrupted by occasional hiccups and I allowed myself to drift into an exhausted sleep. Lulled away by the security of having my men so close and the sound of Hudson's voice in my ear. "We've got you, Isaac. We won't let you go."

When I woke again, I was in Hudson's bed and it was dark. I

could hear voices speaking quietly and there was a soft light coming from the living room, just below the loft. My throat felt scratchy and dry and my eyes were swollen from crying so much. I lay still, waiting for the excruciating pain to take over again, but it didn't. It was still there, but it felt hazy and dull, like it was hovering in the distance, unable to fully touch me. I barely remembered Hudson holding a pill to my lips and telling me to swallow. He'd given me water to wash it down with and then I'd fallen back to sleep.

I climbed out of bed and made my way to the stairs on wobbly legs. I peered down over the railing and my heart ached at what I saw. Hudson was standing near the balcony doors, his arms wrapped around Matt as he rocked him gently back and forth.

"When we found him lying there, unconscious on the bathroom floor, I felt so hopeless, Hudson. I love him and it's killing me to see him in pain, but how can we help if he won't talk to us?" Matt said quietly.

"I know, honey. I want to help him too, but this isn't something we can force him to do. It has to be his decision or we could end up causing more damage," Hudson told him.

Guilt slammed into me as I realized how selfish I was being by not putting myself in their shoes. I could only imagine how much it would kill me to see one of them in pain and wanting to help, but having them turn away from me instead. I knew they had heard me crying late at night, but I'd brushed off their questions, telling myself that they might leave me if they knew the truth. I knew in my heart that was a lie though. I knew Matt and Hudson loved me deeply, and I trusted that they would see me through any obstacle.

The truth of the matter was, I was a coward. I had chosen to hide from my past instead of facing it head-on and dealing with it, and when it all came barreling down, I'd not only been hurt by the crushing weight of it, the two people I loved most in the world had also been hurt.

"I'm an asshole." I hadn't even realized I'd spoken out loud until both men whipped their heads in my direction.

Seconds later they were racing up the stairs and wrapping themselves around me. I nuzzled my face into Matt's neck, breathing his familiar scent deep into my lungs. Hudson's strong chest was pressed against my back and I sighed, cocooned in the warmth and safety of their bodies. That right there was my happy place. The place where the outside world and the demons from my past couldn't touch me. I'd hidden for long enough though. It was time to get everything out into the open.

CHAPTER
Twenty-Three

Isaac

"WE NEED TO TALK," I TOLD THEM, FORCING MYSELF out of their comforting embrace. They exchanged a look that was both cautious and hopeful at the same time and nodded.

We made our way downstairs and Hudson and I each sat down while Matt ran to the kitchen, bringing me back a bottle of water. I gave him a grateful look as I unscrewed the lid and took a long drink. It felt cool and refreshing on my sore throat. I placed the bottle on the coffee table then sat back, staring down at my hands in my lap.

"I owe you both an apology." I held my hand up when they looked like they were going to argue. They didn't look happy, but they allowed me to continue. "I've tried so hard over the last several years to forget about my past and for the most part, I was successful.

I knew it wasn't healthy, but what had happened was just too painful to think about, so I didn't. I hadn't realized though that I was hurting the two of you by not telling you and allowing you to help, and for that I'm sorry."

"You don't have anything to apologize for," Hudson said gently. "Everyone deals with pain in their own way."

"But you're not alone anymore. You have both of us and we'll always be here to listen whenever you're ready," Matt added. I gave them a small smile, so thankful to have them in my life.

"I think I'm ready," I told them. I reached for their hands and clasped them in my own, folding them in my lap then I took a deep breath.

"My story is very similar to the one the boys told today." My eyes widened suddenly and I turned to Matt. He squeezed my hand.

"They're being taken care of. Allison finally got them to eat and CPS was on their way to talk to them when we left. I called and told the caseworker that I would take full responsibility for having a child under thirteen at the center and she agreed to let the boys stay there until something can be figured out." I sagged in relief.

"I'm glad. I feel horrible about what they've gone through," I said.

"You said your story was similar to theirs?" Hudson asked.

"Yes, very much so. I suppose that's what brought everything rushing back. I can usually separate myself from the kids' stories; I have to in order to be capable of doing my job, but theirs was just so much like mine that it took me right back to that place and time that I'd fought so hard to forget." I let go of their hands long enough to grab my water and take another drink, then I reached for them once again and they came willingly.

"My mom died when I was ten years old. She worked at a local clothing store and Dad worked in construction. They got along for the most part, but then there were a few times when I'd wake up to a sound in the middle of the night. I'd lie in bed and hear them arguing. They could get pretty loud and, sometimes, I would hear something that sounded like a slap and then Mom crying. It always scared me because I couldn't understand what was happening or why they were fighting because they never acted that way in front of us. I used to worry that they'd get a divorce like my friend Toby's parents. I quickly learned that there were worse things than divorce." Matt put his arm around my shoulders and pulled me towards him, kissing the side of my head. I closed my eyes and let him comfort me for a moment before I continued.

"They'd been fighting a lot more than usual, waking me nearly every night with their shouting. One morning, I came down for breakfast and Mom had her arm wrapped in a sling. Her bottom lip was swollen and she looked like she'd been crying. I gave her a hug, but it only made her cry harder. She told me to hurry because the school bus would be there to pick me up soon. I told her I loved her right before I ran out the door. That was the last time I saw her alive." I swallowed hard around the lump in my throat.

"She swallowed an entire bottle of pills while we were at school and Dad was at work. By the time we got home, my mom was long gone. I've always wondered if there was something I could've done to try and help her, to stop her before she took her own life," I whispered sadly.

"You were only ten years old, just a child. There was nothing you could've done," Hudson told me. I looked at him, wanting to believe that, but I wasn't sure I could.

"Neither of my parents had sisters or brothers and both were estranged from my grandparents who hadn't approved of them getting married right out of high school. They never really made any friends outside of work so there was no one around to see my father falling apart after Mom died or to help us when he became someone we no longer recognized," I said bitterly.

"Us?" Hudson asked.

"Me and my brother, Zane," I answered. I felt a sharp pain in my chest when I spoke my brother's name out loud for the first time in years. "Zane was a year older than me and I worshiped the ground he walked on. He was funny, played all kinds of sports, and had tons of friends. He was big and strong and everything I wasn't, but he always let me tag along wherever he went.

"Things started to change right after the funeral. Dad went to bed that afternoon and didn't come back out of his room for over a week. Zane and I took turns bringing him food and trying to get him to come out of his room, but he refused to eat and he wouldn't say anything; he just lay there, staring at the ceiling. We were young boys who had just lost our mother, it would've been nice to be able to lean on our dad during that time, but we ended up having to take care of him instead and so we leaned on each other." A cold chill went up my spine as I pictured what happened next.

"A little over a week after we buried our mother, Zane and I were in the kitchen, eating cereal for dinner. We were running out of food and we were talking about how we would need to go to the store if Dad didn't come out of his room soon. I told Zane that I was hungry for mashed potatoes and he said that he would get the stuff and try to make me some, but he knew they wouldn't be as good as Mom's. We didn't know that Dad had come out and was standing in the hall listening. When he heard Zane say Mom's name, it must've set something off in him because he flew into a rage. Dad came storming into the room and slapped Zane across the face, hard enough to leave a handprint. He told us that we were never to speak our mother's name again." Matt squeezed me tighter and Hudson tightened his grip on my hand.

"We couldn't understand what was happening; Dad had never raised a hand to us before. I'd heard him fighting with Mom several times, but he'd always been a pretty good dad to us. It was as if he'd gone into his room as one person and come out a totally different one," I explained.

"It sounds like he had a complete mental breakdown. If that were the case then he really wasn't himself anymore," Hudson murmured.

"Yeah, we basically lost both of our parents on the same day," I whispered. "Dad was never the same after that. He started drinking all the time and the more he drank, the meaner he got. We tried to avoid him as much as possible when he was like that, but the smallest things would set him off and eventually we were getting hit nearly every day. Zane was bigger than me and he would always try to protect me, often taking the brunt of our dad's anger." I winced at the memory of all the bruises and broken bones my brother had endured so that I wouldn't have to.

"It went on that way for years, but despite everything going on at home, Zane continued to excel at sports. He pushed me to keep my grades up, telling me that if I did that, that maybe we both would get scholarships and could go to college and get away from Dad. We kept that as our goal and both of us worked hard to reach it. Zane was my best friend, he was the only one who knew the ugly truth of what was happening inside our home. The only thing he didn't know was that I was gay."

"You didn't think he'd understand?" Matt asked gently. I shook my head vigorously.

"It wasn't that. I knew Zane loved me no matter what and he wouldn't have cared if his little brother was gay. The problem once again was our father. Like I said, he was mean all the time after Mom died, but especially when he was drunk. He loved to call us names while he beat us, anything he could think of to belittle us and try to break our spirits. His favorite name to call us was faggot and he said it with so much loathing and disgust that when I was fourteen and started to realize I was gay, I knew I would have to keep it hidden or he'd kill me. I didn't tell Zane for two reasons; I couldn't risk Dad overhearing me talking about it, and we had so many secrets we were already carrying, I didn't want to add one more to Zane's load."

"Still, it had to be so hard to hide such a huge part of who you were," Hudson said, sounding sad.

"It wasn't all that hard," I told him with a shrug. "I didn't have a normal life so it wasn't like I was bringing anyone home or going out on dates. I was required to come home every day straight after school so there were no opportunities for me to meet anyone. Zane was only permitted to continue sports because the athletic director called and begged Dad and, of course, my father agreed because he couldn't very well let on that he wanted his kids home so he could pound on them." I had trouble holding back the anger in my tone.

"Things continued that way for a long time. Dad kept drinking and hitting us, he eventually lost his job because he'd called in too many times when he was too hung over to make it in. He told Zane and me we would have to get jobs then and, luckily, we both got hired on at the nearby pizza place. It was hard. We were both going to school all day, Zane had practices or games nearly every day, we had homework to keep up with and then suddenly we were expected to hold down a job that didn't end until one in the morning. We were exhausted, but somehow, we managed to hold it together and the job got us out of the house and away from Dad more so that was a plus.

"It somehow got even worse once Dad quit working. I suppose sitting around the house all day gave him more time to dwell on the past, to drink, and to think up ways he could show his hatred towards us. Dad started getting creative then, waiting until we were fast asleep to come in our rooms and attack or catching us as soon as we stepped out of the shower, naked and defenseless. He was a monster who, even in his rage, would be sure not to leave any marks where someone might see.

"One night when I was around sixteen, Zane and I were both asleep in our rooms. I woke up to the sound of Zane screaming and my father shouting vile names at him. There was a loud thumping sound and I wasn't sure what it was until he came into my room next with a baseball bat." Matt sucked in a sharp breath and buried his face in my neck. I could feel him shaking next to me and I knew how hard it had to be for him and Hudson to hear. If anyone ever laid a hand on one of my guys, I'd want to rip them to shreds.

"When it was over and Dad had slunk away somewhere and passed out, Zane came into my room and crawled into bed with me. He was breathing funny and I worried that he had a broken rib, but he was more concerned about me. He made me promise that night that if things ever got that bad again that I'd run. I told him no, that I didn't want to ever leave him, but he wouldn't let up until I promised. Zane was getting upset which was making it even harder for him to breathe so I agreed just so he'd settle down. I promised him that if Dad ever started to beat us as bad as he had that night that I would get away, that I'd run and not look back until I was somewhere safe."

Tears ran down my face as I pictured the look of relief on Zane's face when I made that promise. "It was like as long as he knew I would be safe, then he didn't care what happened to him. That thought had scared me and I'd told him that he needed to promise me the same thing, but he'd passed out from exhaustion and all the pain and horrors of the night.

"Months went by and the beatings continued, but they never got as bad as that night. Zane turned eighteen and graduated from high school. I was terrified that I would be left alone with Dad, but Zane stayed there. He said he'd talked to the college who had offered him a full ride if he played soccer for them and they were willing to wait a year for him. I was so relieved, but at the same time, I felt guilty knowing that he could have been free of Dad, but instead, he stayed there for me. I had turned seventeen and was a senior. We were able to hide some of our pizza delivery tips from Dad and had set that aside so that as soon as I graduated we could get an apartment together somewhere near the college and then start there together in the fall. We never made it that far." Hudson pulled the blanket off the back of the couch and wrapped it around me as I began to shake.

"Do you need to stop, baby?" he asked. I could see how worried they both were, but I needed to get this over with so I shook my head no.

"One day we were all at home. There was no school that day

because of some stupid teacher in-service something or other and our boss said it was slow at work and he didn't need us. Dad had been in his room, sleeping off the bender from the night before. Zane and I were cleaning the house and trying to be as quiet as we could so we wouldn't wake our father. Zane was washing the dishes while I dried them. He handed me a plate and before I could stop it, it slipped from my fingers and crashed to the floor." I closed my eyes, remembering the look of horror that had crossed Zane's face.

"Zane grabbed my arm and we started to run towards the back door. I opened the door and looked back when I felt Zane being yanked backwards by our father. Dad's face was purple, mottled with rage and he threw Zane down on the floor. He began beating him and Zane tried to crawl away. I jumped on Dad's back and hit him over and over, trying to get him to let go of my brother. It was the first time I'd ever fought back and I was terrified, but I had to do something to help Zane. Dad threw me off him and I hit my head so hard on the counter that I saw stars.

"I was dizzy and seeing double of everything. I saw Dad sitting on top of Zane and punching him in the face over and over again. I remember being surprised, because Dad had never hit us anywhere that people could see, and that's when I realized that he didn't plan on stopping that time. He was going to kill Zane." A sob burst from my chest as I relived that terrible moment.

"Zane was barely conscious, but he managed to find me. His eyes had always been the same shape and bright blue as mine, but when he looked at me then, they were dull, like he was barely hanging on. '*Run!*' he screamed at me, but I shook my head no. I couldn't leave him. I managed to get to my feet and I jumped on Dad's back again, hitting and flailing at him with everything I had, but nothing I did seemed to make a difference. '*You promised, now run!*' Zane shouted at me, and then Dad hit him one more time straight in the face. I heard the crack of his nose and teeth and blood went flying." I was sobbing hard then and I wasn't even sure Hudson and Matt could make sense of what I was saying, but I kept talking anyway, needing to purge myself of every last detail.

"Zane stopped moving and there was so much blood. I tried to get to him, to see if he was breathing, but Dad turned on me then and his eyes were black and soulless. He reached for me and I scrambled off his back and towards the door. I looked back at Zane who still hadn't moved and then at my father who had murder in his eyes and I knew it was over. Zane was gone and there was nothing I could do for him, nothing except keep my promise to him. So, I ran. I ran and I ran and I kept going until I was far away from our house and I knew my father couldn't find me.

"I had no idea where to go and I had nothing on me but the clothes I was wearing and the little bit of money I had in my pocket. I made it to a bus station and took a bus as far as my money would get me. I didn't care where that was because at that point, anywhere was safer than home. I ended up in Chicago and I wandered around the streets, trying to figure out what to do. I was terrified. I was seventeen with no money, no friends and I'd just watched my father kill my brother. It was cold out and getting dark. I knew I'd need to find a place to sleep soon and then I walked around a corner and saw a building, all lit up. The sign over the door said *Agape House—A safe place to call home.* I had no idea if they would have room for me or if they'd call the police and send me back to my father, but I was desperate so I went inside." I turned to Matt who had tears streaming down his own face.

"You walked up to me that night and used that same soothing voice you use to put all the new kids at ease and I started crying. I couldn't tell you anything that had happened because I was afraid of being sent back to my dad, but I immediately felt safe with you and that was better than anything I could've asked for right then," I told him.

"What happened with your father?" Hudson asked in a strained voice. He looked angrier than I had ever seen him before, but I could tell he was trying to rein it in. "I'm assuming CPS would've tracked him down and found out what he'd done."

"I don't know, I never saw him again and frankly I was just relieved to be able to stay at the center and never go back to that hell again," I stated honestly. Hudson looked across me to Matt who was staring down at his hands. Matt looked up at us and I could see the defiance in his eyes.

"I never called them, okay?" he said defensively. "I never called CPS. I knew I should, I knew I was required by law and could lose my license for it." His eyes flickered to mine and softened. "But there was something about you, something special. I hadn't allowed myself to feel anything since Sean died, but I felt a connection with you. Maybe I was able to sense that you'd suffered a great loss just like I had, I don't know how to explain it. I just knew that you were different and that whatever had sent you running to me wasn't something you could ever go back to. So, I didn't call CPS. I kept you off the books and I told everyone that you were already eighteen."

"Is that why you always asked me to help out in the office?" I asked.

"That was part of the reason. I had to convince everyone that I'd hired you even though you weren't finished with high school. I'd let other employees stay there before if they needed it so at least I didn't have to make up a story about why you were living there. The other reason was that I just liked being around you. You were always so sweet and kind. You made me happy and I hadn't felt that way in a very long time," Matt admitted. I couldn't help myself, I pounced on him, thanking him in between every kiss that I planted on his face.

"I knew that you had saved me by letting me stay there, but I had no idea the trouble you'd gone through to do it. I owe you my life, literally, because I know that if I'd been sent back, I wouldn't be here today," I told him. Matt smiled at me then glanced nervously at Hudson.

"The laws are in place to try and keep everyone safe, but

sometimes there are situations where we just have to go with our guts. That's what you did, Matt, and it was the right thing to do," Hudson assured him and I watched Matt's shoulders relax.

"I miss Zane so much and I feel horrible that I tried to push him out of my mind for so long," I whispered.

Hudson placed a finger under my chin and lifted my face to his. "Our minds can only deal with so much before something has to give. You had to push it all aside so that you could pick yourself back up and move on. You tried to save Zane, and when you couldn't, you kept your promise to him and saved yourself. There's absolutely nothing for you to feel guilty about and I'm pretty sure if Zane were here, he'd tell you how proud he is of you and how you've turned out." Fresh tears started to flow and they both wrapped me up between them and held me while I cried.

A little while later, Hudson carried me up to bed and him and Matt crawled in on either side of me. We lay there in the dark, just listening to each other breathe, each of us lost in our own thoughts.

"I know the one boy is too young to be at the center for long, but please, promise me that we'll do everything we can to keep them together. I couldn't stand it if those two brothers were separated," I whispered.

Matt kissed the side of my neck. "I promise you, we'll figure something out. I'll make sure they'll get to stay together."

I let out a long sigh of relief and, feeling exhausted from the emotions of the day, I drifted off, cradled between the two men who I knew would never let anything bad happen to me ever again.

CHAPTER
Twenty-Four

Hudson

"It sounds like you're doing really well, Rylie. I'm so happy that the stress of being on the road hasn't caused you to have any slip ups," I told him. He'd asked if we could continue our sessions using Skype while he was on tour and I told him I thought it was a great idea. He'd been gone for over six months, but he'd never missed even one of our weekly sessions.

"It's still stressful, and you and I both know I'll always have times where I have to fight the cravings, but I feel great, I'm more focused than I've ever been and I have so many things to live for," he said, smiling widely. I smiled back at him, so proud of how far he'd come since I'd first met him.

"I'm assuming Lachlan is one of those things," I teased and laughed as Rylie's grin widened even further.

"Yeah, he's the best thing," Rylie answered, his voice gentling at the mention of his husband. "But there's more." I arched an eyebrow at him and waited for him to elaborate. "Oh, would you look at that. We're out of time!" he said with a devious grin.

"Asshole," I grumbled.

"Is that your professional diagnosis, Doc?" Rylie asked, his shoulders shaking.

"Yes, as a matter of fact, it is and I'll be sure to put it in my notes," I informed him haughtily and he burst out into a fit of laughter.

"So, how are things going with your two lovers, you naughty boy?" he purred. I rolled my eyes, but ignored his teasing.

"Things are amazing with both of them. I couldn't imagine finding any two people more perfect for me," I told him.

"I'm so happy for you, you deserve it," Rylie said, sounding more serious than usual. I could tell he had something important to say so I waited quietly. He cleared his throat. "If it weren't for you and Lachlan, I'd probably have died a long time ago in some skeevy motel room. That was the path I was headed down, but because of the two of you, I was able to get back on track and in the end, got a life that's better than I could've ever hoped for. You're more than just my therapist, Hudson. You're one of my very best friends and you deserve to be just as happy as I am."

I swallowed around the knot in my throat that his words had caused. "I feel the same way about you and I'm so glad to have you as a friend."

"Even when I'm forcing you to ride in tiny cars?" Rylie joked, lightening the heavy mood.

"Even then," I chuckled.

"Okay, I better get going. I have a very sexy British man sleeping in the other room and I have plans on how I'd like to wake him." He gave me a wolfish smile and then my screen went dark.

I shut the lid on my laptop and then stood up and stretched, I was still smiling as I walked out of my home office and down the hall to the kitchen. I'd been telling Rylie the truth when I said things were great with me, Matt, and Isaac.

Isaac began seeing a counselor shortly after he told us about his past. It was the same counselor that Matt was seeing and she seemed to be helping them both tremendously. Isaac's nightmares started occurring more frequently which was to be expected after having to dredge everything up. But now, instead of making up excuses, he talked to us about what the nightmares were and let us comfort him. The whole thing had just brought us even closer to each other.

I washed my hands at the sink and then started pulling food out of the fridge. I had a lot to do and only a few hours to get it all done. I'd asked my guys to come over for dinner, but they had no idea that I had planned for this to be a special dinner. A swarm of butterflies took flight inside my stomach when I thought of everything I wanted to say to them. I just hoped they took it well.

A couple of hours later, the food was all prepared and had been put in the oven and I'd cleaned my place. I glanced at the clock on the stove and realized I'd better get a move on if I was going to have time for a shower before they got there.

I cleaned myself quickly and had just finished getting dressed when I heard the front door open. We'd exchanged keys with each other several months ago, making it easier for us all to come and go from each other's homes.

"Oh, wow! Something smells delicious," I heard Isaac say.

"Yum. What is that?" Matt said. They were in the kitchen and I crept up behind them, smiling as they peeked under the lids on the stovetop.

"No need to snoop, I'll tell you." I laughed when they both jumped and turned around to face me, matching guilty expressions on their faces. "It's beef bourguignon with buttered noodles and string beans. I also made a triple chocolate cake for dessert."

"That must've taken you all day," Matt said.

"You're worth it," I responded, moving in to kiss each of them, long and slow.

My cock was aching by the time we stopped, but I made myself because we needed to talk first and I wanted to feed my men. I got dinner out of the oven while Isaac poured the drinks and Matt sliced the loaf of homemade bread I'd made. It felt so natural and domestic and I found myself smiling as I plated the food.

"Everything looks amazing, but is there a special occasion we forgot about?" Matt asked as we sat down at the table.

"Every day with the two of you is a special occasion," I replied sweetly, earning me a grin from each of them.

We talked as we ate. I told them that Aysha had called and asked if we'd keep Nicholas overnight the following weekend so she and Drew could go out of town for a concert. Isaac and Matt's faces lit up as they offered suggestions of fun things we could do with Nicholas. They loved spending time with him and had even taken him to the park a few times when I had to work on a weekend.

We'd finally met Drew when they asked us over for dinner. He was sincere, intelligent, and crazy about my sister, enough to put up with the three of us giving him the third degree. By the end of the night, we'd given him our stamp of approval.

"I have a couple of things I wanted to talk to you guys about," I told them, that nervous jittering starting up again in my gut. I looked at Matt who nodded at me, he knew a little of what I was going to say, but not all of it. Isaac saw the look we shared and his brow furrowed.

"What's going on, guys?" he asked, setting his fork down and giving us his full attention.

"I talked to Matt about this because I wanted his opinion and because I don't like keeping anything from you guys. I asked him not to tell you because I didn't want to say anything before I got some answers," I explained.

"Answers to what?" Isaac asked slowly. I took a drink of water since I suddenly felt like I'd swallowed a mouthful of cotton.

"Answers about what happened after you left home," I said quietly. If I hadn't been staring right at him, I might've missed the slight tensing of Isaac's shoulders and jaw. He took a sip of his own drink and then set it down and looked me in the eyes.

"What did you find out?" he asked. I scooted my chair closer to him, needing him to be within arm's reach.

"I checked police reports first, hoping a neighbor had heard all the screaming and called the police. I hoped they had found your father and arrested him for what he'd done," I told him.

"But that isn't what happened?" Isaac asked sadly.

"I found a police report on your father, but not because they arrested him," I said, hating to have to tell him this part. "It was an autopsy report. Apparently, your father shot and killed himself not long after that night."

Isaac covered his face with his hands and his shoulders began to shake as he cried softly. I knelt beside his chair and put my hand on his back. He turned and threw his arms around me, burying his face in my neck. I smoothed my hands over his hair and Matt began rubbing his back. I hated bringing up the pain of Isaac's past and I was so relieved that he didn't seem to hate me for it.

"Sometimes I think of how different things might have been if Mom hadn't died that day," Isaac said as he sat back up in his chair, wiping his face with his napkin. "So much senseless anger and pain and death followed and maybe none of that would've happened if she'd gotten help or taken us away somewhere with her. But then I would've never met you," he said, looking at Matt adoringly. "And in turn you," he said, giving me the same loving look.

Isaac took our hands and joined them together in his lap like he liked to do. "I just wish Zane could see how everything turned out; how happy I am with you guys and all the love I have in my life." I took a deep breath and Matt and Isaac both turned to look at me.

"Matt doesn't know this part, because I just recently found out.

I made a few phone calls to friends of mine who work at some of the area hospitals. They did some digging for me into medical records for Zane or even any John Does who may have been brought into the morgue."

"And?" Isaac asked, his voice shaking.

"There was no one in any of the morgues matching his age or the description I gave them using the picture in your wallet. Then I asked them to check records of emergency room visits using the description along with what his possible injuries might have been." Isaac's eyes were huge as he stared back at me.

"Did they find anything?" Matt asked.

"It took a long time because there were literally thousands of patient records they had to go through. One of my friends finally got back to me and said they'd found someone who matched Zane's description. Someone dropped him off at the emergency room and left him there alone. He was barely conscious and they had to do emergency surgery to relieve swelling in his brain. They also had to do extensive reconstructive surgery to fix the shattered bones in his cheek and nose, and dental surgery to replace the teeth that he'd lost. Scans of his body showed broken ribs but they were healed so they believed they had happened at a previous date." Isaac's hand was shaking as he covered his mouth and tears poured from his eyes.

"He refused to tell them his name, a nurse made note that he'd said it would be too dangerous to tell them his name. He was in the hospital a month. They tried to get him to stay longer, but he told the same nurse that he had someone he needed to find. He checked himself out of the hospital that same day."

"Oh my God! That's Zane! That has to be Zane, right?" Isaac screeched, grabbing my arms and looking back and forth between me and Matt.

"It sounds like it, baby, but don't get your hopes up just yet," I warned. "I don't want you to be hurt all over again if you find out it's not him."

"I know and I understand, that's why we have to find out for sure," Isaac insisted. "We have to find out."

"We will. I've already called Micah and he's got one of his guys working on it. It's going to be difficult because even if it was Zane, he may not be using the same name anymore, we have no idea where he went after he left the hospital and he may not look the same after all the surgeries. The hospital records said his face was too swollen still when he left to get a good description. But I won't stop until we find out for sure, I promise." Isaac threw himself into my lap and peppered my face with kisses then he turned so he could see Matt too.

"I am honestly overwhelmed. I have no idea what I ever did to deserve you two, but I'm thankful every day to have you in my life. I know you said not to get my hopes up, but I'm going to choose to have hope because it feels a whole hell of a lot better than how I've felt the last few years when I thought about Zane. If my brother is out there somewhere, I'll move Heaven and Earth to find him," Isaac said.

"You won't have to do it alone," Matt said gruffly, wiping tears from his eyes. Isaac pulled him towards us and we shared a long, languid kiss.

We left our dishes where they were and went into the living room where we could all three cuddle together on the couch. We took turns kissing and soon enough we were exchanging blow jobs and enjoying mutual orgasms. As we lay in various heaps on the couch, gasping for air, Isaac spoke up.

"What was the other thing you wanted to talk to us about? You said you had things to talk about, as in plural."

I gazed at both of them, not sure it was the right moment, but as I looked into both of their eyes, happy and sated and still dark from their arousal, I knew that there would never be a more perfect time. I sat up on the couch and I could feel their eyes on me as I reached for my pants that were wadded up on the floor. I heard Isaac gasp as I pulled the small velvet box out of the pocket of my jeans. Their eyes were wide as they stared at me and Isaac had covered his mouth with his hand.

"My life was decent before I met you, I was content in my career and I had my sister and nephew, but there was something missing. I watched my friends fall in love and get married, and I hoped to meet a man and have the same one day. Never in my wildest dreams did I think I'd end up meeting not one, but two people who were absolutely perfect for me. Isaac, Matt, you both have brought more joy and more love to my life than I ever thought possible. You make me happy every day and I want to spend the rest of my life finding ways to make you happy. Will you marry me?"

I lifted the lid of the box and showed them the three matching sterling silver bands inside. I'd had them each inscribed inside with three small hearts all connected to each other. I pulled theirs out and held them up.

"Is marriage even possible for three people?" Isaac asked.

"It wouldn't be a legal marriage, but we could have a ceremony in which we exchange vows. The law and the paperwork isn't what matters anyway. The important thing is the promises we make to each other and the life we choose to build together," I explained.

"I want that. I want a life with the two of you, I want to love you forever and grow old together. Yes, I'll marry you," Isaac said. His smile was breathtaking and I kissed him soundly.

We turned to Matt who had been quiet up until then and I was afraid maybe I had pushed too soon or too far. Matt had been married before and he'd lost his husband. He might not want to get married again.

"Matt, we will only do this if all of us are comfortable with it. If it's too soon, or you never want—" Matt leaned forward and kissed me until my head spun.

"It's not too soon and I do want to spend the rest of my life with you guys. I'm just trying to figure out what to do with these," he said, pulling a small jewelry box from his own pocket.

It was my own turn to gasp as I realized that Matt had been planning on proposing too. We were silent for a few moments and then we were all laughing. We laughed until we couldn't breathe and I had never felt fuller or happier in my entire life.

CHAPTER
Twenty-Five

Matt

I FINISHED PUTTING THE LAST OF MY CLOTHES IN THE BOX AND folded the lid down then looked around my bedroom. The closet stood empty, my bedroom furniture had been taken to the local homeless shelter. All that remained were the boxes on the floor.

After getting engaged, Hudson, Isaac, and I had talked over what our living arrangement would be. It didn't take us long to decide that we should buy a place where we could start fresh, making memories that were just our own. We preferred to live just outside the city, not too far from our businesses, but more private than a condo in the city.

We hired a realtor to do the searching and after a few weeks, she found the perfect house for us. There was an updated kitchen, swimming pool, and media room as well as a large backyard, space for an office, and a master bedroom that was big enough for two California king-sized beds if we wanted them.

My favorite part though was the en-suite bathroom that had a giant rainforest shower with a bench seat in it and a whirlpool bath that all three of us could fit in comfortably. I could picture all the nights we would be able to relax in that after a long day of work; perhaps as we sipped wine and talked about our day.

In fact, as we walked through the house with the realtor, I could picture everything; Christmases, birthdays, anniversaries. That had been what sold me on the house. Everything included in the house was wonderful, but it was the way I could see myself in that home, sharing a long life with the two men I loved most in the world that had been the deciding factor.

A month later we had secured the loan and signed the papers with all three of our names on the title. With very little that needed to be done to get it ready, we were able to begin moving in right away. Isaac told his landlord he wouldn't be renewing his lease and Hudson and I put our properties on the market. Hudson's place sold in a little over a week and my house sold after just three. It had all happened so fast and so easily that it was hard not to believe that it was fate at work.

I glanced at my watch and saw that I had a little bit of time before my guys would be there to pick me up and take the last of my things to the new house. That night would be the first night we all slept there. I picked up the box of clothes and carried it out by the front door then I went back to get another one.

Bending down to pick up the box, the lid popped open and lying inside, on the very top, was my picture of me and Sean on our wedding day. I sat down on the floor and pulled the framed photo from the box. I ran my finger over Sean's jaw, noticing the happiness in his smile and the love in his eyes as he looked at me.

"I remember every single thing about that day. It didn't matter that it wasn't considered legal in the eyes of the law back then, our marriage was real to us and that was all that mattered. I felt like the luckiest man in the world to be marrying you and to have you as my husband. Our life together may have ended way too soon, but the time we had was full of more joy and laughter and love than most people experience in their entire lifetime. You were my first friend and my first love and I will always have a place for you in my heart. It's gotten a little crowded in there since I let Hudson and Isaac in, but they don't mind sharing the space with you," I said with a smile.

"Losing you was the hardest thing I'd ever been through and I didn't deal well with it. I got stuck in the darkness, buried under my grief. I knew you wouldn't have wanted that for me, but I just couldn't seem to find my way out of it. Then Hudson and Isaac found me and they showed me how much I'd been missing by closing myself off from the rest of the world. They taught me that the heart has room for more than one and they taught me how to live again," I told him.

"I'm happy, Sean. They make me happy and I knew you so well, better than anyone else, and I know that you're happy for me wherever you are. I'm going to live my life the way you would have; enjoying one adventure after another, laughing often and loving hard, and when I see you again someday, I'll tell you all about it."

Still smiling, I laid the picture back in the box and closed the lid. I was glad that it no longer hurt when I thought of Sean. I was finally at peace. A noise had me looking up and my smile widened as I saw the two people who had helped me find that peace.

"You okay, honey?" Hudson asked gently, his brown eyes so warm and full of understanding. Isaac was at his side as they both stood in the doorway watching me.

"Yeah, I'm great," I assured them with a bright smile. I was ready to start the next chapter of my life.

We loaded the boxes into both mine and Hudson's cars and then I followed them to our new home. We spent a couple of hours unpacking boxes and deciding where to put everything. It was easier than I had thought it would be to merge all three of our lives into one, but I suppose we all knew how lucky we were to have found each other, so where we put the plates or which section of the closet would belong to whom, really didn't matter. The fact that we had two people we loved, who also loved us, which we got to come home to every night; that was what mattered.

We took a shower together, washing the grime of the day away. We talked and laughed as we took turns soaping each other up and we shared kisses; lots and lots of kisses. We would've loved to have taken things further, but we forced ourselves to stop since the pizzas we'd ordered would be there soon.

After our shower, we got dressed in comfortable sweats and T-shirts since we were staying in the rest of the night. The doorbell rang as soon as we finished putting on the last article of clothing and Hudson ran to the door to get the food while Isaac and I went to the kitchen to get some drinks.

Over dinner we talked about our new house; things we wanted to do to it, changes we wanted to make so it would feel even more like ours. It didn't surprise me that the three of us had similar tastes and ideas because we always seemed to mesh when it came to important things.

I smiled as Hudson described the gazebo he'd like to build in the backyard. I was excited to be making plans with the two of them, planning a future together. I was finally happy and it felt so good. My previous feelings of loneliness and guilt had been replaced with a sense of peacefulness and love and it was all because of the two of them. I wasn't sure they would ever know how grateful I was that they'd come into my life and decided to love me, but I was going to spend the rest of my life showing them.

When we had finished eating, we cleaned up the kitchen and then went to the living room and curled up together on the couch to watch some TV and relax.

"There are so many great things happening, we've bought a house and we're getting married. I feel like celebrating," Isaac announced during a commercial.

"What did you have in mind, baby?" Hudson asked, reaching over and smoothing his hand down Isaac's cheek. Isaac's tongue darted out and wet his lips and blood rushed to my cock when I heard Hudson's deep growl rumbling up from his chest.

"I think we have an awful lot of rooms in this new house that we need to christen," Isaac answered with a seductive grin. "It may take a while so we better get started. What do you think?"

"I think it's pretty obvious what I think," I joked, pointing down to where my erection had tented my sweatpants in an obscene manner. Isaac chuckled.

"You know my favorite place is inside the two of you," was Hudson's response and my body immediately felt like it had been doused with gasoline and set on fire.

Isaac moved so that he was straddling Hudson's lap and I watched as the two of them kissed. I loved seeing them together, witnessing the love and lust between them. It fed the flames of my desire until I was shaking with want. As if they'd read my mind, my lovers reached for me and I joined them, our mouths and tongues mating with each other until I thought I'd go insane with need.

Hudson stood suddenly and Isaac yelped in surprise as he wrapped his arms and legs around the larger man so he wouldn't fall. I reached up and took the hand Hudson offered down to me and he hauled me up from my seat and pulled me up the stairs, still carrying Isaac.

Isaac licked a line up Hudson's neck and then bit down on his ear, causing Hudson to moan, the sound echoing in the dim hallway. Our boy was no longer the innocent virgin he once was. Isaac had learned every little thing that turned us on and he liked to apply those lessons every chance he got.

We barely made it inside the bedroom before Hudson let go of my hand, turned and slammed Isaac against the wall. Their kiss that time was hungry and feral with teeth clashing and tongues demanding more. I was standing at their sides with a front row view of everything going on. Hudson rutted against Isaac, pushing him further up the wall as his mouth moved down the ivory column of Isaac's throat.

Hudson reached a hand out, blindly, and slid it around my waist, yanking me towards them. My hand went to his strong back, feeling the muscles rippling as he thrust his hips against Isaac's. Hudson's hand dipped underneath the waistband of my pants and I groaned as his finger trailed a line through my crease. I arched my back as he found my pucker and circled it, awakening the nerves that surrounded the area. Using just the very tip of his finger, he breached me and I bit down on his shoulder to muffle my cries. It felt so good and I wanted my lovers in me and on me and everywhere all at once.

"I'm going to come if you don't stop," Isaac gasped suddenly and Hudson immediately stilled.

"You're going to come many times tonight by the time we're through with you, but not yet," he ground out. My cock jerked in my pants. I wasn't sure what it was, but my body responded each and every time I heard Hudson use that authoritative tone.

I groaned in frustration when Hudson removed his hand from my pants, but he turned to me, a dark promise in his eyes. "Don't worry, I'll take care of you too."

Hudson stepped back and let Isaac slide down his body until his feet touched the floor. Then he yanked Isaac's shirt over his head in one deft move. We quickly undressed each other, kissing and licking each new piece of flesh as it was revealed until finally, we stood naked, our cocks jutting proudly from our bodies.

My eyes raked over my two lovers, intoxicated by their very different yet very exquisite bodies. Hudson was all smooth, dark skin over chiseled muscle. Isaac was all creamy, pale skin over sleek, defined lines. They were perfect and they were mine. I was delirious with my need to taste them so I dropped to my knees and took them each in hand.

Hudson had a pearly drop of pre-cum beaded at the tip of his dick and I lapped it up with my tongue. It tasted delicious and I slid my tongue into his slit, searching for more. His hand cupped the back of my head and his fingers weaved into my curls, pulling just enough to make my scalp tingle. I swirled my tongue over the broad head of his cock while my other hand worked Isaac's dick up and down. My gaze slid up their bodies and I saw them locked in a heated kiss. Knowing they were pleasuring each other while I pleasured them had my balls aching for release.

I took turns licking and sucking each of my lovers until Hudson stepped away and I turned and devoted all my attention to Isaac. I placed my hands on his hips and sucked him in deeper until my nose was pressed against the trimmed hair at the base of his cock and his dick was nestled deep inside my throat. I swallowed around him and was rewarded with a burst of pre-cum which I drank greedily.

"Oh, God!" Isaac shouted. His cock slid from between my lips, the tip of it red and slick with my saliva. I searched for Hudson and found him kneeling on the other side of Isaac. From the throaty moans above me I could tell that Isaac was thoroughly enjoying the rimming he was receiving.

Wanting to see our young lover come unglued, I refocused my attention on Isaac's cock. My hand wrapped around his base and I pumped my fist up and down his length, feeding it into my mouth. My cheeks hollowed as I increased the suction on the head of his cock. Isaac rocked back and forth between us as I continued to suck him while Hudson rimmed his ass.

Hudson reached between Isaac's legs and wrapped his large hand around my neglected cock and I moaned in relief as he began to jerk me off. Isaac whimpered and his hands delved into my hair, yanking on my curls as his desperation grew. Our baby was close and he needed to come. Hudson must've sensed it too.

"You can come now, Isaac. Come right down Matt's throat. He's starving for it, feed him," I heard him say and I would've come myself if Hudson's fist hadn't tightened around my cock, pushing my orgasm back.

Hudson was right, I was starving for the taste of Isaac's cum and I wasn't disappointed as his cock swelled in my mouth, shooting his creamy goodness all over my tongue. I swallowed every last drop and then licked Isaac's dwindling erection until he was completely clean. I grinned up at him and he gave me a weary, sated smile back, rubbing his hands over my head lovingly.

I immediately missed the feel of Hudson's hand on my cock as he removed it and climbed to his feet. I stood as well and the three of us shared a kiss. Isaac moaned as he tasted himself on my tongue and Hudson sucked it into his mouth, savoring the flavor of our lover.

"Get on the bed, honey. I need to be inside you," Hudson growled at me and I hurried to the bed, eager for the feel of his cock in my ass. "Lie on your back," he commanded.

In our everyday lives, Hudson was patient and kind, always considerate of our feelings, but in moments like this, when it was just the three of us, naked, intimate, and alone in our own bubble, the animal inside him was released and he became bossy and demanding. And. I. Loved. Every. Second. Of. It.

I did as I was told, stretching out with my head on the pillows. Hudson had something else in mind though because he grabbed me by the ankles and pulled me back down to the foot of the bed. I laughed in surprise and he gave me a feral grin. Isaac grabbed a bottle of lube and tossed it onto the bed then crawled up beside me.

We had decided to do away with the condoms several weeks ago after being tested and I wouldn't say I missed them. I loved the fact that we could slide inside each other bare and fill each other with our seed, fully binding us and claiming each other as our own. Hudson had even bottomed for the two of us one night, even though he preferred topping. He said he needed to feel that final connection that made him ours. It was an emotional night and one that I would never forget.

My heart beat rapidly as I watched Hudson pick up the lube and pour some onto his fingers. He leaned down and whispered something to Isaac who licked his lips, his face flushed with arousal. Isaac nodded his head, agreeing with whatever Hudson had said. There was no time to ask what they had been talking about though because Hudson drove his finger inside me, lighting me on fire and stealing my breath.

"Hudson!" I called out and he bent down and kissed me as he crooked his finger just so and suddenly all the synapses in my brain misfired.

He stood back up at the foot of the bed and Isaac took his place, covering my mouth with his own. I reached my arms around him and pulled him towards me, needed him to keep me tethered as Hudson continued to break me apart. Isaac pulled back long enough to pour some lube into his hand and then he reached behind himself. I knew the moment his fingers slid inside his own ass because his eyes rolled up in the back of his head. My cock leaked all over my stomach and I felt like I would explode if they didn't move things along quickly.

Sensing my urgency, Isaac slicked up my cock and straddled my waist. His blue eyes locked on mine and we both gasped as he lowered himself onto me. Hudson peered down at us, watching our mating as he slicked his own cock and my pulse raced as I realized what they'd been planning. They knew that there was no surer way to drive me out of my mind than to have one of them inside me while I was inside the other.

Isaac lay down on top of me and kissed me as Hudson lifted my legs. The head of his cock brushed over my hole and I shivered in anticipation. The stretch and burn was intense as he began to breech me and I had to force myself to relax and allow him to get inside.

"I love you so much," Isaac whispered, his breath ghosting across my lips. I hugged him to me tightly and kissed him thoroughly. Unable to speak, I let my kisses speak for me, conveying to him how much he meant to me and how happy I was to have him in my life.

Finally, Hudson was in as far as he could go, his hips nestled against my ass and I breathed a sigh of relief. He bent down over Isaac's back and the three of us shared a kiss. We were connected in every way imaginable at that moment, our bodies locked together as one and our hearts intermingled. One of us shuddered and it rippled through us all. We looked at each other and I could tell that they were feeling it too. It was intense, it was powerful, it was our souls uniting.

Hudson rocked into me and it pushed my body up the bed. He did it again and I cried out as his cock grazed that perfect spot deep inside me. As our need increased, so did our movements. Hudson stood up and I wrapped my legs around his waist, locking my ankles together behind his back as he thrust inside me.

Isaac sat up too and began to ride my cock up and down, using my body for his own pleasure. The sounds of our slick bodies slapping together and our lust-driven moans filled the air and I felt my balls pulling up tight against my body. I panted loudly, teeth locked together as I tried to hold back my orgasm. It felt so good and I never wanted the moment to end.

Hudson pulled Isaac's jaw roughly towards him and they began to devour each other. He reached down and wrapped his hand around Isaac's cock, pumping it up and down and swallowing Isaac's screams.

Watching the two of them together, the feel of Isaac's tight heat clenching my cock and Hudson's thick shaft stretching me wide and filling me so perfectly was all too much and I shouted their names as I shot my seed into Isaac, my hole squeezing around Hudson's cock with wracking spasms. They followed quickly behind me, Hudson filling me with hot cum and Isaac spraying his all over my chest.

We collapsed on top of each other as the echoes of our orgasms rippled through us like shockwaves after an earthquake. I felt wrecked, totally destroyed, yet at the same time, completely whole. That's what Isaac and Hudson did to me. They took from me, demanding that I give them every part of me; my heart, body, and soul.

Then they filled me back up, giving me every part of them in return until my heart was so full, I thought it would burst.

I floated for a while, barely registering as Hudson got up and turned out all the lights around the house, making sure the doors were locked. Isaac got a warm washrag and cleaned us up and I smiled at him through my haze. They climbed back in the bed and curled up around my sides, their hands finding each other over my chest so we were once again connected.

"Welcome home," I whispered into the dark and then I drifted off to sleep.

CHAPTER
Twenty-Six

Isaac

"Knock, knock, can I come in?" I heard Aysha say through the door.

"It's open," I answered back.

I looked up as the door swung open and smiled. Over the last several months, Aysha had become a sister to me and Matt as much as she was to Hudson. She looked beautiful in a blue silk dress that was elegant yet showed off her feminine curves. She looked happier and healthier than the day I first met her, but I supposed that's what falling in love did to a person. And Drew loved her back just as much. Her eyes sparkled as she looked me over, smiling approvingly at my black tuxedo.

"Well, don't you look handsome. I just wanted to check and see if you needed anything before I headed back down and got my seat." I kissed her on the cheek.

"Thank you, but all I need is the two men who will be walking down that aisle with me," I told her. Aysha's grin widened and she chuckled at me.

"That's almost exactly the same answer they each gave to me," she said. I wasn't surprised at all to hear that we were all on the same page, but it still made me feel warm all over. Aysha's eyes turned serious and she laid a hand alongside my cheek, looking into my eyes.

"You're a good man, Isaac. You've brought so much hope and joy into my life and Nicholas' and for that I thank you, but I want to thank you most of all for loving Hudson the way that you do. He's the best person I know, always so giving and kind. I used to worry that he'd meet someone and they'd take advantage of his goodness, but he found you and Matt instead and I couldn't be happier. You two are exactly right for him because you're compassionate and giving men as well. I know that you three will have a wonderful life together and I'm so glad I get to be there to watch it happen." My eyes were blurry with tears as I wrapped my arms around her in a hug.

"Thank you for accepting and supporting the three of us. My life has become so much richer with you in it," I whispered and she squeezed me tight for a few seconds before she pulled back. We chuckled as we both reached for a tissue and wiped the moisture from our eyes. She took a deep breath and cleared her throat, shaking off the emotions.

"Okay, I'm going to head down now. Are you ready?" she asked.

"I'll be there in just a minute," I told her. Aysha nodded and smiled before shutting the door behind her. I turned back to look in the mirror.

It was finally my wedding day, the day I had dreamed about for years. When I was a young teenager and had first discovered that I liked boys, I used to fantasize that I'd meet a handsome man and he'd fall madly in love with me, marry me, and take me somewhere safe, away from all the pain and anger of my father. Zane would live next door to us with his own family and he and I would run a business together. At night, my husband would hold me in his arms and whisper how much he loved me until I fell asleep.

The reality was a bit different, but some of it was the same. I had two men that loved me instead of one and I worked with them instead of Zane, but thanks to Hudson, I had hope that I might find my brother someday. I wasn't sure if that would ever happen, but the fact that I had hope where there once was none, was enough to make me happy. And I was happy. Sharing my story with Hudson and Matt had released the hold my demons had on me, taking away their power and transferring it back to me. I still felt pain and anger from everything I'd gone through and all the years I'd been cheated out of with my brother, but with the help of my therapist and the support and love of my guys, I was learning how to cope with those feelings.

I looked at my reflection in the mirror one last time and then turned with a smile to go find my men so we could get married. I walked down to the kitchen where we had said we would meet and looked out the window at all our guests. We'd decided to hold the ceremony at our house because we wanted to combine the happiest day of our lives to the place where we would build that life together.

Our friends and family were sitting and talking with one another in the white chairs we had set up for the special occasion. Tables were set up under a tent for the reception afterward and caterers scurried about, making sure everything would be ready for our guests as soon as the ceremony ended. I smiled as I saw that many of the staff and even a few of the kids from the center had shown up, although most of the staff were busy watching over things there, their gift to us so we could enjoy our time together.

Matt's parents had also come. Hudson and I had been nervous meeting them, but they were as kind and gracious as their son and seemed relieved to see Matt so happy. The entire Greene family was there, even Carter and Ryan who had flown in along with Rylie and Lachlan, taking a break from the tour for the day so that they could celebrate with us.

"Hey, beautiful!" I whipped around when I heard Hudson's deep voice and my heart caught in my throat as I looked at him.

His tuxedo was tailored to fit his broad shoulders perfectly and the crisp white shirt he had buttoned underneath showcasing his well-defined chest. I swallowed hard around the lump in my throat as Matt walked in behind him looking just as dashing. I couldn't believe that these two amazing men wanted to spend the rest of their lives with me. I blinked, unable to see past my tears.

Seeing that I was overwhelmed with emotions, they came forward, sheltering me with their bodies like they always did and took turns kissing me and whispering to me how much they loved me until I was able to calm down.

"You both are the most handsome men I've ever seen," I told them. Matt kissed the freckles on my nose and then leaned back and looked at each of us with a smile.

"I can't wait to marry the two of you. Can we hurry up and make that happen?" he pleaded. We all laughed and then I grabbed them each by the hand and walked towards the back door. Nicholas was there and he smiled when he saw his three uncles approach.

"Is it time?" Nicholas asked.

"Yeah, buddy. You do it just like we practiced, okay?" Hudson told him.

Nicholas nodded and then straightened his little body proudly and began walking down the aisle, holding the silk pillow that had our three rings tied together by a ribbon. We'd had trouble deciding which rings to use since Hudson and Matt had both planned on proposing so we finally agreed that we should use one set as our engagement rings and one set as our wedding bands. I was proud of the fact that, so far, we'd always been able to reach a compromise that we all were happy with. I knew there would be bumps in the road along the way, just as there are in any relationship, but I had no doubts that we'd be able to work through them.

As Nicholas reached the end of the aisle and took a seat beside his mother, everyone turned and faced us. In a world that often rejected or ignored that which was different, we were lucky enough to be surrounded by people who loved us and supported us and who wanted to celebrate the love we'd found, regardless of how many it included or the color of our skin. They were happy because we were happy. The people there that day were the definition of love, the definition of family.

The ceremony was short, with each of us taking a turn to vow our love and devotion to each other. It was emotional and beautiful and we were each visibly moved by the time we got to the kiss. There was loud cheering around us from our family and friends as we were announced husbands, but I couldn't take my eyes off my two men long enough to pay attention. Matt, who I'd loved for so long but never imagined could be mine, and Hudson, who had swept in and stolen my heart right out from under me; they were my husbands and I would spend every day of the rest of my life trying to give back all the love they'd given to me.

The reception was next and everyone seemed to have a great time. We made our way around after dinner, visiting with everyone and accepting their congratulations. Caleb and Giovanni were there with their daughter, Sarah, who quickly became friends with Nicholas and the two took off to play with the toys we kept on hand for when Nicholas spent the night with us.

There was a lot of laughter and dancing and when we cut the cake and Matt shoved his piece in my face, he leaned down and whispered in my ear that he would lick it off me later. My face immediately turned red, much to the amusement of our guests who'd been watching the whole thing. Hudson leaned in and swiped his tongue over Matt's bottom lip and Matt shivered, making everyone laugh again.

"Don't worry, I've got your back," he said, giving me a wink.

"Hey! Are you two teaming up against me?" Matt whispered in

mock outrage.

"Only in the way you like," I replied saucily. Hudson laughed while Matt growled in my ear.

"Yeah, I do like that," he admitted then he grabbed both of our hands and led us out to the dance floor for our first dance.

It should've been awkward to try to dance with three people, but as with everything else in our relationship, we found a way to make it happen. Or arms locked around each other, with Hudson pressed against my back and I laid my head on Matt's chest, his heartbeat keeping time with the music. Everything else around us disappeared until it seemed like we were the only three people there.

"I have never been happier in my entire life," I said with a sigh.

"Me either," Hudson added. "I am the luckiest man in the world."

"No, that would be me because I get to be with the two of you," Matt said.

"Okay, I guess we're all pretty lucky," I said with a laugh and they conceded. "Thank you both for showing me what love is," I said, growing serious once again.

"Thank you for sharing your lives with me and for giving me more than I ever dreamed possible," Hudson said in return.

"Thank you for not giving up on me and for showing me that it was okay to love again," Matt said solemnly.

I leaned up and pressed my lips to his and then Hudson did the same. Soon we were locked in an embrace that included all three of us, just how we liked it, exactly as it should be. I knew that we wouldn't always feel the love and support that we felt that day. Some people wouldn't be able to understand how three individuals can fall in love with each other, caring for and supporting one another and building a life together. I felt sorry for those people. I couldn't speak for other triad relationships because I only knew what worked for mine, but as far as my relationship with my partners, it was beautiful, it was real and it was ours.

EPILOGUE

Kathy Greene

S TRONG HANDS LANDED ON MY WAIST AND I FELT RICK LEAN IN and nuzzle his lips against my neck. I giggled because it tickled, but goose bumps raced over my skin for very different reasons. After all these years, the man could still send chills down my spine with just a look or a brush of his hand. I tilted my head so I could give him a kiss and he hummed contentedly.

"Is there anything you need me to do?" he asked.

I looked around the large dining room table at the places that were set. Soon all our children would be there, including their friends who we claimed as our own. With everyone working and having children, or out of the country on tour, it had been awhile since I'd had all my kids under one roof and I was thrilled that they were all able to be at our house for Thanksgiving.

"I think we have everything we need," I answered.

"Good, then we have time for this." Rick spun me around in his arms and dipped me low, making me gasp in surprise before he gave me a long, passionate kiss. I wrapped my arms around his broad shoulders and let myself get lost in the feel of his body pressed against mine.

"Oh my God! They're at it again," I heard Michelle complain.

"You guys, not over the food!" Caleb scolded.

Rick chuckled against my lips and then stood me upright. We turned and faced our children who were wearing smirks on their faces. They liked to pretend that we horrified them, but I knew that seeing their parents so in love made them happy.

"Happy Thanksgiving!" I called out, going to them with my arms open.

I hugged them around the food in their hands, planting kisses on their cheeks and then helped them carry everything into the kitchen. Michelle's husband walked in then, carrying even more food and set it on the island counter. He gave me a hug before telling his wife that he was going to run out and get the last load from the car.

"You better not be referring to my grandbaby as a load," I teased.

Jason laughed. "No, Dad already snatched little Ricky out of the car seat. He said he needed to get some snuggles in before Gram got her hands on him and hogged him for the rest of the day."

"He's a smart man," I admitted. There was no use denying it, since it was the truth. Whenever my grandbabies were around, I made sure to soak up as much time with them as I could. "And where's my sweet Sarah?" I asked, turning to Caleb.

"Right here," I heard Giovanni say from the doorway. I smiled brightly when I saw the little girl in his arms.

"Gram!" Sarah exclaimed when she saw me. She wiggled in her father's arms as she reached for me and Giovanni laughed as he set her down. She ran towards me and I knelt down and held my arms open, pulling her in for a big hug.

"There's my girl," I cooed at her. "Look at what a beautiful dress you have on," I told her and she smiled as she twirled around to show off her dress. Rick walked in then, with his namesake and pride and joy, Ricky, in his arms, smiling smugly and I narrowed my eyes at him.

"You've got about two minutes while I talk to Sarah and then you've got to give him up," I informed him, pointing a finger his way.

Rick laughed and then retreated into the living room, telling Ricky that if Gram couldn't find them then she couldn't take him away. Everyone laughed at that, including me, and then I asked Sarah if she wanted to help me put the name cards on the table.

"Yes!" she answered happily, running to the drawer where she remembered I had put them.

The weekend before she'd come to my house and the two of us made handprint turkeys that we could use as name cards for each person in our family. Sarah had done a fine job of telling me each person that would be at Thanksgiving while I wrote them on the cards. I followed her into the dining room and handed her the cards as she decided where each person should sit.

"Happy Thanksgiving, everyone!" I heard my oldest son say. I looked up and saw Landon and Micah in the doorway and my heart warmed at the sight of them. They were both so handsome and the looks on their faces showed how happy they were.

"Hey, Mom!" Landon called out as he walked into the dining room.

He set the platter of food he was holding down on the table and then gave me a kiss before kneeling down to talk to Sarah, praising her on the beautiful turkeys she'd made. He's going to make such an amazing father someday. I looked up at Micah who was staring down at his husband and I could tell by the soft look in his eyes that he was having similar thoughts to mine. He caught me staring and grinned at me sheepishly.

"Happy Thanksgiving, Mom," he said softly as he bent down to kiss my cheek.

"I'm so glad you're here," I told him, wrapping my arm around his waist. He put his arm around my shoulders and smiled down at me.

Micah had been the most withdrawn of my sons-in-law. He'd been through so much in his lifetime and had only had a brief glimpse of what a loving family behaved like when he'd lived with Giovanni and his parents in high school, so it took him longer to get used to the constant affection our family showed each other. I knew Micah loved us and he showed how much he cared by being protective of all of us, but the fact that he was beginning to hug or kiss us on his own, made me unbelievably happy and I had to fight back my tears so I wouldn't embarrass him.

Carter and Ryan showed up next, looking tired, but happy. They'd been in Europe with the band, but had flown home with Rylie and Lachlan on Lachlan's company jet in order to spend Thanksgiving with us. The tour would be ending soon and I couldn't wait to have my baby back home for longer than a few days.

"Hi, boys! I've missed you both so much," I cried as I hugged them both.

"It's good to be home. I missed you too, Mom," Carter said.

They squeezed me back and then I let them go so everyone else could have a turn. My eyes were watery as I watched Carter and Caleb hug. We were a very tight-knit family, but there was a special bond between the twins that the rest of us didn't share and I knew it had been particularly hard for them to be apart from each other.

My nephew, Morgan, and his husband, Akio, were the next to arrive, followed closely by the newlyweds, Hudson, Matt, and Isaac. They thanked us for inviting them, but I brushed it off, reminding them that they were family now too.

Emma and Mark showed up a few minutes later with my other grandbaby and my namesake, Katherine. I scooped her up in my arms quickly and began kissing her face as Mark helped me tug her heavy coat off. I nuzzled my face into Katherine's neck, breathing in the sweet smell of little girl and making her laugh in the process.

"Rylie and Lachlan will be a little late. They said they had something they needed to do before they could come here," Carter told us.

"I wonder what was up with them. They were acting strangely on the plane, like they were nervous or excited about something," Ryan said.

"Yeah, I know what you mean. If it was just Rylie I would've just chalked it up to the fact that he's always strange," Carter joked. "But Lachlan was acting weird too. Any idea what's going on?" he asked, directing his question to Micah who was close friends with Lachlan.

Micah shrugged his shoulders. "Lachlan told me he had some good news he couldn't wait to tell me, but he refused to say what it was. Said I'd find out when he got home."

"Come to think of it, Rylie was acting very secretive the last time he and I Skyped," Hudson added. "He seemed happy though, so I wasn't concerned. I figured he'd tell me whatever it was when he was ready."

"Well, I'm definitely intrigued now," Rick said. He still had Ricky in his arms and we shared a grin, each of us thrilled to get to spend the day with our children and grandchildren.

"That must be them now," Carter said when the doorbell rang. All eyes were trained on him as he hurried to the door and opened it.

Rylie walked in first. I'd known him for many years and I'd witnessed the struggles he'd gone through. I'd worried about him just like a mother would, and prayed that he'd find his way eventually. I'd been so happy when those prayers had been answered. Rylie had turned his life around after he fell in love with Lachlan and he'd been much happier ever since. Still, I'd never seen him smile as widely as he was when he walked through my door that day.

I stared in surprise as Dylan and Max, the two young brothers I'd gotten to know and love at Agape House, walked in behind him, followed quickly by Lachlan who was wearing a grin that matched his husband's.

"What's going on?" Isaac asked and I saw the hopeful look he gave Rylie.

"We know everyone here has met these two guys, but Lachlan

and I would like to formally introduce our sons, Dylan and Max. Lachlan was able to pull some strings despite the holiday and we just came from the courthouse, the adoption became official about an hour ago," Rylie said, his voice cracking at the end.

Everyone was quiet in the room and then Isaac spoke up and his voice sounded shaky as tears swam in his eyes. "You mean they get to stay with you? They get to stay together?"

"They're ours," Lachlan confirmed, smiling down at the two boys who gazed up at him like he'd hung the moon. "They'll be raised together in a loving home from now on." Matt put an arm around Isaac and kissed the side of his head, whispering something in his ear. Isaac nodded his head and smiled up at him.

Everyone moved at once then, hugging, kissing, and congratulating the new family. I swallowed around the lump in my throat, but couldn't stop the tears that were streaming down my face. I couldn't have picked a better couple to raise those boys.

"So, this..." Hudson said as he approached Rylie. Rylie nodded his head.

"Yeah. The other things I have to live for," he answered. Hudson pulled him in for a tight hug and whispered something to him about how beautifully he'd painted his portrait. I didn't understand what that meant, but I heard the fierce pride in Hudson's voice and saw the happy tears in Rylie's eyes.

"It seems that we have even more to be thankful for than we'd realized. Welcome to our family, boys," Rick said. Max and Dylan looked around at all of us with wide eyes, but they were grinning all the same. I knew we were a lot to take in all at once, but in time, they'd get used to us.

"Who's ready to eat?" I asked and everyone shouted at once.

Laughing, I led them into the dining room where the food covered every available inch of space on the table. No one would leave hungry, that was for sure. Rick and I grudgingly handed the children back to their parents who promised to give them back as soon as they were finished eating.

Rick grabbed a couple extra chairs for Dylan and Max then everyone settled into their assigned seats, families intermixing according to Sarah's plan and I noticed that she'd seated herself right next to me. I kissed the top of her head as I sat down next to her and she grinned up at me. Rick stood at the head of the table and we all bowed our heads as he said grace then everyone was laughing and talking as they passed the food around, filling their plates.

I looked around at the people gathered there to celebrate Thanksgiving with us. We'd been through an awful lot over the past few years, some good and some bad. We'd been sad when Caleb had left to study abroad, but he'd returned to take the job of his dreams and in doing so, met the love of his life.

We'd been worried sick when Carter had been trapped in a fire at Romero's, but Ryan had pulled him to safety and we'd all stood by his side as he struggled through physical therapy to repair the damage done to his hand, not sure if he'd ever play his guitar again. Carter was strong and determined though and he'd regained the strength needed in his hand and we'd all been there to celebrate his first sold out concert.

We'd agonized over whether or not Landon would pull through after being kidnapped and shot by an insane woman, thankful that Micah had been there to rescue him and get him to safety quickly. Landon had survived though and I couldn't remember ever seeing him as content and happy as he was since falling in love with Micah.

We'd made it through all those moments intact and we'd gone on to celebrate many happy occasions as well. Each of my boys married their soulmates, Caleb and Giovanni adopted Sarah. My girls, Emma and Michelle, had given me two other grandchildren to love and dote upon. I was sure it wouldn't be long before Landon and Micah added to our family and perhaps Carter and Ryan too, once the tour wound down.

Rylie had faced his demons and come out smiling, giving

Lachlan someone to love again after losing his brother. Morgan had found someone he could trust and depend on with Akio, and Hudson, Isaac, and Matt had found a love that, despite what society may think, I knew was strong and true and would last forever.

I smiled as I looked around at my family. While some of them may not biologically be mine, they were the family of my choosing, the family of my heart. I had claimed them and I loved them as if they were my own. My eyes met my husband's from across the table and my breath caught in my throat at the love I found staring back at me.

We shared a smile. We'd been married long enough that I knew we were thinking the same thing. There was no possible way for us to know what life had in store. I was sure there would be struggles and surprises along the way, but whatever happened, we would always be strong because we would always have each other. We were family and there was no love more powerful than that.

The End ???

Coming December 2017…join the Greene family one more time as they celebrate Christmas together.

Also, follow me on Facebook or join my group, Annabella's Sexy Souls to find out about my upcoming projects, including Zane's story.

AFTERWORD

Agape (pronounced like uh-gop-A) love is the highest form of love. It embraces a universal, unconditional love that transcends and persists regardless of circumstance.

When I started this series, I wanted to write about a family that loved and accepted each other unconditionally, regardless of age, race, sexual orientation or circumstance. The Greene family live their lives as an example of agape love. Sure, they have their ups and downs, moments where they're frustrated or even angry with each other, what family doesn't? But at the center of it all is their love and commitment to each other and that never wavers.

I also wanted to include a LGBTQA youth center that would extend agape love beyond that of a family, reaching out to help those who have been cast aside, hurt, lost or broken and giving them a place where they could feel understood, accepted and loved for who they were.

Writing this series has been an incredible journey for me. Not only has it provided a fun, creative outlet for me, it's also taught me to be stronger and braver than I ever thought I could be. It's taken me on adventures, brought me joy and a sense of purpose while introducing me to countless new friends that I might have never met had I not started writing.

So, I thank you all for your encouragement and support, your friendship and love throughout this journey. I hope that you will join me as I take off on my next adventure and I encourage you to practice agape love in your own lives. Show others that they are loved and cared for because of who they are and exactly how they are, without limitations.

ACKNOWLEDGEMENTS

As always, my first thanks go to my family; my husband, my children, my siblings and my parents. You have stood by my side from the moment I started dreaming up the Greene family. You offered your support, your wisdom and your encouragement and none of this would have become a reality without you. I love you guys. You are my heart and soul.

Thank you to Aimee for teaching me, guiding me and encouraging me to give writing a chance, but mostly, I thank you for being my friend. I can't wait to show the world what we can do when we join forces.

Thank you to Deena for being my rock and my best friend. Through every change we've had in our lives, our friendship has never faltered. I know that no matter what, we will always have each other's backs. You are the best friend I could've ever asked for.

Thank you to Jenn, my PD for being my best friend and my sister by heart. Somehow, in this huge, crazy world, we were lucky enough to find each other and I will be thankful for that every day of my life. We've had a lot of fun together, but we've also been there to support each other through some darker moments. I will always be there for you no matter what.

Thank you to my team: Pam Ebeler of Undivided Editing, Jay Aheer of Simply Defined Art, Judy Zweifler of Judy's Proofreading, Stacey Blake of Champagne Formats and my beta readers; Lee Rey, Melissa McIntyre, Jenn Gibson, Allison Hopfazel, Meredith King, Lori Greis, Wendy Lynn, Nemerald and Jodie Temple-Harding. Writing this series has been an amazing journey from beginning to end and I've been very blessed to have the same people working with me and encouraging me throughout the entire process, while adding a few new friends along the way. You all have shown me more support, encouragement and enthusiasm than I could ever repay you for. Thank you all from the bottom of my heart.

ABOUT THE
Author

I am married to my high school sweetheart who let's face it, is a saint for putting up with me all of these years. Together we have been blessed with the chance to raise two amazing human beings and so far we haven't screwed it up; I'll let you know for sure later. I am a business owner and spend more time laughing than actually working most days. I love watching movies, cooking, going to the beach and spending time with my family and best friends. I am an obsessive reader who is a complete sucker for a good love story, but loves to feel a broad range of emotions throughout a book. I think real life is hard enough and so my books offer twists and turns, but always with a happy ending.

I love to hear from my readers. You can reach me at:
Twitter
twitter.com/annabellamicha1

Facebook
www.facebook.com/profile.php?id=100011438515157

Annabella's Sexy Souls
www.facebook.com/groups/233274880449097

Blog
www.annabellamichaels.blogspot.com

www.ingramcontent.com/pod-product-compliance
Lightning Source LLC
Chambersburg PA
CBHW030405020726
47493CB00003B/946